The Great Divide:

When Earth Lost Its Shadow

By

Rafael McCrary

© 2025 Rafael McCrary

All rights reserved. This book was created with the assistance of AI tools but has been reviewed, edited, and curated by the author. No part of this book may be reproduced, stored in a retrieval system, or transmitted in any form or by any means—electronic, mechanical, photocopying, recording, or otherwise—without the prior written permission of the author, except in the case of brief quotations for reviews or academic use.

Contents

Chapter 1: Fractured Lines 4

Chapter 2: A Dissonant Harmony 25

Chapter 3: The Vanishing 51

Chapter 4: Earth Without Shadows 69

Chapter 5: Adjusting to Noctivara 97

Chapter 6: Survivors Saving Survivors 122

Chapter 7: The Fractured World 142

Chapter 8: Bridging the Divide 174

Chapter 9: The Next Step 203

Chapter 10: Unity in the Shadows 227

Chapter 1: Fractured Lines

The neon "Bar & Grill" sign cast a soft, wavering glow over the crowded sidewalk, where the scent of grilled food lingered. The hum of overlapping conversations mixed with the soulful notes of a street musician's saxophone, creating an ambiance that felt lively yet distant. Inside, the bar buzzed with laughter, the clinking of glasses, and the occasional burst of cheers when a dart hit the bullseye.

At a corner table, Maya sat, her posture relaxed but her expression tight, almost unreadable. Her fingers lightly traced the condensation on her glass, her gaze fixed somewhere in the middle distance. Across from her, Ethan leaned back in his chair, arms crossed. His easy grin—so often his shield—had faded, leaving behind a vague defensiveness in his eyes.

"It's not just a joke, Ethan," Maya said, her tone cool but steady. There was no anger in her voice, just the weight of repetition. "It's a pattern. The little comments your friends make, the things they let slip, and the way you laugh it off like it doesn't matter. Do you have any idea what that feels like?"

Ethan shifted in his seat, brushing a hand through his hair—a nervous habit she knew too well. "Maya, they're just jokes. You know they don't mean anything by it."

She didn't respond immediately. Instead, she let the silence stretch between them, her gaze settling on him now, sharp and unwavering. "You really think that's enough? That their intention erases the impact? Ethan, those things they say…they chip away at people like me. And you, of all people, should understand that."

Ethan exhaled sharply, his brow furrowing. "People like you?" His tone was incredulous, almost offended. "Maya, I'm not exactly some golden boy with a free pass in life. Do you know what it's like to walk into a room and have everyone look at you differently because of the color of your skin? To be told you don't belong?"

Maya leaned back slightly, folding her arms. "I do, Ethan. But what you're missing is that your experiences don't cancel out mine. They're not the same. And when it comes to anti-Blackness, you don't get it. You think because you've faced racism, you can't perpetuate it. But when you sit there and let those comments slide, you're proving otherwise."

Ethan's mouth opened, but no words came out. She saw it in his face—that mix of defensiveness and something quieter, harder to admit. Guilt, maybe. Or confusion. He glanced away, out toward the bar, where a group of friends were laughing loudly at something none of them would remember tomorrow.

Liam, sitting to Ethan's left, cleared his throat. "Uh, maybe this is something worth talking about—like, really talking about," he said cautiously, glancing between them. "It's not exactly black-and-white."

Ethan turned to Liam, his frustration spilling over. "Liam, you don't need to turn this into one of your debates, okay?"

Maya's laugh was soft, almost inaudible, but it cut through the noise. "You always do that," she said, more to herself than to him. "Shut people down when the conversation gets uncomfortable."

Elena, who had been silently fidgeting with her napkin, finally spoke up. "So...does this mean we're skipping another round of drinks?" Her attempt at lightening the mood fell flat, her voice barely rising above the din of the bar.

Maya stood abruptly, her chair scraping against the floor. The sharp sound drew a few curious glances from nearby tables, but she didn't care. "I'm done," she said, grabbing her bag from the back of the chair. Her voice remained calm, but inside, a storm raged as her steps carried her swiftly out the door.

"Maya—" Ethan began, reaching out as if to stop her, but she shook her head, silencing him with a look.

"Goodnight," she said, her tone final. She didn't wait for a response, didn't even look back as she made her way through the crowd and out the door.

The cool night air hit her like a wave, though it did little to quiet Ethan's words echoing in her mind. She paused beneath the neon sign, the saxophonist's music curling around her like smoke. For a moment, she just stood there, watching the blur of cars and people moving through the night. The city felt distant, like she was floating somewhere just outside of it.

She wasn't angry—not anymore. Anger would have required energy, an emotional investment she didn't have to give. What she felt now was quieter, heavier. It was disconnection, the kind that made her wonder how two people could share a life and still live in entirely different worlds.

She took a deep breath, the night air sharp in her lungs. And then, with no particular destination in mind, she walked away from the glow of the bar and into the shadows of the city.

As Maya walked home, the cool night air did little to quiet the echo of Ethan's words. Inside the bar, Ethan slumped back in his chair, dragging his hand through his hair. "I'm not saying it doesn't matter. I'm just saying—why does it have to ruin everything? We were having a good night," he muttered, barely loud enough to be heard over the noise.

Liam's head snapped up, his gaze cutting through the table like a blade. "Because it is, Ethan. It always has been." His voice was steady but carried an edge sharp enough to silence the others. "You think this is about you being uncomfortable? Imagine what it's like to walk through the world knowing your discomfort could cost you your life—or your dignity—every single day."

Ethan frowned, his mouth opening slightly, but Liam didn't give him the chance to respond. "Ethan, have you thought about what Maya's up against? Black women face workplace discrimination three times more than anyone else. And don't even get me started on healthcare or housing or how they're overpoliced just for existing. Maya's not making this up."

Elena hesitated, her voice soft. "But isn't she just... I don't know, being overly sensitive about the jokes?"

Liam turned to her, his expression softening but his tone unwavering. "No, Elena. She's not. The 'jokes' you're talking about? They're microaggressions—death by a thousand cuts. It's not just one comment or one laugh. It's the cumulative effect of constantly being reminded you're other. That you don't belong."

Ethan leaned forward, his expression defensive now. "But I do get it, Liam. I've dealt with racism too. You think it's easy being the only Indian guy in the room sometimes?"

Liam didn't back down. "And yet, here you are, Ethan, using that as a shield. Like it exempts you from having to listen. Your experiences don't invalidate hers—they don't even begin to compare. Anti-Blackness is its own beast, and instead of standing by her, you're brushing it off because it's easier for you."

The table went silent for a moment, the weight of Liam's words pressing down on all of them.

Finally, Liam leaned back, his expression softening just slightly. "Look, Ethan. You love Maya, right? Then listen to her. Not just her words, but what's underneath them. Because if you don't... you're going to lose her. And you'll deserve to."

The apartment was unnervingly quiet when Maya stepped inside, her heels clicking sharply against the hardwood floor. The faint scent of lavender lingered, mixing with Ethan's cologne—a bittersweet reminder of the life they had tried to build together. She slipped off her shoes and dropped her bag by the door, sinking into the couch as if the weight of the night had finally caught up with her. The TV screen stared back at her, dark and empty.

The sound of the door opening broke the stillness. Ethan walked in, his footsteps hesitant, as if he was crossing some invisible boundary. "That was... quite the exit," he said, his attempt at humor falling flat.

Maya didn't turn to look at him. "Good. Maybe they'll start asking why."

Ethan sighed loudly, frustration evident in his voice. "Can we just—talk? Like adults?"

Her laugh was sharp, almost cruel in its brevity. "Oh, sure. Maybe I should sign up for obedience classes while we're at it. Learn how to sit pretty and smile so I stop making everything about race. Would that make it easier for you?"

The Great Divide: When Earth Lost Its Shadow

"That's not what I'm saying," Ethan snapped, his voice rising before he caught himself. He stepped closer, tension radiating off him. "Why does it always have to come back to this? We're married, Maya. I'm not your enemy—I'm your husband. I don't know how to fix this," he admitted quietly. "But I don't want to lose you."

Her head tilted slightly, her gaze finally cutting toward him. "Husband?" she repeated, her voice low and icy. "Then why does it feel like I'm doing this alone? Why did you marry me if you can't stand to hear me speak my truth? What does our love even mean to you if I can't feel safe with you?" As the words left her mouth, a pang of sorrow followed. How had their love, once her sanctuary, become this?

Ethan hesitated, the words choking him. "You know... this. The constant... need to point out every little—"

"Microaggression? Racism? Disrespect?" she cut in, her voice quiet but biting. "Yeah, Ethan, that's what this is. It's the air I breathe. The ground I walk on. It's not me bringing it up—it's the world slamming it into my face every damn day. And you don't notice because you don't have to."

He raised his hands, pacing now. "I'm trying, Maya. I'm here. I'm listening. Do you think it's easy for me to feel like I'm failing you every time we argue?"

"Listening?" she scoffed, shaking her head. "No, Ethan. You're defending yourself. There's a difference. And I'm tired of fighting for scraps of understanding from the one person who's supposed to get it."

Ethan stopped pacing, his eyes searching hers. "So... what are you saying? That I'm not enough for you?"

Her expression softened, but her voice remained even. "I'm saying I need space. To think. To breathe. Because right now? I feel like I'm drowning."

"Maya—" he began, his voice cracking, but she raised a hand, halting him mid-sentence.

"Goodnight, Ethan," she said firmly, her words cutting through the tension of the moment. She turned away, her stomps clashing with the hardwood floor as she walked toward their bedroom. Behind her, she heard the faint shuffle of Ethan shifting his weight, but he didn't follow. The gap between them felt wider than the hallway she now crossed.

Once inside the bedroom, the silence closed in around her like a heavy blanket. She moved to the closet, pulling out her suitcase with deliberate care. But as she stood there, her hands resting on the handle, a memory surged to the surface—sharp and clear, unshakable.

It had been six months ago, on the balcony of their apartment. Ethan had been sipping whiskey from a crystal tumbler, his gaze fixed on the city skyline like a man staking claim to his kingdom. Maya had just returned from a panel where she'd been invited to speak as a rising entrepreneur in tech. That night, she had felt invincible—like all the late nights and sacrifices had finally paid off. She had thought Ethan felt the same.

"You killed it out there," Ethan had said, smiling in that way that had once made her feel seen. He handed her a glass of wine and clinked it against his. "To my superstar girlfriend. Thirty Under 30 and everything."

She had laughed, a little giddy, as she leaned against the railing. "Feels like the first time people are really seeing me, you know? Not just what I do, but what I'm capable of."

Ethan's smile had faltered, just for a moment. "Well, you're the perfect face for it," he had said, swirling his whiskey. "Smart, talented, beautiful—and let's be honest, you check all the boxes."

Her laugh caught in her throat. "What do you mean by that?"

"You know," he said casually, as if stating the obvious. "Black, female, in tech. They need people like you for the optics. It's not a bad thing," he added quickly when he saw her face change. "It's just... the reality."

The reality. The words hung between them like a brick wall. His comment stung, not just because of what he'd said, but because she had thought he would understand better. As an Indian man, he'd faced his share of racist comments and subtle exclusions. But he didn't seem to recognize how much heavier her burden was—or maybe he just didn't want to.

"Do you really think that's why I'm here? That my success isn't earned?" she asked, gripping the railing tightly as the skyline blurred before her.

Ethan sighed, rubbing the back of his neck. "Maya, I'm not saying you don't deserve it. I'm just saying it probably helped."

"Helped," she repeated, the word tasting bitter on her tongue. She left the balcony then, and the conversation dissolved into an uneasy silence, one they never fully addressed again.

The memory clung to her like a shadow as Maya stood in their bedroom, packing her suitcase. The argument, the sting of Ethan's words, and the silence that followed swirled in her mind, fueling her resolve. She zipped the bag closed, the sound sharp in the quiet room, and rolled it toward the door. Each movement felt heavier than it should, as if the act of leaving carried a weight she wasn't yet ready to set down.

Ethan was in the hallway, leaning against the wall, his arms crossed. His expression was a mix of frustration and sadness. "Where are you even going?" he asked, his voice low.

She paused, looking around the apartment. The art on the walls, the throw pillows she had picked out, and the coffee mugs they fought over every morning—all reminders of a life that felt impossibly distant. "I don't know yet," she said finally, her voice steady. "But I can't stay here tonight."

In the living room, she hesitated, phone in hand. Her thumb hovered over a booking app, but instead, she swiped to her contacts and dialed Jamal. He picked up on the second ring.

"Maya? It's late. What's going on?"

Her voice cracked. "I just... needed to hear a friendly voice."

Jamal, her older brother and her anchor in moments like this, didn't hesitate. "You're always welcome here. Jean Louis and I just finished dinner. Want to come over?"

Maya hesitated, picturing Jean Louis's calculating gaze. He was kind, but his pragmatic outlook could be exhausting when all she wanted was comfort. Still, the thought of being anywhere but here won out. "Yeah," she said softly. "I'll be there in 20."

Twenty minutes later, Maya found herself in Jamal's warm apartment. Jean Louis greeted her with a glass of chilled viognier, his French accent soft and disarming. "Maya, it's good to see you. Jamal mentioned you've had a rough evening."

She sank into the couch, letting the plush cushions embrace her. "It's been... a night."

Jamal sat beside her, his face etched with quiet concern. "Do you want to talk about it?"

"Not everything," she admitted. "But Ethan... he doesn't get it. He doesn't understand the weight of what I deal with. And worse, he doesn't want to try."

Jean Louis leaned forward, his blue eyes thoughtful. "It can be difficult to bridge those gaps, even with good intentions. In France, we view these issues differently, but that doesn't always mean it's better."

Maya glanced at him. "What do you mean?"

"Privilege is quieter in Europe, but no less insidious," he explained. "I've had to confront it myself, being in a relationship with Jamal. Sometimes, it's about learning to sit with discomfort without getting defensive."

Jamal nodded. "That's true. But Maya, you don't have to carry this alone. You've always been the strong one, but even the strongest people need to breathe."

She exhaled deeply, feeling some of the tension ease. "Thanks. Both of you."

An hour later, Maya left Jamal's apartment, her suitcase rolling behind her. Their words lingered as she walked down the quiet street, the crisp air biting at her skin. It wasn't closure, but it was something—a reminder that she didn't have to go through this alone.

Finally, she booked a temporary hotel room, her fingers moving decisively over the screen. The room was small but comforting, a sanctuary where she could finally breathe. She pulled out her phone again and opened her group chat with Jamal and Sophie.

Maya: London. Next week. You in?

Jamal: Now why didn't you ask this when you were here? You know I'm always down. Details.

Sophie: I'll clear my schedule! Let's talk when I see you.

Maya stared at their replies for a moment, then typed back.

Maya: Just need to get away. We'll talk when I see you.

She placed her phone on the nightstand, feeling a flicker of relief. This was her step forward—not perfect, not final, but hers. Somewhere far from here, a new chapter awaited. And this time, she was ready to write it.

The next morning, Maya checked into the Commodore Perry Estate, a quiet sanctuary in the heart of Austin. The suite's elegant blend of old-world charm and modern luxury offered a welcome pause from the chaos. She set her suitcase on a velvet bench and walked to the window, letting the peaceful scene ease her restless mind.

Her phone buzzed with an incoming call, and she didn't need to check the screen to know who it was.

"Peninsula again?" Jamal's familiar voice teased as she answered.

"Commodore Perry," Maya corrected, smirking as she perched on the edge of the bed. "But maybe both someday. You really invade my privacy with Find Friends."

"It's not invading if you left location sharing on," he shot back, laughing. "So, what's up? You sounded off last night."

Maya leaned back against the headboard, the smile fading as her thoughts turned serious. "It's Ethan. But it's not just him—it's everything. Work. Expectations. That constant uphill climb just to be seen as legitimate. Sometimes, I feel like I'm fighting a battle he doesn't even know exists."

The Great Divide: When Earth Lost Its Shadow

Jamal's voice softened. "He's not walking the same path, Maya. He can't see the world through your eyes. That doesn't mean it's okay, but it means the weight you're carrying—he'll never fully grasp it. The question is, are you okay with that?"

Maya let out a long breath, staring at the textured ceiling. "That's the thing. I don't think I am. And the more I try to explain, the more it feels like I'm talking to a wall."

"You've always been the one to teach people how to meet you where you are," Jamal said. "But that only works if they're willing to learn. Maybe you need to decide if Ethan's willing—or even capable—of doing that."

His words hung in the air, heavy and unspoken, as she mulled them over. Finally, she changed the subject. "What about you? You mentioned a tricky case—something about a reverse discrimination claim?"

Jamal sighed, the sound heavy with frustration. "A White executive claiming diversity quotas cost him a promotion—it's the kind of case that makes you wonder if we've made any real progress. The company's got receipts proving he wasn't qualified, but he's framing himself as the victim."

Maya frowned. "And you're stuck representing him?"

"Yup," Jamal said. "I don't get to choose my clients. And I hate everything about this case—how it feels like a personal attack on the progress we've made. But here's the thing: cases like this are bigger than one person. It's about the precedent they set. If I don't handle this right, it could undo years of work in diversity and inclusion."

Maya could hear the tension in his voice, the weight of the dilemma pressing down on him. "That's why you're one of the best," she said gently. "Because you can see the big picture, even when it's hard. But you don't have to do it alone, Jamal."

He let out a quiet laugh. "I can always count on you for a pep talk."

"It's what I'm here for," she replied. "Now, tell me—how's Jean Louis? Still planning your wedding in his head?"

The next morning, Maya joined Jamal at their favorite café, the light-filled patio buzzing with the hum of Austin's eclectic energy. He was already seated, dressed sharply in a tailored blazer, his tablet open to a page of legal notes. When she approached, he waved her over, sliding a coffee across the table as she sat.

"You look better," he said. "Sleeping in luxury suits you."

Maya smirked, taking a sip of the perfectly brewed latte. "It wasn't just the hotel. Talking to you helped."

"Flattery will get you another croissant," he teased, gesturing to the pastry basket. But his smile faded as she glanced at his notes. "Okay, spill. How bad is this case messing with your head?"

Jamal leaned back, his expression hardening. "Honestly? It's making me question why I'm even doing this. I went to law school to fight for people who didn't have a voice—not for someone who thinks equity is oppression."

Maya studied him, noticing the way his hands fidgeted with the edge of the table. "You know why you're doing this, Jamal. Don't let one client make you doubt that."

He looked at her, a shadow of doubt in his eyes. "Sometimes, it feels like I'm just treading water. Like no matter how hard I fight, there's always another case, another uphill battle. And I'm tired, Maya."

Her gaze softened. "You can be tired, but don't forget who you are. You're the same person who made it through Rollins' class at UW. Remember that day with Dred Scott?"

Jamal groaned, but a faint smile tugged at his lips. "Don't remind me."

The University of Washington's School of Law lecture hall buzzed with heated debate. Professor Rollins, a sharp-eyed woman in her sixties, stood at the front, pointing toward the words Dred Scott v. Sandford on the screen.

"So," she began, her voice slicing through the chatter. "This case ruled that Black Americans, whether free or enslaved, could not be citizens of the United States. Thoughts?"

Jamal, seated near the middle, felt the pressure of every eye fixed on him. He gripped his pen, trying to keep himself steady.

"Mr. Graham," Rollins called, her tone expectant. "Care to share your perspective?"

Jamal hesitated, then stood. "Well, first off, this case was never about justice—it was about maintaining a system that dehumanized an entire group of people. And the fact that it took nearly a century to overturn speaks volumes about how deeply ingrained that system was."

A hand shot up in the front row. A classmate, red-faced and eager. "But wasn't it just a reflection of the time? You can't judge historical figures by modern standards."

Jamal bit back a sharp response, keeping his tone measured. "We don't judge them by modern standards. We judge them by the consequences of their actions. The ruling wasn't just a reflection of its time—it shaped the lives of millions. Ignoring that is how we end up repeating history."

The room grew quiet, the weight of his words settling over the class. Rollins nodded, her expression contemplative. "Thank you, Mr. Graham. A poignant reminder that the law doesn't exist in a vacuum."

"You didn't walk out because you knew you belonged there," Maya said firmly. "And you still do. This case isn't about the client, Jamal—it's about the fight you've been in since UW. Don't lose sight of that."

Jamal shook his head, laughing softly at the memory. "I still can't believe I didn't just walk out that day."

The café hummed with life as the late-morning crowd swirled around them, but for Maya and Jamal, the rest of the world seemed to fade into the background. It was how it always felt when they talked—an unspoken understanding that their connection was constant, no matter how chaotic life became.

"You always know what to say, sis," Jamal said, the tension in his shoulders easing.

"It's a gift," Maya teased, nudging his arm. "Now, tell me when you're landing in London. I need my favorite lawyer there."

Jamal grinned. "Let me get through this case first. Then I'm all yours."

As they lingered over their coffee, Jamal tilted his head toward her. "So, what's next for you? After London, I mean. You're not running from everything forever, right?"

Maya smiled wryly. "No, I'm not running. Just recalibrating. London's more about reconnecting with myself—figuring out what I actually want. Work is steady; I've got a new funding round coming up, and I'm working to expand the pipeline for Black and brown talent in biotech. But the personal stuff... that's where I need to put in the effort."

Jamal raised an eyebrow. "Is it just Ethan? Or have you been putting yourself on the back burner for too long?"

She paused, the question hitting closer to home than she'd expected. "It's not just Ethan," she admitted. "I've been so focused on proving myself in an industry that barely lets me in the door, I haven't stopped to ask if I even want to be in some of these spaces."

"Do you?" Jamal asked, his voice soft but probing.

"I don't know," Maya replied honestly. "I love what I've built, but sometimes it feels like I've tied my identity so tightly to success that I've forgotten who I am without it. And Ethan... he doesn't understand. He thinks my achievements are just wins. But for me, they're proof that I deserve to exist in spaces that weren't made for people like me."

Jamal nodded slowly, his face contemplative. "You deserve to exist, period. You don't have to prove that to anyone, least of all Ethan. And if he doesn't see that..." He let his words trail off, unfinished but clear.

Maya sighed, leaning back in her chair. "It's hard, you know? Admitting that something you've invested so much in might not be the right fit. Whether it's a relationship, a company, or a vision of yourself—it's terrifying to let go."

"But letting go isn't failure," Jamal said softly. "It's growth. And you've never been afraid of that."

The two siblings parted ways an hour later, Maya feeling lighter but still lost in thought. She spent the afternoon wandering through the city, her mind drifting between past choices and future possibilities. By evening, she found herself back at the hotel, sipping wine on the terrace as the city lights flickered to life.

Her phone buzzed on the table. It was Ethan.

Maya stared at the screen, her thumb hovering over the green icon before letting the call go to voicemail. She needed space—not more half-hearted apologies or attempts to justify his actions.

Instead, she texted Jamal:

Maya: Dinner tomorrow? I need to hear more about this case.

He replied almost immediately:

Jamal: Only if you pick the place. And make it fancy. You've got Commodore Perry money.

Maya chuckled softly, setting her phone down. Despite everything swirling in her life, she was grateful for Jamal's steady presence. He had his own struggles, but he always found time for her.

They met at Aba, a chic Mediterranean restaurant with a sprawling patio and a menu that could've been plucked from a food magazine. Jamal arrived early, scrolling through his tablet while sipping an Old Fashioned. Maya joined him a few minutes later, her outfit sharp and effortless, radiating the quiet confidence she had honed over years of being underestimated.

"Alright, big spender," Jamal teased as she sat down. "What's the occasion?"

"No occasion," Maya replied, picking up the menu. "Just thought we could both use a good meal after the weeks we've had."

The Great Divide: When Earth Lost Its Shadow

Jamal smirked. "Fair enough. I'm not complaining if you're paying."

As they ordered and settled into the warm ambiance, Maya steered the conversation back to Jamal's case. "So, tell me more about this tech exec. What's his angle?"

Jamal leaned back, his expression hardening. "He's been with the company for years, and his performance has been... fine. Not stellar, not terrible. But when a leadership position opened up, they gave it to a younger, Black woman instead of him."

"And he assumes it's because of her race," Maya said, her voice tinged with frustration.

"Exactly," Jamal replied. "Never mind that she's twice as qualified, with a track record that puts his to shame. He's convinced the only reason he didn't get the promotion is because of the company's diversity initiatives. He keeps throwing around terms like 'meritocracy' and 'reverse racism' like they're magic words."

Maya rolled her eyes. "Classic. So, what's your strategy?"

Jamal sighed, stirring the ice in his drink. "Honestly, I'm walking a tightrope. I have to defend him because it's my job, but I also have to challenge the idea that diversity initiatives are inherently unfair. It's exhausting."

"Sounds like it's more than just exhausting," Maya said, watching him closely. "You're questioning whether this is the kind of work you want to do, aren't you?"

He hesitated, then nodded. "Yeah. I went into this field to fight for equity—to make workplaces better for people who've been excluded for far too long. But this case... it's making me feel like a cog in the same machine I've been trying to break down."

Maya reached across the table, squeezing his hand. "You're not a cog, Jamal. You're the one steering the damn machine. And even if this case sucks, it doesn't erase the good you've done—or the good you'll keep doing."

Jamal smiled faintly, her words bolstering him in a way few others could. "Thanks, sis. I needed that."

As they lingered over dessert, the conversation shifted. Jamal tilted his head toward her. "So, what's the plan after this? Heading straight back to work?"

Maya hesitated, swirling the last of her latte. "Not yet. I'm going to London next week."

Jamal raised an eyebrow. "London? That's sudden."

"Not really," Maya said, a small smile tugging at her lips. "London's been calling me for months. I need a change of scenery—somewhere that doesn't feel like a constant reminder of who I'm supposed to be. Plus, Sophie's been nagging me to visit, and I figured some time with friends might help clear my head."

Jamal nodded thoughtfully. "London's got that vibe. Just don't let Sophie talk you into one of her six-hour gallery tours."

Maya chuckled softly. "I'll try, but you know Sophie."

Jamal smirked but quickly caught himself, his expression shifting. "Speaking of news, did you hear about the travel system crash today?"

Maya frowned. "No. What happened?"

"Global chaos," Jamal said, scrolling through his phone. "Every major transportation system—planes, trains, even shipping—just shut down this morning. Networks went offline, and no one knows why. People are stranded everywhere."

Maya's eyebrows shot up. Her mind drifted, uncomfortably linking the chaos outside to the cracks forming in her own life. Everything felt so fragile.

"Cyberattack is the popular theory," Jamal continued. "But some experts think it was just an overload or a perfect storm of system failures. Either way, airports, train stations, even docks are packed. It's like the world's on pause."

Maya shook her head slowly. "That's... eerie. One glitch, and everything stops. It feels so fragile."

"Because it is," Jamal said. "It's a reminder of how fragile everything is, Maya. One glitch, and the world grinds to a halt."

"Great. Just what I needed—existential dread to go with my latte," Maya said dryly, though a flicker of unease passed through her.

"It's probably nothing," Jamal said with a shrug. "We'll forget about it in a week."

But as the conversation drifted to lighter topics—memories from their childhood, plans for Maya's London trip, and Jean Louis's increasingly extravagant ideas for a future wedding—Maya couldn't quite shake the nagging feeling that things were shifting in ways she couldn't yet grasp.

Later that evening, as Maya stood by the window of her suite, the city lights flickered like restless thoughts she couldn't quite chase away. The quiet luxury of the room gave her space to think, but her mind refused to settle. Her conversation with Jamal played on a loop, his words cutting through her usual defenses.

"You don't have to prove anything to anyone, least of all Ethan," he'd said.

It was a sobering thought, one that left her feeling as untethered as the city lights blinking below her window.

She turned away from the window and picked up her phone. The screen glowed softly as she scrolled through her group chat with Sophie and Jamal. She paused on her last message:

Maya: London. Next week. You in?

The thought of London felt like a breath of fresh air. The city's rhythm was nothing like Austin's, and being surrounded by Sophie's eclectic group of friends might give her the perspective she needed. Maybe there, with the distance and the noise of another world, she'd find some clarity.

The distant hum of the city seemed sharper, its usual rhythm unsettling rather than comforting. She couldn't explain it, but the air felt heavier, like a quiet tension building just out of reach. Shaking off the thought, she slipped under the covers, exhaustion pulling her into uneasy sleep.

What she didn't know was how much more the world was about to shift.

Chapter 2: A Dissonant Harmony

The taxi trundled down a rain-slicked London street, its headlights scattering across fragmented pools of water. Maya sat stiffly in the back seat, one hand clutching the strap of her favorite Louis Vuitton bag, the other pressed against the cold glass window. The city's constant hum surrounded her—an intricate orchestra of car horns, distant sirens, and pedestrian chatter. London always seemed to pulse with its own unique rhythm, a rhythm Maya admired but rarely felt in sync with.

As the taxi pulled up in front of a narrow, ivy-covered townhouse, Maya let out a slow breath. Relief and trepidation churned in her stomach. Sophie had insisted on hosting her, as she always did, eager to wrap Maya in her whirlwind energy. But the weight she'd been carrying for months—grief, anger, exhaustion—seemed to amplify the emotional risk of even the smallest kindness.

Dragging her suitcase over the cobblestones, Maya paused to take in the townhouse. The bright red door stood out like a cheerful defiance against the dreary gray evening. She reached for the knocker, but before her hand could connect, the door burst open, and Sophie spilled onto the stoop like a human firework.

"Maya!" Sophie's voice rang out, joy lighting up her freckled face. She wore a flowing patchwork dress that ignored both season and logic, her auburn curls bouncing as she flung herself forward to wrap Maya in a bear hug.

"You're finally here!" Sophie exclaimed, stepping back but still gripping Maya's arms. "You look fantastic. Clearly, traveling agrees with you."

Maya smiled faintly, the corners of her mouth betraying her exhaustion. "Thanks. You, uh... still look like Sophie."

Sophie smirked. "I'll take that as a compliment!" Without giving Maya a chance to protest, she grabbed the suitcase. "Come on, let's get you inside. Jamal's in the kitchen whipping up his famous tea. He swears it cures everything—jet lag, bad moods, even heartbreak."

Maya followed her into the house, immediately enveloped by the warmth of Sophie's space. It was as much a reflection of her personality as her words: unapologetically bold and vibrant. The walls were a riot of color—Sophie's own photography interspersed with protest posters and an eclectic mix of art prints. Bookshelves groaned under the weight of well-worn novels, radical manifestos, and political essays. A faint crackle came from a corner where a vintage record player spun a jaunty Ragtime tune.

"This place..." Maya shook her head, letting her eyes wander. "It's like stepping into your brain."

"Messy but brilliant?" Sophie teased, breezing toward the kitchen. "That's the goal."

Before Maya could reply, Jamal appeared in the doorway, carrying two steaming mugs. He was a steady contrast to Sophie, his calm energy grounding the vibrant chaos around him.

The Great Divide: When Earth Lost Its Shadow

"Hey, Maya," he said with a quiet smile, handing her one of the mugs. "Not sure how you survived the latter part of the week without me, but welcome to London."

Maya smirked faintly, holding the warm mug between her hands. "Barely made it," she replied. "And don't worry, your absence was not noted—Jean Louis filled in with wine and unsolicited advice."

Jamal chuckled, settling into the chair across from her. "Sounds like him. And you? Doing okay?"

She hesitated, her eyes drifting over the vibrant chaos of Sophie's living room. "Trying to be. It's... better. Distance helps."

Jamal nodded, his expression softening. "Sometimes you need space to see things clearly. You've been in fight mode since your rose gold glasses were removed, Maya. You're allowed to step back for a minute."

From the kitchen, Sophie's voice broke through, teasing and light. "Is this tea time or therapy? Don't hog her, Jamal—I'm next."

Jamal's lips twitched into a faint smile. "You'd think she'd mellow out after all these years," he murmured, his tone warm with affection. "But seriously, Maya—whatever you need while you're here, you've got it. Whether it's Sophie's chaos, my steady hand, or just silence, we're here-ish."

Maya let herself relax into the moment, the weight of his words settling around her like a protective shield. "Thanks, Jamal," she said softly. "And thanks for picking up last week. I really needed that."

"Who else are you going to call? One of your flighty best friends or a brother who knows it all?" he said, his voice steady and sincere. "Though next time, let's skip the existential crises and go straight to dinner. Or croissants. Something less emotionally taxing."

Maya laughed, the sound lightening the room. "Deal."

Sophie appeared from the kitchen, a plate of mismatched cookies in her hand. "Alright, enough brooding. We're here, together, and that's all that matters." She plopped down beside Maya, nudging her shoulder. "Now spill. What's the plan for London? Are we doing galleries, rooftop bars, or both?"

Maya shook her head, the corners of her mouth twitching upward. "I'm just here to breathe, Sophie. No six-hour art tours."

Jamal smirked. "See? She knows better."

Sophie gasped in mock offense. "You're both so rude! But fine. Breathing it is. With a side of fun."

As the conversation swirled around her, Maya felt a small knot in her chest begin to loosen. This wasn't a solution—not yet. But it was a start. And for now, that was enough.

Jamal's voice cut through the volume of Sophie's record player, gentle but probing. "You've got that look again."

Maya blinked, turning toward him. "What look?"

He tilted his head slightly, studying her. "The one where you're here, but not really. What's going on?"

Her gaze fell to her tea, the steam curling upward in soft tendrils. She hesitated, her fingers tracing the edge of the mug. "Nothing. Just... memories."

Jamal nodded, as if waiting for her to elaborate but knowing better than to push. "Funny thing about memories," he said quietly. "They're always there, even when you think you've moved past them. But sometimes, looking back helps you figure out what's next."

Maya sighed, her lips curving into a faint, humorless smile. "Always the philosopher."

"Only when it counts," he replied lightly. But his tone shifted as he added, "Where'd your head go, Maya? You can tell me."

Her gaze shifted, landing on a framed photograph near the window. It was Sophie at her most Sophie: standing in the center of a crowd, megaphone raised triumphantly, her auburn curls wild with determination. The photo was unmistakable—Harborville.

Maya felt the memory slam into her with the force of a rogue wave, pulling her under before she could catch her breath. That day had been a turning point for Sophie, an awakening. For Maya, it had been something far heavier: survival.

She stared at the photo, her throat tightening. "That rally... Sophie always called it the day she found her voice. For me? It was the day I realized mine will never matter."

Jamal's brow furrowed, his silence urging her to continue. But Maya couldn't bring herself to say more. The past was clawing its way to the surface, vivid and raw.

The room around her seemed to fade, the edges of Sophie's vibrant world dissolving as the memory took over. She was back in Harborville, the heat of the summer sun pressing down, the weight of the moment nearly suffocating. The chants, the signs, the faces—they all came rushing back, as real and as unrelenting as they had been that day.

It had been the summer of Harborville.

The news had been impossible to avoid. Footage of torch-carrying white supremacists marching through the streets had sparked a national outcry. For days, the headlines were filled with their hateful slogans, their smug faces illuminated by flames. When a counter-protester was killed, Maya's simmering anger hardened into quiet resolve.

She'd been visiting Jamal at his university that week, where he was buried in textbooks for his course on race and law. The walls of his small apartment were stacked with casebooks on employment and labor systems, the kinds of injustices they had both grown up witnessing firsthand. Maya had found him at the kitchen table, highlighting passages with the same focused intensity he brought to every problem he wanted to solve.

"Jamal," Maya said, holding up her phone with a flyer on the screen. "There's a solidarity rally downtown this weekend. We have to go."

Jamal set down his pen, glancing at the flyer. His brow furrowed. "You know it's going to be tense, right? The police will be there in full force. It could turn ugly."

"And what's the alternative?" Maya asked, her voice gentle but firm. "Staying home and pretending this doesn't affect us? That we're safe?"

Jamal leaned back, rubbing his temples. "We aren't safe, and you know that. I'm just saying... We've seen what happens when tensions boil over. I want to go, but we have to be smart about it."

Maya softened, placing her hand on his arm. "We'll be smart. But we have to show up. If we don't, who will?"

Jamal sighed, his shoulders relaxing slightly. He rarely argued with Maya when her tone was like this—not sharp, but steady, anchored in her unwavering belief in doing what was right.

On the morning of the rally, Sophie had been the wild card. She arrived unannounced, a bright scarf tied around her head and a canvas bag slung over her shoulder, filled with water bottles and granola bars. She greeted them both with a determined smile.

"I'm coming with you," Sophie said firmly, setting the bag down on Jamal's kitchen counter.

Maya blinked at her in surprise. "Sophie, you don't have to—"

"Yes, I do," Sophie interrupted, her tone resolute. "This is too important to sit out."

Maya glanced at Jamal, who shrugged slightly, his expression unreadable. Maya turned back to Sophie and nodded, choosing not to argue. She knew Sophie's heart was in the right place, even if her enthusiasm sometimes felt disconnected from the deeper realities of what they were walking into.

The rally began peacefully. A sea of people filled the square in Harborville's historic downtown, their voices rising in unison with chants that echoed off the old brick buildings. Maya stood between Jamal and Sophie, gripping her sign that read, Justice Is the Bare Minimum. For a moment, she felt a surge of hope. The unity of the crowd, the rhythm of their chants—it was powerful, almost healing.

Sophie held her own sign, Silence Is Violence, her voice loud and unwavering as she joined the chants. Maya glanced at her and saw the fire in her eyes, a passion that was undeniably genuine. It was easy to forget, in moments like this, that Sophie had the privilege of seeing this as a choice. Maya and Jamal didn't have that luxury.

As the sun dipped lower in the sky, the mood shifted. A group of counter-protesters appeared at the edge of the square, their presence like a storm cloud rolling in. Maya's chest tightened as she spotted the Confederate flags and crude, hand-painted symbols of hate. The jeers from the group grew louder, their venomous words cutting through the rally's chants.

"Stay close," Jamal murmured to Maya, his tone low but steady. Maya nodded, instinctively reaching for his arm. She had seen this before—the energy of a protest changing in an instant, the thin line between solidarity and chaos.

Sophie, however, surged forward, her scarf trailing behind her like a flag. "No! We can't let them intimidate us!" she shouted, her voice ringing out above the crowd.

"Sophie, wait!" Maya called after her, panic rising in her throat. She pushed through the throng, her heart pounding as she fought to reach her friend.

It happened so quickly. A shout, a shove, the crackle of a police radio. Maya turned just in time to see Sophie stumble backward, her face pale with shock as an officer stepped between her and the advancing counter-protesters. The officer's hand rested on his baton, his posture stiff and unyielding.

"You need to move," the officer said, his voice cold and detached.

"But they're the ones—" Sophie began, her voice breaking with indignation.

"Move, now," the officer barked.

Maya reached Sophie just in time, grabbing her arm and pulling her back into the crowd. Sophie resisted, her eyes blazing. "Maya, we can't just leave! This is why we're here!"

"And getting arrested—or worse—won't change that!" Maya said, her voice firm but soft.

"Sophie, listen to me. You can walk away from this. I can't. Jamal can't."

Sophie froze, her breath catching as Maya's words sank in. For a moment, the noise of the rally faded into the background, leaving only the sound of their uneven breathing.

Jamal appeared beside them, his face grim. "We need to go," he said quietly, his tone leaving no room for argument.

Maya nodded, her grip on Sophie's hand tightening as they maneuvered through the crowd, away from the rising tension. Behind them, the chants grew louder, angrier, as the counter-protesters pressed closer. Maya didn't look back.

Even then, Jamal had been the steady one—the anchor Maya could rely on when the chaos threatened to pull them under. She hadn't understood it fully at the time, but she saw it now: Jamal had always been playing the long game.

Maya blinked, the vivid memory fading. She set her tea down, her fingers curling into the fabric of the couch. Sophie's voice cut through the haze as she reappeared, balancing a plate of cookies and another mug.

"Maya, you're doing it again," Sophie teased, flopping onto the couch beside her.

"Doing what?"

"Getting all broody and serious," Sophie said, nudging her playfully. "Relax, tonight's going to be incredible—you'll see."

Maya managed a faint smile. Sophie's optimism was relentless, almost disarming. But Maya couldn't forget Harborville, or the way their friendship had been tested that day. The photograph lingered in her peripheral vision like a ghost of the past, a reminder of all the conversations they still hadn't had.

"We'll see," Maya said quietly, reaching for a cookie. "Let's see if this play is as life-changing as you say it is."

Jamal, who had been listening quietly from the corner, caught Maya's eye. His steady presence was like an anchor in the swirl of Sophie's energy. Whatever the night held, Maya knew he'd be there to steady her.

The theater was a relic of London's gilded age, its facade adorned with intricate carvings that seemed to whisper secrets of a bygone era. Inside, the scent of polished brass, old wood, and the faint tang of red wine mingled in the air. It was a place that held stories—many untold, some forgotten. Maya walked slowly, taking in the vaulted ceilings and ornate chandeliers. The space seemed to hum with anticipation, but to her, it felt layered with contradictions.

"Isn't this place incredible?" Sophie asked, leaning in close as they navigated the bustling crowd. Her voice was tinged with awe, her eyes sparkling as she gestured toward the intricate molding above. "It's been here since the 1800s. Imagine all the stories it's seen."

Maya nodded absently, her attention drifting to the people around her. The audience was a vibrant mix—a reflection of London's multicultural heartbeat. Yet, beneath the surface, Maya couldn't help but notice the subtle divides. Who came dressed in tailored coats and carefully chosen jewelry versus those who had arrived in practical, worn layers? Who spoke in polished accents and easy confidence, and who shifted quietly, navigating the space with an air of caution?

She caught snippets of conversation as they passed through the crowd. A young couple discussing the symbolism of the production, a trio of older patrons reminiscing about the theater's golden days. There were moments of warmth, but also of discomfort—a misplaced comment, a lingering glance that suggested someone didn't quite belong.

Maya's chest tightened. Spaces like these always made her feel both visible and invisible. The theater itself was stunning, but it carried with it the weight of a history that hadn't been written for people like her. She wondered how many of the "stories it had seen" were stories of exclusion.

Sophie's voice broke into her thoughts. "Oh! Let me introduce you to everyone," she said, her enthusiasm boundless.

They reached their seats in the middle of the orchestra section, and Sophie began her introductions like a host at a dinner party. "This is Claire—she's an artist specializing in installation work. Raj is a community organizer. And Shanti, over there, is an urban historian. Total genius."

Maya smiled politely as she greeted each of them, but her thoughts remained elsewhere. The introductions felt curated, like Sophie was assembling pieces of an idealized puzzle—a group that reflected the diverse, socially aware world she aspired to inhabit. It wasn't that Sophie's intentions weren't genuine, but sometimes, it felt like she was trying to present a version of herself to the world that didn't fully account for its messier truths.

"Nice to meet you," Maya said softly, though her tone carried a hint of detachment.

Sophie didn't seem to notice, already launching into a conversation with Claire about the theater's architecture. Maya took her seat and let her gaze wander. The stage loomed ahead, stark and industrial, with backdrops that hinted at the stories waiting to unfold. She exhaled slowly, trying to shake off the weight pressing down on her.

The house lights dimmed, and a ripple of quiet fell over the audience. The opening notes of a piano filled the air—haunting and deliberate. The stage was set with sepia-toned projections of tenement buildings and gritty streets, interwoven with abstract industrial imagery. Actors moved like shadows through the set, their voices rising in a melody that carried both pain and resilience.

The play began in the early 20th century, its narrative intertwining the lives of Black musicians, immigrant families, and wealthy industrialists. Maya leaned forward slightly, drawn into the stark portrayals of systemic oppression. The characters' struggles were visceral and unflinching—a Black pianist pouring his soul into music, only for a white impresario to steal both his work and his dignity; an immigrant mother sewing late into the night, her hands raw and blistered, trying to keep her children fed.

Maya felt the stories echoing in her chest, their weight pulling at memories she tried not to revisit. The Black musician's plight brought to mind people she knew back home—brilliant but boxed in by systems designed to exploit their brilliance. The immigrant mother's quiet desperation reminded her of neighbors who had fought for years just to scrape by, only to see their victories overshadowed by unrelenting struggle.

The narrative shifted abruptly, jolting the audience into the present. The sepia tones disappeared, replaced by vivid projections of modern cityscapes. Spoken word performers took the stage, their words raw and biting. They called out police brutality, cultural appropriation, economic disparity, the ghosts of the past haunting the present in new forms. The rhythm of their voices was relentless, each line landing like a blow.

Maya's hands gripped the edges of her seat. She glanced at Jamal, who sat rigid beside her, his jaw clenched and his brow furrowed. His reaction mirrored her own—an uncomfortable familiarity with the pain the performers laid bare.

By the time the final note rang out, the audience rose to its feet, their applause thunderous. Sophie was one of the first to stand, clapping enthusiastically, her face alight with inspiration. Maya, however, remained seated, her hands folded tightly in her lap.

Sophie turned to her, her voice brimming with emotion. "Wasn't that incredible? It's just so important to acknowledge our privilege and do the work to be better."

Maya glanced up at her, her expression unreadable. "Acknowledgment is easy," she said coolly. "The work is harder."

The restaurant was small and intimate, its dim candlelight casting uneven shadows over the mismatched plates and scarred wooden tables. A low murmur of conversation filled the space, punctuated by the occasional clink of cutlery. Outside, London's streets pulsed with energy, but here, in the subdued warmth of the restaurant, the group felt momentarily distanced from the outside world.

Maya sat between Sophie and Jamal at the long wooden table, her hands wrapped around a glass of wine she had yet to taste. She listened in silence as Sophie animatedly recounted her favorite moments from the play, her voice rich with excitement. The evening had begun with lighthearted chatter, laughter, and shared stories, and Sophie thrived in the lively atmosphere—expressive, assured, and steering the conversation with ease.

"I mean, that scene with the piano player?" Sophie leaned forward, gesturing with her fork. "The way they used silence to emphasize his loss—it was brilliant. Absolutely haunting."

Claire, seated across from her, nodded slowly. "It's incredible how they took something historical and made it feel immediate. Like... you can't watch that and not feel compelled to do something."

Jamal, who had been quiet until now, glanced at Maya as if to gauge her response. She arched an eyebrow but remained silent. He held her gaze for a moment—a quiet reminder to pace herself, to wait for the right moment. But as the conversation deepened and the wine kept pouring, Maya felt frustration creeping in, curling tight in her chest.

Claire traced the rim of her glass with one finger, her voice turning thoughtful. "I just keep thinking about how crucial this moment feels," she said. "Everything is connected in ways we can't ignore. It's overwhelming, but also... it makes you want to believe change is possible."

"Inspiring?" Maya's voice was quiet but sharp, slicing through the conversation like a blade. "Maybe for some. For others, it's exhausting."

The table fell silent. Sophie's gaze darted to Maya, her smile faltering. Claire set her glass down with a small frown. "Well, isn't awareness the first step?"

Maya leaned back in her chair, her expression unreadable. "It's not the last," she said evenly. "The play was about lives

The Great Divide: When Earth Lost Its Shadow

being torn apart by systems designed to do exactly that. Applauding it doesn't dismantle those systems."

The words lingered, dense and unshaken. Sophie shifted in her seat, her fingers twisting in her lap. "But isn't that why we're here?" she asked softly. "To learn, to grow?"

Maya exhaled, her tone easing just slightly. "Learning is step one, Sophie. Growth takes action."

Jamal leaned forward, his voice steady as he cut through the rising tension. "What Maya's saying is that art is a catalyst, not a solution. Being moved by a performance doesn't mean the work is done. It's just the beginning."

Sophie nodded slowly, her confidence visibly wavering. "But isn't it important to start somewhere? To use that feeling as motivation?"

As Maya spoke, Sophie felt a sting of discomfort. It wasn't the first time she'd been reminded of how different their experiences were. But the longer she listened, the more she realized discomfort wasn't something to resist—it was something to learn from.

"Sure," Maya said, her tone steady now. "If it leads to something real. But too often, it doesn't. People clap, they feel good about themselves, and then they go back to their lives. Nothing changes."

Claire's discomfort was unmistakable. She shifted in her seat, tucking a strand of hair behind her ear as if searching for a way to pull the conversation back to safer ground. "I guess it's just... it's hard to know where to begin," she said, her voice hesitant. "There's so much that needs to change."

Jamal's gaze softened as he met her eyes. "You start where you are," he said. "You use what you have. It's not about solving everything at once—it's about making an impact."

Claire tilted her head, her brows drawing together. "But what if you don't even know where to begin? What if it just feels... too big?"

Jamal glanced at Maya, something unspoken passing between them. He turned back to Claire, his voice steady. "It's always going to feel like too much. That's the nature of the fight. But the key is realizing that small actions create momentum—if you're intentional."

Maya studied him, her frustration momentarily giving way to curiosity. His words struck a familiar chord, echoing something deeper. It wasn't the first time Jamal had spoken about the long game, but tonight, she found herself wondering if there was more to it than she'd ever realized. She tucked the thought away, deciding to ask him later.

Sophie's usual buoyancy had dimmed, but she wasn't ready to let the conversation end. "Maya," she said carefully, "isn't there something to be said for people trying? Even if it's imperfect? If someone like Claire is moved enough to have this conversation, isn't that progress?"

Maya exhaled, setting her glass down. "Trying isn't enough if it stops at words, Sophie. The play ends, the lights come up, and nothing outside this room changes. That's what frustrates me."

Sophie's face fell, and she started to respond, but Jamal spoke first. "Maya's not saying the effort isn't valuable," he said gently. "She's saying it can't stop there. If it does, it's not effort—it's performance."

Claire stiffened slightly, her discomfort shifting into defensiveness. "That feels unfair," she said, her tone tightening. "Some of us are doing the best we can. Not everyone can just throw themselves into activism."

Maya's gaze softened, her voice losing its earlier sharpness. "I'm not asking everyone to go all in. I'm asking people to be honest about what they're willing to do—and what they're not."

The table fell silent again. Maya turned to Sophie, her tone gentler now. "I know you're trying. And I do appreciate that. But sometimes, it's hard to explain what it's like to live inside the system we're talking about. To know it wasn't built for you—that it's actively working against you."

Jamal broke the silence, his voice thoughtful. "It's a long game," he said. "And we all have different roles to play. What matters is that we keep playing."

Sophie nodded slowly, her earlier exuberance subdued. "I'll keep trying," she said quietly. "I promise."

As the group drifted apart outside the restaurant, Sophie lingered near the doorway, her scarf shifting in the crisp night air. Maya and Jamal walked ahead, their figures dissolving into the glow of the streetlamps. Sophie hesitated, her earlier confidence replaced by a gnawing sense of inadequacy.

Maya's words echoed in her mind: "Learning is step one. Growth takes action."

She pulled her coat tighter, as if shielding herself from the weight of that truth. Was she doing enough? Did her efforts truly make a difference, or were they just another way to quiet her own guilt? The questions pressed in, leaving her more unsettled than she wanted to admit.

Finally, she exhaled, her breath curling into the night. Maybe tonight had been uncomfortable, but that discomfort felt necessary. Urgent. She resolved to start with what she could control—listening more closely, asking herself harder questions. It wasn't everything, but it was a beginning.

Sophie leaned forward, her hands clasped on the table. "But Maya, isn't there something to be said for people trying? Even if it's imperfect? If people like Claire are moved enough to have this conversation, isn't that progress?"

Maya sighed, her grip tightening around her glass. "Trying isn't enough if it stops at words, Sophie. The play ends, the lights come up, and nothing outside this room changes. That's what frustrates me."

Sophie opened her mouth to respond, but Jamal spoke first, his tone quiet but firm. "Maya's not saying the effort isn't valuable. She's saying it can't stop there. If it does, it's not effort—it's just talk."

Claire bristled. "That feels unfair. Some of us are doing the best we can. Not everyone can just dive headfirst into activism."

Maya's gaze softened slightly. "I'm not asking everyone to dive in headfirst. I'm asking people to be honest about what they're willing to do—and what they're not."

Sophie looked between them, her expression pained. "But isn't having these conversations part of the work?"

"It's part of it," Jamal said, his voice measured. "But it's not the whole picture. Conversations like…"

Maya leaned back, exhaling slowly. "You don't know how many times I've had this conversation," she said, her voice softer now. "And how many times it's led nowhere. I'm tired of hoping it'll be different."

Sophie reached out, placing a hand on Maya's arm. "I'm listening," she said quietly. "Even if it feels like I don't get it, I'm trying."

Maya glanced at Sophie, her expression softening. "I know you are. And I appreciate that. But sometimes it's hard to explain what it feels like to live inside the system we're talking about. To know it wasn't built for you, and that it's actively working against you."

The table fell silent again, the heaviness of Maya's words settling over them. Jamal reached for his water glass, breaking the tension with a quiet, reflective statement. "It's a long game," he said. "And we're all playing different roles. What matters is that we keep playing."

Sophie nodded slowly, her buoyant energy dimmed but not extinguished. "I'll keep trying," she said, her voice almost a whisper. "I promise."

The air outside was sharp and crisp, carrying the faint tang of rain that always seemed to linger in London. Maya stepped out of the restaurant ahead of the group, her arms crossed tightly against the cold. The laughter and chatter spilling from the door behind her felt like an intrusion on the quiet unease that had settled in her chest.

Jamal followed a few paces behind, his hands tucked into his jacket pockets. He had been silent for most of the evening, his calm presence a counterpoint to the tension between Maya and Sophie. Now, as the group said their goodbyes and went their separate ways, Maya turned to him.

"Walk with me?" she asked, her voice softer than usual.

Jamal nodded, falling into step beside her. They moved through the quiet streets, the glow of street lamps reflecting off the slick pavement. The hum of distant traffic was the only sound between them at first, but the tension from the dinner lingered, unspoken but palpable.

Finally, Maya broke the silence. "You were quiet at dinner," she said, glancing at him.

As they walked, the city's familiar hum surrounded them, a mixture of distant car horns, echoing footsteps, and murmured conversations. Above them, the streetlights flickered intermittently, casting long, uneven shadows on the pavement. Maya glanced up at the hazy night sky, her gaze catching a faint streak of light—a shooting star, or perhaps just the flash of an airplane. It was impossible to tell.

"Do you ever feel like we're just... chasing something we'll never catch?" she asked, her voice quieter now. The words hung between them, fragile and unguarded.

Jamal followed her gaze upward, his expression thoughtful. "All the time," he admitted. "But that's why you have to keep moving. Even if the path isn't clear."

The faint light in the sky faded, swallowed by the haze, but its brief spark lingered in Maya's thoughts as they continued walking.

"I said my piece," Jamal replied, his voice calm but even. He didn't look at her.

"You said the safe thing," Maya countered, her tone not accusatory but insistent. "You could've pushed harder."

Jamal exhaled, his breath visible in the cold night air. "Not every conversation needs to be a fight, Maya. You've got to meet people where they are."

Maya stopped walking abruptly, turning to face him. Her voice sharpened. "And where's that? Comfortable in their privilege?"

Jamal paused, studying her with a patience that only made her frustration grow. "I know you're angry," he said finally, his tone steady. "But not everyone is ready to dive in headfirst. I wasn't. You know that."

The Great Divide: When Earth Lost Its Shadow

Maya's expression softened slightly, though the tension in her posture remained. "You've never told me why, Jamal. Why you didn't take the activist route after law school. You were better at it than me. People listened to you."

Jamal looked down, his shoulders slumping slightly. The question had lingered between them for years, unspoken but ever-present. Now, in the cool quiet of the London streets, it demanded an answer.

"It wasn't that simple," he said finally, his voice quiet. "And I think you already know why."

Maya shook her head, taking a step closer to him. "I don't, Jamal. All I know is that you were brilliant at it—better than I ever was. And then you just... stopped."

He looked at her then, his eyes filled with a mix of weariness and resolve. "It's not about stopping," he said. "It's about deciding where you're most useful. That's what Simmons helped me understand."

Maya frowned, tilting her head. "Simmons? Your professor?"

Jamal nodded, a faint smile tugging at the corner of his mouth. "Yeah. He... let's just say he gave me some clarity."

Maya raised an eyebrow, sensing the beginning of a story she'd never heard before. "What kind of clarity?"

Jamal sighed, glancing away. For a moment, it seemed like he wasn't going to answer. Then he spoke, his words measured and deliberate.

"Let me tell you about the spring of my senior year."

It had been the spring of Jamal's senior year, and the campus was alive with protests. Another unjust verdict had shocked the nation, and students poured into the quad to demand change. Jamal found himself at the forefront of the movement, not because he sought leadership, but because people naturally gravitated toward his calm presence.

The rally that day had been one of the largest in the school's history. Hundreds of students filled the square, their voices rising in unison, their signs a patchwork of demands for justice. Jamal had felt the raw power of collective action, the surge of hope that came with standing together against something so deeply wrong. But beneath the adrenaline was an ever-growing burden—a gnawing doubt about whether they were moving the needle.

After hours of marching and chanting, Jamal returned to his small apartment off campus, his body aching and his mind buzzing with unanswered questions. He sank into the couch, staring blankly at the stack of books on his coffee table: legal texts, historical analyses, and activist essays. Each one offered solutions, but none seemed big enough to dismantle the systems they were up against.

A knock at the door broke his reverie. When Jamal opened it, he found Professor Simmons standing on the stoop, holding a worn leather briefcase. Simmons was a wiry, older man with thinning white hair and wire-rimmed glasses that always seemed slightly askew. He taught civil rights law and had spent decades litigating landmark cases, but his demeanor was unassuming, almost awkward.

"Thought I might find you here," Simmons said, stepping inside uninvited but not unwelcome. He glanced at the books on the table and gave a faint smile. "Heavy reading for a heavy day."

Jamal closed the door and leaned against it, crossing his arms. "What are you doing here, Professor?"

Simmons set his briefcase down and shrugged. "I was at the rally. Saw you leading the chants." He paused, his eyes narrowing slightly. "You looked good out there. Confident. People listen to you."

Jamal didn't reply. He moved to the couch and sat down, his posture tense. "It doesn't feel like it's enough," he said after a moment. "We chant, we march, but the system's still there. It doesn't change."

Simmons pulled up a chair, sitting on its edge with his elbows resting on his knees. "That's the thing about systems," he said, his voice low and measured. "They're like rivers. They don't just stop because you throw a rock in. But sometimes, if you throw the right rock, you can change the flow."

Jamal frowned, rubbing his temples. "I don't think I'm throwing the right rocks. What's the point of all this if nothing moves?"

"Ah," Simmons said, leaning back in his chair. "The age-old question: protest or policy? Immediate action or long-term strategy?" He gave a small, wry smile. "I've been asking myself that same question for forty years."

Jamal glanced at him, surprised. Simmons rarely talked about his own experiences, preferring to focus on teaching. "And what did you decide?"

Simmons shrugged. "Both are necessary. But you can't do everything. You have to figure out where you're most effective. Some people are born to be in the streets, rallying the troops. Others are better off in the courtroom, where they can make the rules bend—sometimes even break."

He gestured to the books on Jamal's table. "You've got the mind for the latter. You see the bigger picture. The structure. If you wanted to, you could be in the rooms where the decisions get made, where the laws get written. And that's not nothing, Jamal."

Jamal felt a pang of discomfort. "It's not that simple, though. Isn't that just working within the system we're trying to tear down?"

"It can be," Simmons admitted. "But it doesn't have to be. Working within the system doesn't mean you agree with it. It means you understand it well enough to dismantle it. It's like playing chess. If you don't know the rules, you can't win."

Jamal leaned forward, resting his elbows on his knees. "And if I lose?"

Simmons chuckled, a dry, quiet sound. "You will, sometimes. But losing a game doesn't mean the board disappears. You reset and play again. The point is to keep showing up."

As Simmons left that evening, Jamal sat staring at the books on his table. The path Simmons had laid out felt daunting, almost impossible. But as the night wore on, he began to see the truth in it: changing the flow of the river might be slow, but it was work worth doing.

For weeks after that conversation, Jamal wrestled with the decision. He loved the immediacy of activism, the fire and solidarity of standing shoulder-to-shoulder with others who shared his convictions. But he couldn't shake Simmons' words. The idea of dismantling the system from within felt daunting, almost impossible—but also logical in a way that Jamal couldn't ignore.

By the time graduation arrived, Jamal had made his choice. He enrolled in law school, focusing on employment and labor law with a concentration in race and systemic inequities. It wasn't a decision he took lightly, and at times, it felt like a betrayal of the movement he had once led. But deep down, he believed it was the right path—not for everyone, but for him.

Jamal exhaled slowly, his breath visible in the cold night air as he finished recounting the story. He and Maya had stopped walking, standing beneath a flickering streetlamp. Maya was quiet, her arms crossed as she considered his words.

"Do you ever regret it?" she asked, her voice soft.

"Sometimes," Jamal admitted. "There are days when I miss the energy of the rallies, the feeling of being part of something bigger. But I don't regret the decision itself. I know what I'm working toward. And I know it's going to take time."

Maya nodded, her expression thoughtful. "You've always been better at seeing the long game. I don't know if I could do it."

"You don't have to," Jamal said gently. "The world needs people like you, Maya. People who remind the rest of us what we're fighting for."

She gave him a small, wry smile. "And people like you to figure out how to actually win."

"Exactly," Jamal said, chuckling. He glanced at her, his tone softening. "You know, you're doing more than you think. Don't forget that."

For the first time all night, Maya felt the burden on her chest ease slightly. They started walking again, the tension between them replaced by a quiet understanding.

As they neared Sophie's townhouse, Maya slowed her pace, her thoughts swirling. Jamal's words echoed in her mind: "The point is to keep showing up."

She didn't have all the answers—she wasn't sure she ever would—but maybe that wasn't the point. Maybe the fight wasn't about clarity or perfection. Maybe it was about refusing to give up, even when the odds felt insurmountable.

At the door, she turned to Jamal, her expression softer now. "You're right," she said quietly. "It's not about fixing everything at once. But... I need to figure out where I can make the biggest dent."

Jamal smiled, the faintest hint of pride in his eyes. "You will," he said simply. "You already are."

Maya thought about the night—a blend of moments that didn't quite fit together yet somehow carried a strange rhythm, like a dissonant harmony waiting to resolve.

Chapter 3: The Vanishing

The hum was the first thing Maya noticed—a low, soothing vibration that seemed to emanate from everywhere and nowhere at once. It wrapped around her senses, steady and rhythmic, like a heartbeat she didn't recognize as her own. Her eyelids fluttered open to the soft glow of the room, pulling her out of a disjointed haze. The walls around her pulsed faintly, smooth and gleaming, as though alive. She sat up slowly, her head spinning as if gravity had shifted.

"Jamal?" she croaked, her voice rough and barely above a whisper.

Movement flashed in her peripheral vision, drawing her focus to a figure nearby. Jamal, his broad shoulders unmistakable even in the strange light, was stirring awake on a similar platform. His groggy expression mirrored her own disorientation.

"Maya," he murmured, blinking hard as he rubbed his temples. "What the hell…" His voice trailed off as he took in their surroundings. "Where are we?"

She swung her legs over the edge of the platform, her bare feet touching the smooth, cool floor. The sensation was unfamiliar but oddly pleasant, like stepping onto polished glass. She scanned the room, instincts sharpening despite the fog in her mind. "I don't know," she said finally, her tone clipped, "but this isn't Earth."

The air felt different—lighter, cleaner—carrying an almost imperceptible hum. There was a faint luminescence to the room, the light source indistinguishable yet soothing. Every breath seemed to clear her head, sharpening her awareness.

Maya pressed her toes harder into the floor. It pulsed faintly beneath her, almost imperceptibly. The strange rhythm felt alive. She hesitated, leaning toward Jamal. "Does this feel... wrong to you?"

Jamal pushed himself upright, his feet landing softly on the glowing floor. "Everything feels wrong, Maya. But we're breathing. That's a start."

Before Jamal could say more, a doorway melted open across the room. Maya froze. The door hadn't slid or swung—it had dissolved into the wall, seamlessly disappearing. A tall figure stepped through, humanoid but unmistakably alien. Her radiant skin shimmered like liquid opal, shifting hues with each movement. Her elongated features were serene yet commanding, and she wore a flowing garment that rippled with the same luminescence as the walls.

"Welcome," the figure said, her voice resonant and calm. "My name is Zara. I am here to guide you."

Maya and Jamal exchanged wary glances. Jamal stood slowly, placing himself slightly in front of Maya in a protective gesture. She ignored it and stepped forward, her chin tilted up in defiance of the fear clawing at her chest.

"Guide us where?" Maya demanded, her voice steady despite the chaos swirling inside her.

Zara's lips curved into what resembled a smile. "To understanding. To healing. You have been chosen to join us on Noctivara—a sanctuary where you can grow, thrive, and lead."

"Chosen?" Jamal's voice carried an edge of suspicion. "By whom? For what?"

Zara stepped closer, her shimmering skin shifting to a soothing blue. "Your resilience is extraordinary. Your stories of survival have echoed across the stars. We observed the suffering on your planet and could no longer stand by. You, and others like you, have been brought here as part of the liberation. Together, you will help create a future of hope—for yourselves and for the universe."

Maya's mind raced, the words clashing with her instincts. She wanted to trust Zara's calming presence, but the enormity of what was happening made her bristle. "What gives you the right to decide that for us?" she asked, her arms folded tightly across her chest.

Zara's expression softened, her skin shifting to a faint green. "It was not a decision made lightly, Maya. But the choice to leave oppression behind—to create something better—is yours to make."

Before either of them could respond, the hum intensified slightly, and Zara gestured toward the open doorway. "Come. There is much to show you."

Maya glanced over her shoulder, noting other figures emerging from similar chambers in the corridor. Their faces were diverse, their expressions a mixture of awe, fear, and confusion. Snatches of conversation in different languages filled the air, their emotions creating a complex symphony of human experience.

Jamal leaned closer to Maya as they walked, his voice low and steady. "This is bigger than us."

She nodded, her gaze scanning the crowd. "But what do they want from us?" Her words felt heavy, as though the answer might break them.

The corridor opened into a vast observation deck. Gasps rippled through the group as they took in the sight before them. The transparent walls revealed Earth, suspended in the infinite blackness of space, vibrant yet fragile. Maya gripped the railing tightly, her chest tightening as the enormity of their absence hit her.

"We're just... gone," she whispered.

A voice beside her, thick with an accent, broke through her thoughts. "Gone, yes." The speaker, a wiry man with dark eyes, gestured around the room. "Look at us—so different. What connects us?"

Another figure chimed in, a woman clutching a small gold pendant at her neck. "Maybe we're the expendable ones. No one will miss us."

"That's not true," Jamal interjected firmly, stepping forward. "Every one of us mattered to someone. I left my boyfriend behind. He'll notice. He'll care."

The murmurs around them grew louder, rising like a wave of confusion and despair. A young man whispered a prayer in a language Maya didn't recognize, while an older woman clutched a photograph, her trembling hands pressing it to her lips. The emotions in the room were palpable—a quiet storm of grief, awe, and fear.

Maya turned to Jamal, her voice unsteady. "But what happens to Ethan now? What happens to the people we left behind?"

Jamal's hand rested on her shoulder, grounding her. "And what about the world?" His voice carried, drawing more attention from the group. "What happens to the world we left behind?"

A middle-aged man with a salt-and-pepper beard stepped forward from the back. "Is that why you took us?" he demanded, his voice thick with emotion and anger. "You took us without asking. How can you justify that?"

Zara appeared, stepping onto a raised platform in the center of the room. Her shimmering form caught the ambient light, casting faint reflections on the transparent walls. Her skin shifted to a muted gold as she spoke, her tone steady yet laced with solemnity. "We understand your fear, your grief. But know this: what awaits you here is not captivity. It is freedom—freedom to rebuild, to lead, and to thrive."

"Freedom?" A younger woman's voice rose, sharp and incredulous. "You call this freedom? You ripped us from our lives, our families. I didn't ask for this!" Her fists were clenched, her face flushed with anger. "And you expect us to just... accept it?"

Zara turned to face the woman directly, her light dimming slightly as though in acknowledgment of the pain. "I understand your anger," Zara began, her voice softer but firm. "What you see as a rupture will become a bridge. Your departure is not the end of your bonds. Those you love—your families—are here, aboard this vessel."

The room froze. Then a ripple of shocked murmurs swept through the crowd, faces lighting up with disbelief and tentative hope. Maya's breath caught in her throat, her grip tightening on Jamal's arm.

"What do you mean, they're here?" someone called out, their voice trembling. "Where? When can we see them?"

Zara raised a hand, her expression calm but tinged with sorrow. "You will see them—if you remain as you are. If your lineage holds to the harmony that brought you here. This is a reunion for those who carry the threads of shared heritage, a chance to rebuild as one people. But..." Her gaze swept the group, her luminous skin flickering with an almost imperceptible shift. "If your identity diverges from that bond, if it has been diluted beyond recognition... then the reunion you seek will not come."

The room erupted into a cacophony of disbelief and outrage.

"What the hell does that mean?" a man shouted, his fists clenched. "Diluted? Are you saying we don't deserve to see our families if we don't meet some... some standard?"

A woman near the back called out, her voice thick with defiance. "Who are you to decide who we are? Who's worthy?"

Zara's light grew brighter, silencing the crowd. "It is not about worth," she said, her voice tinged with an emotion that almost sounded like regret. "It is about preserving what must endure. The bonds that brought you here are sacred. They must remain strong to guide the future of Noctivara. Choices made in the past have consequences. Those who no longer align with the essence of this unity cannot be part of its rebuilding."

Maya's heart sank, the weight of Zara's words pressing down on her. "So that's it?" she said, stepping forward, her voice trembling but loud. "If we don't fit some perfect definition, we're just... cut off? No second chances?"

Jamal placed a hand on her shoulder, his jaw tight. "This isn't unity," he said, his voice cold. "This is division."

Zara stepped down from the platform, her tone softening as she addressed them directly. "I know these words are difficult to hear. But this is not a punishment. It is a call to rise—to prove that what you carry within you is strong enough to withstand the tests ahead. For those who do, the reunion you long for will come."

The man with the salt-and-pepper beard shook his head, his face etched with anger and grief. "Hope? Hope doesn't bring my family back. It doesn't fix this... this cruelty."

Zara's gaze remained steady. "No, it does not. But hope is the foundation upon which everything else is built. Without it, there is nothing."

The room fell silent, the air thick with a mixture of despair and determination. Maya exchanged a long look with Jamal, the enormity of their situation pressing down on them both.

The group was ushered into a central chamber, its walls glowing faintly, the light pulsating in rhythm with the ship's hum.

Zara luminous form radiating a soft, steady light that cast subtle patterns across the walls.

"You are the first," she began, her voice calm but commanding enough to stifle the murmurs in the room. "The first to join Noctivara, to help shape what it will become. Your strengths, your stories, your humanity—these are what we need to forge a new beginning."

The room erupted. Voices overlapped in a chaotic mixture of confusion, fear, and anger.

"What do you mean, the first?" a young man demanded, his voice sharp with skepticism. "Are we your experiment?"

"Why us?" a middle-aged woman with graying hair added, her arms crossed. "You didn't ask—you just took us."

Zara's glow shifted to a tranquil blue, her expression unchanging as she met their questions. "You are not experiments. You are pioneers. Each of you carries something unique— a story that can inspire. You were chosen because you survived, and because you can lead."

A scared man near the center scoffed. "Survived? You say that like it's some kind of gift. Do you know what it cost us to survive?" His voice cracked with emotion as he added, "You call this a choice, but you gave us none."

Maya stood near the back with Jamal, her arms crossed tightly. "She's spinning a fairy tale," she whispered, her voice low and cold. "And it reeks."

"Probably," Jamal murmured, his eyes scanning Zara and the room. "But what if it's not? What if this is our shot to do something better?"

Maya's lips thinned, her skepticism unrelenting. "What if it's just another lie? Leaders on Earth said the same thing, and all they did was take. How do we trust her?"

Zara raised her hand, and the room fell into uneasy silence. Her glow brightened slightly, her voice calm yet resolute. "This is your opportunity to rise beyond survival. To become something greater. Together, we can create a world where no one is othered, where every voice matters."

A younger woman, barely out of her teens, spoke up, her voice trembling but loud enough to carry. "And what about what we left behind? Are we supposed to just forget? My friends, my cat - they need me!"

Zara stepped forward, her expression softening as her glow shifted to a warm gold. "You will never forget. The memories you carry, the bonds you forged—they are your compass. But the choice is yours: to cling to the past or to honor it by building a future worthy of those you left behind."

For a moment, silence filled the room, heavy with indecision. Then the scarred man stepped forward again, his voice hard with doubt. "That's easy for you to say. You're not the one who's lost everything."

"I have lost," Zara replied, her tone briefly faltering before regaining its strength. "And I understand your fear, your grief. But know this: what awaits you here is not captivity. It is freedom—freedom to rebuild, to lead, and to thrive. Your departure is a ripple, not an end."

Maya turned back to Zara, her grip tightening on the railing. "You keep saying this is freedom," she said, her voice low and steady, "but freedom doesn't come without trust. And trust isn't something you can take. It has to be earned."

Zara met Maya's gaze, her glowing skin shifting to a soft lavender—a gesture Maya now recognized as empathy. "You are right. Trust must be earned. And I am prepared to earn it. But that begins with you choosing to take the first step."

Maya again exchanges a long look with Jamal, the enormity of their situation pressing down on them both.

Around them, the group remained tense, whispers of hope and dissent mingling in the air.

Maya turned to Jamal, her voice low and firm. "They're hiding something. I don't know what, but they are. And until we know, I'm not trusting anyone."

"Agreed," Jamal said, his tone hardening. "But maybe we use this. If they're lying, we figure out why. And if they're not..." He let the words hang, his expression unreadable. "We figure that out too."

Maya nodded, her gaze lingering on Earth's distant glow. Whatever lay ahead, it wouldn't be simple. But one thing was certain—this fight wasn't over. Not yet.

The images dissolved, leaving only the hum of the ship and the faint glow of the panels.

"I will not lie to you," Zara said, her gaze steady. "There will be challenges. This is not a utopia—it is a chance to create something new. But it will require courage, collaboration, and trust."

A man near the back of the group stepped forward, his brow furrowed. He was older, with salt-and-pepper hair and a weariness in his eyes that spoke of hard-earned wisdom. "You say we've been chosen, but what makes us so special?" he asked, his voice steady.

Zara's expression softened, her skin shifting to a pale gold. "You are special not because of what you are, but because of who you are. Each of you has faced adversity and risen above it. Your resilience, your ingenuity, your capacity for hope—these are the qualities that make you capable of shaping this world."

The man nodded slowly, his skepticism tempered but not erased. A younger woman beside him, her arms crossed tightly over her chest, interjected, her voice sharp. "Resilience? Hope? That sounds nice, but we didn't sign up to be anyone's inspiration. Some of us just wanted to live, not rebuild your broken world."

The scarred man stepped forward again, his jaw clenched. "You talk about building something better, but better for who? I've heard promises like yours before—politicians, preachers, bosses. They all say it's for the greater good, but the ones doing the building are always the ones carrying the load. What makes this any different?"

A murmur of agreement rippled through the crowd. Zara inclined her head, her tone unwavering. "You are right. None of you asked for this. But consider this: the worlds you left behind were fractured, teetering on collapse. Here, you have the chance to do more than survive—you have the chance to thrive. That is why you were chosen."

A man with a thick accent, his voice rough and raw, stepped forward, his fists clenched at his sides. "You talk about thriving, but what if we don't want your world? What if we just want to go back to what we know, to the people we love?"

Zara's light dimmed slightly, and for a moment, she looked almost human in her sadness. "I understand that yearning. But there is no going back. What lies behind you is gone. What lies ahead is yours to create."

Maya's hands curled into fists at her sides. "Gone?" she echoed, her voice rising. "You talk like you know what we've lost, but do you? Do you know what it feels like to watch your world be torn apart, to know everything you've built could vanish in a heartbeat?"

The room fell silent, all eyes on Zara. Her golden glow flickered as she stepped closer to Maya, her voice gentle but resolute. "No, I do not know. But I have seen the aftermath of loss. I have seen what happens when the chance to rebuild is rejected out of fear. And I have seen what can be achieved when it is embraced."

Maya turned away, her throat tight. Her mind lingered on Zara's words, pulling at memories she'd tried to leave behind. She thought of her grandmother's hands, calloused and strong as they smoothed the pages of a family photo album. "They don't tell you everything in school, baby," she'd said. "But you come from survivors. Remember that." The photographs had shown it all: sharecroppers under a blazing sun, marchers holding signs, her own mother standing proudly in front of a house she'd fought to keep.

Her grandmother's words echoed now, louder than Zara's. "You come from survivors." But how many times did survival mean losing something first?

She turned to Jamal, her voice trembling. "What if we're just repeating it all?" she whispered. "The fighting, the surviving. What if nothing changes?"

Jamal met her gaze, his brow furrowed. "Then we fight to make sure it does." His voice was quiet, but there was steel in it. "We've survived worse. We've built from nothing before. Maybe this time we get to build it right."

Maya's throat tightened, her emotions a tangled knot of fear, grief, and a flicker of hope she couldn't fully extinguish. "And if we fail?" she asked, her voice barely audible.

Jamal's hand rested lightly on her shoulder, grounding her. "Then we fail trying. Together."

Around them, the murmurs in the room began to soften, uncertainty mingling with the first stirrings of resolve. The salt-and-pepper-haired man spoke again, his tone quieter now. "You're asking us to trust that this is worth it. To risk everything for a future we can't even see yet."

Zara nodded, her voice steady. "I am. And I will be here to guide you every step of the way. But the choice is yours. This new beginning cannot be built on compulsion—it must be born of your will."

The room fell quiet, the weight of Zara's words settling over the group like a heavy blanket. Maya exchanged a long look with

Jamal, the enormity of their situation pressing down on them both.

Later, the group was escorted to individual quarters—small but comfortable spaces with walls that pulsed softly in time with the ship's hum. Maya sat on the edge of her platform, staring out at the stars visible through a narrow window. The vastness of space felt suffocating, a constant reminder of how far she was from everything she'd ever known.

A soft knock on the frame of her doorway broke her thoughts. Jamal leaned against the wall, his arms crossed. "You okay?" he asked, his tone gentle but searching.

Maya shrugged without looking at him. "Define 'okay.'"

He gave her a wry smile, stepping inside and perching on the edge of the small table opposite her. "Fair point."

They sat in silence for a moment, the hum of the ship the only sound between them. The unspoken weight of their situation filled the air like a heavy fog. Finally, Maya broke the silence, her voice barely above a whisper.

"What if Zara's right?" she asked, her eyes still fixed on the endless expanse of stars. "What if this is a chance to do something better? Something that matters?"

Jamal sighed, running a hand over his face. "I don't know, Maya. Maybe it is. But I also know that nothing comes without a cost. We've been given 'opportunities' before, remember? They always come with strings attached."

"Yeah," Maya said bitterly. "Strings they only show you once you're too tangled to fight back."

He nodded, his jaw tight. "Exactly. I keep thinking about what Zara said, how they 'chose' us because of what we've been through. Like it's some kind of badge of honor. But surviving isn't the same as thriving. We've spent our whole lives surviving, Maya. What's the cost this time?"

Her gaze dropped to her hands, fingers nervously picking at the seam of her pants. "You think they're lying?"

"I think they're not telling us everything," Jamal replied. "And that scares me more than if they were outright lying."

Maya looked up, her voice laced with a mix of fear and determination. "Then we need to figure it out. We need to ask the right questions, push back if we have to. I'm not going to sit here and let them decide our future for us."

Jamal studied her for a moment before nodding. "Agreed. But, Maya..." He hesitated, his voice softening. "If this really is what they say it is... if we really can make something better... don't let the past stop you from seeing it."

Maya's brow furrowed as she met his gaze. "And what if it's not better? What if it's just another version of the same thing we've always had to deal with? Promises that don't mean anything?"

"Then we fight," Jamal said firmly. "We fight like we've always fought. But maybe—just maybe—it's worth giving it a shot first."

Maya let out a shaky breath, turning back to the window. The stars felt cold, indifferent, like they were watching and waiting to see what she would do. "I want to believe it," she admitted. "I really do. But trusting someone like Zara? Someone who can just... take us like this? It doesn't sit right."

Jamal moved to sit beside her, his shoulder brushing hers. "You don't have to trust her right now. Hell, I don't. But trust isn't the same as hope. We can keep our guard up and still hope this isn't all for nothing."

Maya gave him a sidelong glance, a faint smile tugging at her lips. "When did you become the optimist?"

Jamal chuckled softly. "Let's just say one of us has to be, or we're both screwed."

Her smile faded as she returned her gaze to the stars. "Maybe," she said softly, her voice tinged with doubt. "But I'm not trusting anyone until I know for sure. If we're going to do this, we do it on our terms."

"Always," Jamal said, his tone firm. "No matter what, we stick together. We figure this out. And if they're hiding something..." He paused, his voice darkening. "They're going to regret ever bringing us here."

Maya leaned into him slightly, her hand brushing his. "You're a good brother, you know that?"

He smirked, nudging her lightly. "Yeah, well, you're stuck with me."

For the first time since waking, Maya felt a flicker of something that wasn't fear. It wasn't quite hope—but it was something.

The hum of the ship deepened, a low vibration that seemed to reach into Maya's chest. The walls around them shifted, their faint luminescence intensifying as if the entire vessel were alive and responding to some unseen force. Zara stood at the edge of the platform, her radiant form casting elongated shadows across the chamber.

"We are approaching Noctivara," she announced, her voice steady but carrying a weight that silenced the murmurs of the group. "Prepare yourselves."

Maya's stomach churned. Her hands clenched at her sides, though she wasn't sure if it was from fear or anticipation. Around her, the abductees exchanged wary glances. The tension in the room was palpable, a quiet storm of unspoken doubts and whispered prayers.

"Prepare for what?" someone called out, their voice cracking. "What happens when we get there?"

Zara's skin flickered, her hues shifting momentarily to a pale lavender. "You will understand in time," she said, her tone soft but offering no comfort.

The lights in the chamber dimmed, leaving only the glow of the walls and Zara's luminous form. Maya's breath quickened as the hum grew louder, more resonant, almost deafening. The floor beneath her seemed to shift, the faint pulse of the ship synchronizing with her heartbeat.

"Jamal..." she murmured, her voice trembling. "I don't know about this."

Jamal placed a hand on her shoulder, grounding her. "We don't have a choice, Maya," he said quietly. "But whatever happens, we face it together."

The far wall of the chamber began to dissolve, revealing a vast, panoramic window. Gasps rippled through the group as the view outside became clear. Noctivara loomed before them, a shimmering sphere suspended in the void. It glowed with soft, ethereal light, its surface an intricate blend of greens, blues, and silvers. It was beautiful, impossibly so. But the perfection unsettled Maya, like a painting so flawless it felt unnatural. Her stomach churned. *What are we walking into?* she thought. *If it looks too good to be true, it probably is.*

Before Zara could answer, the ship shuddered violently. The hum shifted to a higher pitch, sharp and grating, and the lights flickered. Panic erupted in the chamber as the abductees stumbled, their cries filling the air.

"Stay calm," Zara called out, her voice cutting through the chaos. Her form brightened, radiating a brilliant white light that momentarily blinded Maya. "This is merely—"

Her words were drowned out by a sudden, deafening silence. The hum stopped. The lights went out. For a moment, there was only darkness, thick and oppressive.

Then, with a jarring clarity, the ship was flooded with a crimson glow. A voice, mechanical and alien, reverberated through the chamber, its tone devoid of emotion.

"Warning. System disruption detected. External interference is imminent."

Maya's chest tightened. She grabbed Jamal's arm, her nails digging into his sleeve. "What does that mean?" she asked, her voice barely above a whisper.

"I don't know," Jamal said, his eyes wide and darting. "But it doesn't sound good."

Zara's glowing form dimmed, her hues darkening to an uneasy gray. Her gaze flickered toward Noctivara, the shimmering planet growing larger in the window. For the first time, Maya saw hesitation in her alien guide—a crack in the otherwise serene facade.

"The approach is unstable," Zara said, her voice softer, almost to herself. "This was not expected."

The ship jolted violently, and the red light grew brighter, bathing the chamber in an eerie glow.

Zara's gaze darted between the group and the planet outside, her glowing form now dimmed to a pale gray. "Stay together," she commanded, though her tone betrayed a flicker of uncertainty. "Whatever happens next, stay together."

Maya wasn't listening. Her gaze was locked on the planet, its shimmering surface rippling like water under a restless wind. For a moment, she thought she saw faces in the glow—faint, ghostly, watching. A shiver ran down her spine.

The voice returned, mechanical and emotionless: "External interference confirmed. Emergency protocol initiated."

"Hold on to something!" Jamal shouted as the ship jolted again, sending several abductees sprawling to the floor.

The ship began to descend, the hum growing into a roar. Noctivara loomed larger, its beauty now overshadowed by a dark, foreboding glow.

Chapter 4: Earth Without Shadows

Ethan sat slumped at the kitchen table, the ghost of Maya lingering in every failed attempt to recapture her presence. The plate before him was a disaster—watery grits paired with undercooked chicken, a lumpy sauce, and cornbread muffins that resembled sad, misshapen rocks. Frustration tightened his jaw as he shoved the plate away, his appetite obliterated. The air carried the acrid scent of failure, a pungent reminder of his growing despair.

Her recipe had vanished. Just like her playlists. Just like the videos of her laughing during their vacations. Even the song she used to belt out from the shower—wildly off-key yet somehow irresistibly sexy—was nowhere to be found. Ethan had scrolled through his music library for hours, each fruitless search another gut-wrenching blow.

"Gone," he muttered bitterly. "Like the world finally succeeded in erasing her."

His stomach grumbled in protest, but he ignored it. Instead, he reached for a bag of chips on the counter, hoping for a quick fix. The crinkle of plastic was oddly reassuring—a familiar sound in a world that felt increasingly foreign. But as he pried the bag open, his fingers met nothing but stale air. Empty.

A hollow laugh escaped him. Of course. Yet another Black invention disappeared without a trace.

The kitchen, once their sanctuary of shared jokes and experimental recipes, felt vacant. The clatter of pots and pans—once the prelude to a night of laughter and indulgence—now echoed like a ghost of what had been. Even the chair across from him, where Maya used to sit with her crooked grin and teasing remarks, seemed accusatory in its emptiness. The suffocating weight of it settled in his chest.

Desperate for distraction, he turned on the news. It only deepened his discontent. Anchors debated The Great Divide, their sterile phrasing doing nothing to dull the horror of mass disappearances. Black communities across the globe had simply vanished. Families shattered. Economies buckled. Culture... evaporated. And nobody seemed to have any answers.

At first, the world had responded with panic—governments scrambling to explain the impossible, reporters hesitating to name the phenomenon outright. But as days stretched into weeks, something more insidious took root. Stripped of the historical scapegoat that upheld the racial hierarchy, the foundation of power trembled.

Ethan had noticed the shift in news cycles—the way politicians and thought leaders fumbled for new targets, desperate to fill the void. Crime statistics were hastily re-examined. Entire industries—fashion, music, sports, even food—were left hollow, exposed for the cultural exploitation they had long profited from. The machinery of oppression hadn't ceased; it had merely sputtered, struggling like an engine starved of fuel.

It was as if the world had slipped into a quiet, collective crisis: Who would they blame now?

In America, the response was swift. Without Black bodies to bear the weight of systemic inequality, new scapegoats were conjured almost overnight. Hostility toward immigrants exploded. Surveillance expanded in communities that had once been overlooked. Prisons—once overflowing with Black men—suddenly had new quotas to meet.

And yet, none of this was addressed in plain terms. The media tiptoed around the truth, disguising reality behind vague phrases like shifts in economic patterns and unforeseen social consequences. But the truth was too raw to name aloud: the racial construct could not exist without a bottom. And now, that bottom was gone.

Ethan clenched his fists. They weren't grieving the loss of Black people. They were grieving the loss of the role Black people had played in upholding their power.

His thumb hovered over Maya's contact, her familiar smile frozen in the tiny photo on his screen. For a fleeting moment, he thought of calling—of hearing her voice, even if only through a voicemail. But the weight of her absence hit him like a gut punch. He set the phone down, his chest tightening with helplessness.

Outside, the streets felt eerily quiet, as if the city itself had lost its heartbeat. The coffee shop where Maya used to get her morning latte had closed indefinitely. The neighborhood jazz bar where they had shared their first date was shut down, its marquee blank and lifeless like a forgotten relic. The hair salons, the food trucks, the community centers—places once brimming with warmth and movement—were now either shuttered or hauntingly deserted.

It wasn't just the people who had disappeared. It was the life they brought with them.

He had ignored the little things—the moments when Maya had asked for understanding instead of solutions. There had been a voicemail once, one he hadn't listened to until it was too late. Now, its memory loomed large, a cruel reminder of how much he had failed to see her.

His thoughts drifted to Jean-Louis, Jamal's boyfriend, who had been tirelessly advocating for answers. Ethan had seen him at the vigil, standing strong in the rain, his voice unwavering as he spoke of love, loss, and justice. Jean-Louis had taken his grief and transformed it into action, becoming a rallying point for so many who were still searching for hope.

Ethan, by comparison, felt useless. While Jean-Louis was out there leading vigils and organizing protests, Ethan was here—staring at ruined grits and stumbling through memories. His inaction felt like a betrayal—not just of the love he had shared with Maya but of everything she had stood for. She had believed in making the world more just, more equitable. And yet here he was, paralyzed by his own helplessness, his so-called privilege doing nothing to close the chasm between what he wished he could do and what he was actually doing.

Shame clawed at him, raw and relentless. He wanted to do something—anything—to make her proud. But every time he tried, the void she left behind swallowed him whole. Jean-Louis's strength only underscored Ethan's own paralysis, a cruel mirror reflecting all the ways he had failed to rise.

He let the phone slip from his hands and leaned back in his chair, staring at the ceiling. The silence wrapped around him, dense and suffocating. He shut his eyes, hoping to block it all out, but the quiet only magnified the emptiness.

Without Maya, even the smallest sounds—the creak of a chair, the distant hum of traffic, the faint whir of the fridge—felt hollow.

And worse, so did he.

The Great Divide: When Earth Lost Its Shadow

The collapse was both deafening and eerily quiet.

It roared in the crashing markets, the flailing governments, the protests swelling into riots. But it also whispered—in the small absences, the unspoken voids creeping into daily life, undeniable yet never directly acknowledged. Without Black communities, the foundation upon which so much of the world had depended—often without recognition—was crumbling.

At the university, Dr. Helena Grant stood frozen at the front of her lecture hall, grief tangled with confusion. The absence of Baldwin, Hurston, and Morrison wasn't just a loss of voices—it was the erasure of history, a wound that left her struggling to guide her students through a world she no longer recognized.

"I don't understand," she murmured, flipping through her notes. "These readings were here. I built this course around them."

Her students exchanged uneasy glances, their confusion reflected in her panicked expression. A young woman raised her hand hesitantly.

"Dr. Grant, wasn't today supposed to be about Toni Morrison?"

Helena nodded, her fingers tightening around the podium. "Yes. Yes, it was. But... it's gone."

The room fell into a heavy silence, the void settling over them like an unspoken reckoning. History itself felt fractured, as if someone had carved out entire chapters, leaving gaping holes where understanding should have been. Without these voices, Helena realized, the syllabus wasn't just incomplete—it was meaningless.

In a downtown club, a DJ stared at their empty playlist, frustration bubbling into anger. Tracks that had once shaped generations—jazz, hip-hop, blues, soul—were missing. The intricate beats of J Dilla, the sultry smoothness of Sade, the electrifying anthems of Beyoncé—gone.

They scrolled through their music library, searching desperately for something to fill the silence. On the dance floor, the patrons shifted awkwardly, their movements stiff and disconnected. The DJ settled on a generic track—mechanical, lifeless, unable to spark the energy that had once made the club pulse with life.

"Where's the good stuff?" someone shouted from the crowd. "Play some Coltrane! Some Aretha!"

"I would if I could!" the DJ yelled back, their voice cracking. "It's just... gone."

The crowd began to thin, disappointment thick in the air. The absence of rhythm, of soul, drained the room, leaving the club as hollow as the beats now playing.

Even industries that had thrived on Black ingenuity were unraveling. At a high-profile fashion house, a design team sat around a table cluttered with uninspired sketches. Their creative director paced back and forth, her frustration pressing into every clipped footstep.

"This isn't working," she snapped, gesturing at the uninspired designs. "Where's the edge? Where's the innovation?"

A junior designer hesitated before speaking. "A lot of what we've drawn from... it's gone."

"What's that supposed to mean?" the director barked.

The Great Divide: When Earth Lost Its Shadow

"Streetwear. Afro-Caribbean patterns. Hip-hop culture," the designer explained. "We've always... borrowed. And now... it's just not there."

The director slammed a hand on the table. "So what are we without it?"

Silence settled over the room. They all knew the answer but couldn't bring themselves to say it aloud. The fashion industry, long built on appropriating Black culture, was now floundering without the creative spark it had exploited for so long.

The tech sector was unraveling, too. Servers crashed, algorithms failed, and communication systems sputtered. Engineers scrambled to patch the problems, but every solution was a bandage over a widening gap.

In a sleek boardroom, the CEO of a major tech firm paced in front of his senior staff, frustration carving deep lines into his face. "What's happening? How are we still down? I thought our systems were foolproof."

A lead engineer hesitated. "Much of the technology we rely on—fiber optics, signal processing, telecommunications advancements—was pioneered by Black innovators. Shirley Jackson, James West, Mark Dean... Without continued contributions, we're seeing cracks we never anticipated."

The CEO blinked, uncomprehending. "You're saying we can't function without them?"

The engineer didn't answer. He didn't need to. The silence was loud enough.

The collapse rippled outward, touching every corner of society. Hospitals faced devastating shortages as the loss of countless Black doctors, nurses, and researchers crippled healthcare systems. Schools floundered without the educators who had fought tirelessly for underserved communities. Activist networks—the backbone of social justice movements—dissolved, leaving a void where leadership and vision had once stood.

For centuries, the world had extracted Black labor, creativity, and resilience while refusing to value Black humanity. Now, in their absence, the systems that had taken so much without giving back were laid bare—hollow, fragile, and unsustainable.

Rain fell steadily on the vigil, but the candles refused to die. Hundreds gathered in the city square, their faces illuminated by flames that flickered defiantly against the encroaching darkness. The scent of rain mixed with melted wax and smoke, clinging to the air like the grief that settled over every heart.

Jean-Louis stood at the center, gripping the microphone as if it were his last tether to this world. The sharp angles of his face were cast in shifting shadows, his pain raw, etched deeply into his expression—but his voice was steel.

"They've taken our mothers, our fathers, our children," he began, his words cutting through the steady patter of rain. "We've lost teachers, healers, innovators, and dreamers. Their absence is not just our loss—it's the world's unraveling."

A murmur rippled through the crowd, rising like a slow wave. Some nodded; others lifted their candles higher, their faces streaked with rain and sorrow. Jean-Louis's words struck deep because they rang with truth. His grief, once personal, had grown into something larger—a righteous fury, a purpose that refused to be extinguished.

He gestured toward the empty space beside him, where Jamal should have been. "I want you to remember—this is not just about numbers. It's not just about missing census records or economic collapse. This is about people. About love. About families. About voices that were never meant to be silenced. We cannot—will not—let them disappear without a fight."

A woman in the crowd sobbed softly. A man clenched his fist, his candle trembling in his grasp. Some lowered their heads in prayer. Others stood rigid, their gazes locked on Jean-Louis, their rage mirroring his own.

"This isn't just about mourning," Jean-Louis continued, his voice faltering for the briefest moment. He swallowed hard, straightening, his gaze sweeping over them. "It's about fighting. Fighting to remember them. Fighting for their legacies. Fighting to bring them back."

The flames flickered as the wind picked up, but the candles stayed lit—just as the applause that erupted from the crowd refused to be stifled. Some clapped, others cheered, and a few lifted their voices in chants that surged like wildfire through the square. The energy of the moment swelled—a fragile unity forged in shared loss and defiance.

Ethan stood at the edge of the crowd, his body rigid, his grip tightening around the umbrella as rain slid off its edges. The applause rang through the square, but instead of lifting him, it weighed him down. He watched Jean-Louis on the platform, shoulders squared, his words igniting something vital in the people around him.

And then there was Ethan. Standing there. Silent. Invisible.

Jean-Louis had found purpose in the wreckage of devastation. He had taken his pain and turned it outward, wielding it like a weapon against injustice. Ethan had done the opposite. He had retreated, drowning in grief and helplessness.

Watching Jean-Louis now, composed and commanding in the rain, made Ethan's shame feel suffocating.

He thought of Maya—how she would have stood beside Jean-Louis, her voice cutting through the storm, her presence unwavering. She would have fought for every stolen life, every shattered dream, every soul left behind. And she would have expected Ethan to do the same.

But he wasn't. He couldn't. He didn't know how.

His throat tightened as guilt and longing twisted inside him. He wanted to step forward, to join the crowd, to do something—anything—that mattered. But he remained still, his feet planted as if the ground itself held him back. His umbrella sagged beneath the relentless downpour, shielding him from more than just the rain. It was a flimsy barrier between him and the people who refused to surrender. Water streamed off the edges, dripping onto his shoes like the tears he couldn't afford to shed.

"This isn't just about mourning," Jean-Louis's voice rang out again, clear and defiant above the storm. "It's about fighting."

Ethan's grip tightened around the umbrella's handle until his knuckles ached. He wanted to believe he could fight—for Maya, for their future, for all of them.

But right now, all he could do was stand there—an outsider on the fringes of something greater than himself.

The cheers swelled, the energy of the square rising into a furious roar. Ethan lowered his head, turned away, and stepped into the rain. Jean-Louis's words lingered in the air behind him, trailing him like shadows in the dark.

The Great Divide: When Earth Lost Its Shadow

In the cold glow of his office, Liam sat amid scattered papers that formed an incomplete but deeply troubling picture. Stolen documents hinted at secretive dealings between Earth's leaders and the Noctivara. Phrases like "trade-off scenarios" and "targeted interventions" leapt off the pages, but the specifics remained maddeningly elusive.

The Noctivara—an alien race whose name now carried an ominous weight in Liam's mind—had approached Earth's governments with an offer that only led to more questions. Meeting notes referenced a proposed "societal adjustment", yet the objectives were murky, the implications unsettling.

Liam's stomach tightened as he read on. Global leaders had debated in hushed, high-level discussions, their concerns buried beneath layers of cold, bureaucratic language. But beneath the formal tone, an unmistakable unease bled through. The transcripts didn't depict a unified front or a decisive course of action. Instead, they read like the record of a fractured debate—a desperate scramble to retain control.

One section stood out: a transcript from a meeting between Earth's leaders and Noctivara representatives. The humans had pressed for clarity on the aliens' objectives, but the answers were evasive, laced with grand proclamations of "advancement" and "global equilibrium" but devoid of tangible details. Then, at one critical moment, a leader had raised the most urgent question:

Why was it necessary to take entire communities?

The Noctivara's response was chilling in its brevity:

"Your people's survival depends on this."

Liam exhaled sharply, rubbing his temples as a wave of nausea rose in his throat. The proposal was grotesque, and the deeper he dug, the more its logic unraveled. If the Noctivara's technology was as advanced as they claimed, why not offer it freely? Why the secrecy, the selective disruption?

And why had Earth's leaders—even in desperation—entertained such a dangerous proposition?

Except... had they?

The next document, buried in a folder labeled **CLASSIFIED: INTERNAL DISPUTE**, painted an even murkier picture. There were notes detailing factions within the leadership—some urging caution, others advocating swift acceptance, and a few resisting outright. Yet the final decision was unclear. Had the Noctivara proceeded without full agreement?

One line, scrawled hastily in the margin of a briefing, sent a shiver through him:

"We have no assurances they will uphold their end. Is this coercion disguised as collaboration?"

Liam's eyes narrowed. Coercion. The word hung in the air like a blade.

Had the Noctivara manipulated Earth's leaders into compliance, dangling catastrophe over their heads like a guillotine?

Or worse—had they lied outright, using promises of salvation as a smokescreen for something far more sinister?

His gaze fell on one last document, a heavily redacted report from an unnamed source. The few legible sentences referenced "discrepancies in the Noctivara's stated goals" and flagged "the unexplained targeting of Black communities, whose contributions are foundational to Earth's resilience."

Then, a final line that turned his blood cold:

"The cultural void they create could destabilize global systems far beyond their stated objectives."

The Great Divide: When Earth Lost Its Shadow

Liam leaned back in his chair, his breath unsteady as the weight of the revelation pressed down on him.

This wasn't negligence.

This was something far worse.

But where did the true betrayal lie? With Earth's governments, who might have bartered away humanity for power? Or with the Noctivara, who had orchestrated this nightmare from the shadows?

Or both?

Whatever the truth was, it wasn't just about Earth's leaders failing Black communities—it was about the horrifying possibility that Earth itself had been outmaneuvered by forces it barely understood.

The crowd stirred, a murmur rising like a slow wave. Some nodded in solemn agreement, while others lifted their candles higher, their faces streaked with tears and rain. Jean-Louis's words struck deep because they rang with undeniable truth. His grief, once deeply personal, had transformed into something greater—a relentless fury, a purpose that refused to be extinguished.

"This isn't just about mourning," he continued, his voice faltering for the briefest moment. He swallowed hard, then straightened, his gaze sweeping the crowd. "It's about fighting. Fighting to remember them. Fighting for their legacies. Fighting to bring them back."

The flames wavered as the wind picked up, but the candles held, just as the applause that rippled through the crowd refused to be silenced. Some clapped, others cheered, and voices rose in chants that spread like fire through the square. The energy surged—fragile yet unyielding, a unity forged from shared loss and defiance.

But not everyone in the crowd was an ally.

Near the back, Jean-Louis caught sight of a cluster of figures, their faces obscured beneath dark hoods, their gazes locked onto him. He recognized their stance—the tense shoulders, the quiet, simmering hostility. He knew the look of men who resented change, who feared the shifting tides of power.

One of them spat onto the ground near his feet before turning and vanishing into the shadows.

A slow chill crept down Jean-Louis's spine. He had known this fight would not come without opposition.

The Great Divide had not only left an absence in culture, economy, and daily life—it had fractured identities, exposing the fault lines of those who had built their sense of self on dominance over others. Some had come to understand the truth, standing beside Jean-Louis, mourning the disappearance of an entire people. But others—too many—clung to their inherited privilege with desperate, grasping fingers, searching for someone else to blame.

As the vigil drew to a close, Jean-Louis stepped down from the stage. Mourners approached him, some thanking him for his words, others sharing stories of loved ones lost. He listened, nodding, offering what comfort he could.

But his mind was elsewhere.

He was being watched.

He felt it in the way the air shifted, in the unseen eyes tracking his every move.

Turning onto a side street, he saw them. Three figures lingering beneath a streetlamp, their silhouettes stark against the dim glow. One stepped forward, his face partially swallowed by shadows.

Jean-Louis clenched his fists, his heart hammering in his chest.

"You think you're some kind of leader, don't you?" the man sneered. "Stirring up trouble. You're making people angry."

Jean-Louis's breath remained slow, measured. "People should be angry."

The man chuckled, low and cold. "Yeah? And what do you think happens when they get angry enough?"

Jean-Louis didn't answer. The threat hung heavy in the air.

But he also knew something else: he wasn't afraid.

He took a step forward, his stance unwavering despite the tension thickening around them. His voice was low but steady, sharp as steel.

"If you're trying to scare me, you'll have to do better than vague threats in the dark."

He let the words settle, watching the subtle shift in the man's posture—the flicker of hesitation, the slight adjustment of his footing, the way his fingers twitched at his sides.

The man's grin faltered. He muttered something under his breath, a weak attempt to save face, then jerked his head toward the others. They hesitated before backing away, slipping into the shadows where cowards belonged.

Jean-Louis exhaled, his pulse steady. His hands were still clenched, but not from fear—from resolve.

This wasn't the first threat. It wouldn't be the last. But if they thought whispered warnings would break him, they were dead wrong.

Because he wasn't just fighting for himself. He was fighting for the ones they had tried to erase. For the voices they had silenced. For the people they wanted the world to forget.

And he wasn't stopping. Not now. Not ever.

Jean-Louis stared at the documents spread before him in the dimly lit café, his favorite painting of Maya Angelou speaking to James Baldwin hanging nearby. His jaw tightened, a vein in his temple pulsing as his hands clenched into fists on the table. The carefully controlled demeanor he typically maintained fractured beneath the weight of what he had just read.

Across from him, Liam shifted uneasily in his chair. The café was nearly empty, the occasional clink of coffee cups and the low murmur of conversation creating an unsettling contrast to the gravity of their discussion.

"They knew," Liam said quietly, his voice thick with shame. "And they let it happen."

Jean-Louis's response was a low, simmering growl, raw with fury. "They didn't just let it happen. They turned away. They chose comfort over courage." His dark eyes burned as he met Liam's gaze. "It wasn't ignorance—it was indifference."

Liam swallowed hard, guilt gnawing at him. "Some of them pushed back," he said, though even to his own ears, the words rang hollow. "There were those who hesitated, who questioned the Noctivara's motives. It wasn't unanimous."

Jean-Louis snorted, a bitter smile tugging at his lips. "And yet, here we are. Does it matter if some hesitated when they still let this unfold?" He jabbed a finger at one of the papers. "This isn't just betrayal—it's abandonment. They let entire communities vanish. And for what? Promises? Hope? Lies dressed up in pretty speeches?"

Liam had no answer. He felt like a coward sitting across from Jean-Louis—a man who had lost everything yet still radiated purpose. Jean-Louis's fire was relentless, a force that Liam both admired and feared. It was a stark contrast to his own quiet, analytical approach, which now felt woefully inadequate.

Jean-Louis sat back, his gaze darkening as he studied both the documents and Liam. His fury, though tempered, burned with a smoldering determination. "We can't just expose this," he said, his voice quieter but no less intense. "It's not enough to tell people their governments were complicit. We need to mobilize. We need to prepare them for the truth."

Liam frowned, his fingers running along the edge of a folder. "What do you mean by 'prepare'? If we release this information strategically, public outrage will be enough to force accountability."

Jean-Louis shook his head. "No. You're thinking like a politician. Outrage is temporary, and governments are experts at deflection. They'll find a scapegoat, spin a narrative, and bury the real story. The truth isn't something you just drop on people and hope for the best. You have to prepare them to act."

Liam's brow knitted. "Act how? The protests are already escalating—people are angry, scared. If we provoke more unrest without a clear direction, it could spiral out of control."

Jean-Louis leaned forward, pressing his hands against the scattered papers on the table. "Exactly. That's why this energy needs to be directed before it burns out or fractures. People need to grasp what's at stake—not just for Black communities, but for everyone. This isn't just about betrayal; it's about survival. The Noctivara deceived them—or worse, manipulated them into submission. If they didn't act now, who was to say the Noctivara wouldn't come back for more?"

Across from him, Liam nodded slowly as the picture became clearer. Jean-Louis was right—this wasn't just about uncovering the truth. It was about rallying people into a movement strong enough to stand against both Earth's leaders and the Noctivara.

"We'll need resources," Liam said, his voice measured. "Contacts, platforms, a way to spread this information without alerting the very people trying to keep it buried. I have some connections, but if we're going to make this work, we need a strategy."

Jean-Louis pressed his lips into a thin line. "I'll handle the groundwork. I know people who will fight tooth and nail for this. But we need more than protests and speeches. We need undeniable proof that the Noctivara misled us—that this was never about some grand galactic favor. People need to see exactly what's been taken from them."

Liam hesitated, his gaze drifting over the documents again. There was still so much they didn't know. "If we push too hard without the full picture—"

"This isn't just about survival," Jean-Louis interrupted, his voice edged with urgency. "It's about reminding them who built this world. Without us, their systems—everything they claim as theirs—collapses."

Liam sat back, a mix of exhaustion and exhilaration churning inside him. Jean-Louis's conviction was electric, but the risks were staggering. The backlash, the danger—it would be relentless. And yet, as he met Jean-Louis's gaze, his resolve solidified. This wasn't just about exposing lies. It was about fighting for a future that was slipping through their fingers.

The Great Divide: When Earth Lost Its Shadow

"Alright," Liam said finally. "Let's do this."

Jean-Louis gave a sharp nod, his expression grim but unwavering. "No half-measures. We're all in."

The café settled into a hush as their conversation tapered off, but the silence between them wasn't empty. It pulsed with determination, an unspoken understanding that they were about to step into a battle far greater than either of them had ever faced.

The world unraveled around him, the void expanding with each passing day. Ethan felt it everywhere—in the quiet streets where laughter had faded, in the hollowed-out syllabi stripped of Black voices, in the lifeless clubs where once-vibrant rhythms now rang thin and vacant. The absence wasn't just noticeable—it was suffocating, pressing in on everything.

Maya's voice echoed in his mind, an unrelenting refrain: "If you're not part of the solution, Ethan, you're part of the problem." The words burned, not because they were cruel, but because they were true. He had spent too long ignoring the fractures in the world, too long dismissing the warnings Maya had tried to show him. Now, those fractures had split into chasms, swallowing everything he once believed.

He had seen enough. The protests, the disappearances, the slow erosion of Earth's soul—it was all connected. For weeks, he had immersed himself in conspiracy forums, obscure archives, and half-buried government reports. The deeper he dug, the clearer the pattern became. One name surfaced again and again, a whisper threading its way through the cracks of history: the Noctivara.

Late one night, after piecing together fragments of evidence that formed a grim portrait of complicity and cover-ups, Ethan found himself standing outside the penthouse of a former colleague. Harold Beckett had once been a rising star in the tech world, his fortune built on exploitative labor disguised behind sleek marketing campaigns. Now, Harold was only a shadow of the confident mogul Ethan had known.

Inside, Harold poured himself a whiskey with shaking hands, the ice clinking against the glass. The pristine luxury of his apartment had given way to disorder—empty bottles lined the counter, and discarded paperwork sprawled across the coffee table. He gestured for Ethan to sit, but Ethan remained standing, arms crossed tightly.

"You don't get it, Ethan," Harold muttered, his voice frayed with desperation. "They were essential. And now, without them, the whole system's falling apart."

Ethan's eyes narrowed, his fists tightening at his sides. Essential? His voice was quiet, but there was a sharpness to it, cutting through the air like a blade. "You mean the people you exploited. The ones you undervalued, ignored, and discarded—until their absence became too big for you to deny."

Harold flinched, taking a nervous sip of his drink. "It's not like that. I... I didn't know this would happen. I didn't—"

"Didn't know?" Ethan's voice sharpened, his restrained fury finally breaking free. "No, Harold. You didn't care. That's the difference. You built your empire on their backs, and now you're panicking because the people you treated like disposable parts were the ones actually keeping it running."

Harold's gaze flicked toward the window, his jaw tightening. "You don't understand what it's like, Ethan. The pressure, the expectations. You do what you have to do to survive in this world."

"And they didn't have to survive?" Ethan shot back. "Maya warned me. She warned all of us, and we ignored her. But you—" He jabbed a finger at Harold. "You had the power to change things. You could've pushed back, even tried. Instead, you fed the system. And now you're paying the price."

Harold set his glass down with a sharp clink, his face pale. "You think this is easy for me? Watching everything I've built collapse?"

Ethan leaned in, his voice dropping to a cold, measured tone. "Good. It should hurt. Because for them—for Maya and everyone else—it wasn't just business. It was survival. And now they're gone, Harold. The world is unraveling, and all you can think about is yourself."

Harold slumped into the chair, rubbing his temples as if trying to erase the conversation. "It's too late, Ethan. The damage is done. What do you want from me?"

Ethan straightened, his jaw tight. "I want you to admit the truth. That people like you—like us—let this happen. That we were part of the problem."

Silence thickened between them, heavy and unrelenting. Harold's eyes darkened with something—shame, perhaps—but he said nothing.

Ethan exhaled sharply, turning away. "You're right about one thing, though. It is too late for you. But it's not too late for me."

As he reached the door, Harold called after him, his voice hollow. "What are you going to do, Ethan? You can't fix this."

Ethan paused, glancing back over his shoulder. "Maybe not. But I can make sure they're not forgotten. And I can make damn sure people like you never get the chance to rebuild the world they destroyed."

He stepped into the hallway, the door slamming shut behind him. For the first time, his anger wasn't just rage—it was resolve, pushing him forward. He didn't have all the answers, but he had purpose.

If you're not part of the solution, Ethan, you're part of the problem.

He was done being the problem.

The city was on fire—both metaphorically and literally.

Smoke curled into the night sky, thick and suffocating, rising from shattered storefronts like the collective cries of thousands who had taken to the streets. Buildings burned, their skeletal remains glowing orange against the darkness. Sirens howled through the chaos, a discordant wail of desperation as police forces and military units clashed with civilians.

The streets—once vibrant with culture, music, and life—had become a war zone.

It had started as a march.

A peaceful protest.

A call for truth.

But truth had never come easily.

Thousands had gathered in the city square, a restless tide of people demanding answers. *Where are they? Bring them back!* The words were painted across banners, chanted in unison, shouted from rooftops. The crowd swelled, their patience thinning with each passing hour of silence from the authorities. Frustration hardened into fury.

Then the first tear gas canister was fired.

Panic erupted. White smoke billowed, burning lungs, blinding eyes, forcing bodies to scatter. But they did not flee. They fought. Anger swallowed fear. Bottles shattered against riot shields. Trash cans were overturned and set ablaze. Windows splintered. Stores were looted. The rage simmering beneath generations of oppression was now an unrelenting force.

Somewhere in the chaos, Ethan found himself trapped between two worlds—a man without direction, caught between the past and the future, standing at the heart of something far bigger than himself.

He hadn't planned to be here.

He hadn't planned for any of this.

Yet, as he watched the city burn, he realized he had never truly been outside of it. He had simply ignored it.

A young woman stumbled past him, pressing a soaked bandana to her mouth, her eyes raw from the gas. Her half-open backpack was filled with medical supplies—a protest medic, pushing against the tide of violence. She glanced at Ethan, desperation flashing in her gaze.

"You standing there or you helping?" she demanded.

Ethan blinked.

Then, without thinking, he ripped the scarf from around his neck, drenched it in a nearby puddle, and pressed it against his mouth before following her into the storm.

Ethan's Breaking Point: The Last Voicemail

Ethan staggered home, the acrid scent of smoke clinging to his clothes, his hands still stained with the young man's blood. He collapsed onto the couch, his head pounding, exhaustion pressing down on him like a crushing weight.

His phone lay on the table, screen cracked, barely holding together after the chaos of the riot. He picked it up, his thumb hesitating over the screen.

Then he saw it—a voicemail from Maya.

The timestamp sent a chill through him. Weeks before she disappeared.

His heart pounded against his ribs as his thumb hovered over the play button.

Finally, he pressed it.

Her voice filled the room, soft yet exasperated. It was the voice he hadn't realized he had been aching to hear.

"I never asked you to save me, Ethan. I just wanted you to see me."

The message ended. Silence rushed back, thick and suffocating. But her words lingered, slicing through him with an unexpected sharpness.

I just wanted you to see me.

He sank onto the edge of the couch, the phone slipping from his hand.

She had told him—time and again—but he hadn't listened. Not really. He'd been too caught up in preserving the illusion of stability, believing that keeping his head down would keep them safe. But safety had been a lie, and his silence had cost them everything.

"I'm sorry," he whispered, his voice cracking. "I should've listened. I should've seen you."

Tears burned at the edges of his vision, but he blinked them away. Crying wouldn't bring her back. Regret wouldn't mend what had been shattered. But her words had sparked something in him—a clarity that had eluded him for too long.

She didn't need me to save her. She needed me to stand with her. To fight beside her.

He stood, his mind sharpening. He couldn't bring her back, but he could fight for her. For all of them. The files he'd gathered, the connections he'd made—they weren't just scraps of information anymore. They were weapons. Tools to expose the truth, to hold those responsible accountable.

Outside, the city raged, flames dancing in the reflection of his window. Somewhere in the chaos, people were still fighting—for answers, for justice, for hope.

It was time to join them.

Not just for the truth.

For redemption.

Ethan grabbed his coat, the fire inside him burning hotter than the inferno outside. He cast a final glance at his apartment—the remnants of a life he could never return to.

"This is for you, Maya," he murmured. "And for everyone they took."

With one last look, he stepped into the night, ready to fight.

The Great Unraveling

The world was coming apart, the void stretching wider with every passing day.

Ethan felt it everywhere—in the hushed streets where laughter had vanished, in the hollow syllabi where Black voices had been erased, in the lifeless clubs where rhythms once pulsed with energy but now lay flat and forgotten.

The absence was suffocating, pressing against his chest like a force he couldn't escape.

Maya's voice echoed in his mind, sharp and unrelenting:

"If you're not part of the solution, Ethan, you're part of the problem."

Not a question. A truth. One he had spent too long avoiding.

For years, he had convinced himself that things would balance out, that change took time, that progress was slow but inevitable.

But there was no balance left.

Only collapse.

He had seen enough.

The protests.

The disappearances.

The slow, relentless unraveling of the world.

For weeks, he buried himself in conspiracy forums, classified government files, and whispers from those too afraid to speak openly. The deeper he dug, the clearer the pattern became.

A single name kept surfacing.

The Noctivara.

And now, late one night, after piecing together fragments of evidence, reports, and testimonies, Ethan found himself standing in front of the penthouse apartment of Harold Beckett.

Once a tech mogul. A visionary. A man who built his fortune on the backs of others.

Now, a ghost of his former self.

Harold poured himself a whiskey with shaking hands, the ice clinking against the glass.

The room was in disarray—empty bottles, discarded paperwork, the remnants of a life spiraling into collapse. He gestured toward the chair across from him, but Ethan didn't sit.

"You don't get it, Ethan," Harold said, his voice edged with desperation. "They were essential. And now, without them, the whole system's breaking down."

Ethan's fists tightened. His breath remained slow, controlled.

"Essential?" His voice was quiet, but sharp enough to cut. "You mean the people you exploited. The ones you ignored, dismissed, undervalued—until their absence became too big for you to deny."

Harold flinched, his grip tightening around the glass. "It's not like that. I—I didn't know this would happen. I didn't—"

"Didn't know?" Ethan's voice rose, the anger he had swallowed for too long now breaking free. "You didn't care. That's the difference."

His pulse thundered in his ears.

Maya had tried to warn him. She had tried to warn all of them. But they hadn't listened.

And Harold?

Harold had profited.

"You had the power to change the system," Ethan said, his voice edged with steel. "You could have tried. You didn't. Instead, you fed it. And now you're paying the price."

Harold set his glass down with a sharp clink, his face drained of color. "You think this is easy for me?" His voice was hollow. "Watching everything I've built collapse?"

Ethan leaned in, his expression unyielding. His voice, cold. "Good."

The single word landed like a strike.

"It should hurt," Ethan continued, his breath steady. "Because for them—for Maya, for Jamal, for every person you and people like you discarded—this wasn't just business. This was survival. And now they're gone. And the world is crumbling."

He let the silence stretch between them, let Harold sit with the weight of it.

Finally, Harold slumped back in his chair, rubbing his temples as if he could erase the moment. "It's too late, Ethan," he muttered. "The damage is done. What do you want from me?"

Ethan straightened, his jaw set. "I want you to admit the truth. That people like you—like us—let this happen. That we were part of the problem."

Silence.

Harold's eyes darkened with something—shame, regret, fear—but he didn't speak.

Ethan exhaled sharply, turning away. "You're right about one thing, though." His voice was quieter now, but still razor-sharp. "It is too late for you."

He reached for the door, his fingers curling around the handle. "But it's not too late for me."

Harold's voice followed him as he stepped into the hallway. "What are you going to do, Ethan? You can't fix this."

Ethan paused, glancing back over his shoulder. "Maybe not." His gaze hardened. "But I can make sure they're not forgotten. And I can make damn sure people like you never get to rebuild the world you destroyed."

Then he walked away, leaving Harold behind in the ruins of the empire he had built on borrowed time.

For the first time, Ethan's anger felt like momentum.

He didn't have all the answers.

But he had a purpose.

And if you weren't part of the solution, you were part of the problem.

This fight wasn't just Jean-Louis's. It was his.

Chapter 5: Adjusting to Noctivara

The air shimmered as the group stepped off the transport, their eyes widening to take in Noctivara's breathtaking radiance. Even breathing felt different here—each inhale tingled with a gentle electric charge, as though the very atmosphere carried both warmth and energy. For a moment, they stood in stunned silence, captivated by the world before them. Sunlight glinted off crystalline rivers that wound through rolling valleys, while towering, organic structures stretched skyward, their surfaces pulsing with hints of bioluminescence. It was as if every molecule of this planet had been shaped with intent, existing in a state of perfect harmony.

A soft murmur broke the quiet before Zara could speak.

"It's almost as if the planet is welcoming us home," Leon whispered, his voice trembling with awe.

Amina nodded, her eyes bright with wonder. "I can feel its heartbeat, echoing our own."

Zara led them forward, moving with a quiet grace that seemed attuned to Noctivara's rhythm. The settlement unfolded before them like a living entity—structures of shifting light and color responded to the gentle breeze, shimmering in iridescent hues of pink, blue, and gold. Pathways of smooth, living material wove between self-sustaining farms, where vines coiled around trellises and fruit-bearing plants thrived without barriers. The entire scene felt like a seamless collaboration between architecture and nature, a testament to the Noctivara's deep commitment to coexistence.

"Noctivara was designed as a sanctuary," Zara said, her voice carrying both warmth and conviction. She turned to face them, her gaze unwavering. "Here, you can grow unburdened—free from the systems that oppressed you. This is your second chance to build a world where you belong."

Her words settled over them, and a quiet but earnest conversation broke out.

"But can we truly leave our past behind?" Marcus asked, his tone caught between hope and doubt.

"Is it really possible to start fresh?" Tonya murmured, her voice hesitant.

Zara met their questions with a confident smile.

"Every ending paves the way for a new beginning. Trust in the journey."

Her words fell into the silence like stones into still water, sending ripples through the group. Some faces flickered with cautious optimism, while others grew more pensive, weighed down by the enormity of what had been lost—and what might be found.

At the rear of the group, Maya lingered, her fingertips grazing the petals of a low-hanging blossom. The flower radiated a gentle glow, its soft light spilling over her hand in a quiet pulse of reassurance. Yet, despite its beauty, an ache nestled deep in her chest. She glanced at Jamal. His expression—tight with worry—mirrored her own. He met her gaze and gave a quick nod. A silent promise.

She wasn't alone in this.

As they moved deeper into the settlement, the air buzzed with life. From every corner of Earth—once divided by oceans and borders—people now mingled, sharing stories and forging new bonds. A chorus of languages wove together into a shared rhythm of resilience, underscored by the bright laughter of children chasing glowing orbs that drifted just out of reach. Joy flashed in their eyes, momentarily freeing them from the shadow of the planet they had left behind.

Amidst the merriment, a young child called out cheerfully, "Look! It's like the stars have come down to play!"

Another replied, "And they're inviting us to dream big!"

But Maya, even as she admired the happiness around her, felt the ache of Earth's absence pressing against her chest. The planet that had birthed them was gone, and no amount of majesty or novelty could ever fill that void.

They arrived at the cultural hub, a dome-like structure that pulsed with a steady, comforting luminescence. Its exterior shimmered with swirling patterns reminiscent of Earth's auroras, and upon entering, Jamal's breath caught. Inside, it was as if humanity's past and present converged in a single, glowing space. Shelves and displays showcased artifacts carefully salvaged or painstakingly re-created: paintings, sculptures, recordings of ancient songs, and digital archives capturing the voices of long-lost communities. Videos played on curved screens, telling stories of resilience and defiance, each one a testament to the perseverance that had defined Earth's Black cultures. Every inch of this place spoke of endurance, of a history that refused to be forgotten.

Jamal traced his fingers over the edge of a carved wooden mask, his voice hushed. "Look at these artifacts," he murmured to a nearby curator, who offered a knowing smile. "They remind me that no matter how far we travel, our roots remain here, intertwined with every beat of our hearts."

The curator nodded, replying, "Our history is the foundation upon which we build our future."

As Jamal wandered, a soft scraping sound caught his attention. He followed it until he saw an alien seated cross-legged on the floor, carefully carving into a wooden panel. Their features were elegant, their eyes flecked with shifting color, as if reflecting unseen constellations. Something about their posture spoke of both confidence and calm. Jamal's gaze was drawn to the intricate lines and swirls emerging beneath the carving tool—so precise they seemed almost alive. He hesitated, unsure whether to interrupt, but the alien looked up, meeting his eyes with a warm, knowing smile.

"Your energy carries stories," said Omari, his voice melodic, flowing like a river. "Would you share one with me?"

Jamal rubbed the back of his neck, suddenly self-conscious. "I wouldn't know where to begin."

Omari set down his carving tool and gestured toward a nearby console that glowed softly, invitingly. "Then let's begin in the middle," he said, his voice gentle yet certain. "This archive preserves Earth's Black cultures—memories, histories, art. Would you help me expand it?"

Before Jamal could respond, another voice drifted from behind a display case.

"I have a story to share, too," said a soft-spoken archivist, stepping forward with a weathered photograph clutched in her hands. "It's a story of struggle, but also of triumph. We must remember every detail."

Jamal and Omari exchanged glances, their expressions reflecting both determination and understanding.

Jamal's gaze lingered on the console, its soft glow reflecting in his eyes. A quiet weight settled over him—the unshakable feeling that the voices of those he'd lost were urging him forward. Slowly, he nodded. Together, he and Omari approached the console, gathering stories and recollections from fellow abductees. Each tale became a piece of something larger, an unbroken chain of memory and resilience. With every entry, Jamal felt a small piece of his burden lift—replaced by the understanding that in preserving the past, they were shaping the future.

Later that evening, Maya sought a moment of solitude near a waterfall that cascaded under the silvery glow of Noctivara's twin moons. The air was soft against her skin, carrying the scent of alien blossoms and cool minerals. She settled onto a smooth rock at the water's edge, knees pulled in tight. The waterfall mesmerized her, each droplet catching the moonlight until the spray shimmered like falling stars. She let her mind drift, finally allowing thoughts of Ethan to surface.

A gentle voice broke the stillness.

"The water sings of old sorrows and new beginnings, doesn't it?"

Maya turned slightly, finding a wanderer who had been meditating nearby. She managed a small smile.

"Yes," she murmured. "It carries the echoes of everything we've lost, and yet, promises something more."

The stranger studied her for a moment before offering a knowing glance. "In every goodbye, there is a hidden hello. Hold onto that hope."

Maya exhaled slowly, letting the words settle.

She could still see Ethan's smile in her memory, feel the warmth of his hand in hers. They had loved each other fiercely, but Earth—fractured by inequality, violence, and desperation— hadn't given them the space to dream. Her fingers drifted to her stomach, where new life took shape, a miracle she was still learning to accept. The thought that Ethan might never know about the child cut deep, sharp as a blade laced with regret.

"He tried," she whispered into the hush of the water, her voice trembling with the weight of longing. "He really tried. But trying isn't always enough."

For a moment, she closed her eyes, wrestling with the ache in her chest. The waterfall's gentle roar became a lullaby, offering a bittersweet solace. Noctivara was supposed to be a fresh start, but she couldn't help wondering—would the child someday ask about Earth? About the father they would never meet? The unanswered questions circled her thoughts, pulling her between sorrow and the fragile hope that she might protect this new life from the shadows she herself could never escape.

A soft voice from behind startled her. "You speak as if every drop of water holds a secret. "Maya turned to see a figure emerging from the dim light—a fellow traveler named Rina.

"Maybe sharing those secrets could ease the burden," Rina added gently. Maya hesitated before nodding. "Perhaps. But some secrets are too heavy to tell. "Rina reached out, giving her hand a reassuring squeeze. "Then let us carry them together."

Maya rose and made her way back through the settlement, her path lit by soft, shifting hues that rippled along the walkways. The ambient glow cast a tranquil atmosphere, but beneath its beauty lay an ever-present hum—an energy that pulsed through the very architecture of Noctivara. As she entered the administrative center, she was met with sleek corridors lined with faint, pulsing veins of light, each rhythmic pulse a reminder that this place was unlike the world they had left behind.

The Great Divide: When Earth Lost Its Shadow

Turning a corner, Maya halted abruptly. Just ahead, two Noctivara stood locked in an intense exchange. Though their language was foreign to her, their stiff postures and clipped gestures made the tension unmistakable. One of them, his voice edged with authority, barked, "We cannot ignore the strain any longer!" His counterpart's response was measured, deliberate. "But unity must prevail, even in discord." Though Maya didn't understand their words, the urgency behind them sent a shiver down her spine.

She pressed herself against the wall, heart hammering, straining to catch any clue that might give meaning to their conversation. A few terse remarks later, the pair parted, heading in opposite directions without another glance. The air in their wake felt charged, unsettled.

Maya lingered, unease coiling in her gut. Noctivara's serene exterior, so carefully projected by Zara, now seemed thinner, more fragile. The harmony that had once felt so seamless now carried an undertone of something else—something unspoken.

That evening, as the group gathered for their meal, Maya sought out Zara. She measured her words carefully.

"Noctivara is beautiful," she said, her voice even despite the unease curling in her chest. A brief pause, then—"But beauty can mask fractures. Is everyone here as united as you claim?"

A fellow traveler, one who had been observing just as closely, spoke softly. "I've seen the smiles, but also the guarded glances. What binds us together if not the courage to acknowledge our scars?"

Zara's expression remained serene, her smile unwavering, though something in her gaze sharpened. "Belief isn't always necessary for progress," she replied. "Unity, however, is."

A brief silence stretched between them before another voice from the gathering added, "And sometimes, unity is only real when we confront those fractures."

The words lingered in Maya's mind long after the conversation had ended. What did Zara's version of unity truly mean? Was it a bond forged in shared purpose, or a fragile peace maintained by suppressing dissent?

As she sat with these thoughts, Noctivara's enchanting glow remained unchanged, its shimmering rivers and living structures as breathtaking as ever. And yet, the deeper she looked, the more she sensed that paradise—no matter how luminous—always concealed cracks beneath its surface. Still, a part of her clung to hope. Perhaps, here in this strange and radiant world, they could carve out a second chance. Or perhaps, like every utopia, Noctivara would prove to be something else entirely—something far more complicated than they had imagined. Only time would tell.

A hushed conversation unfolded near the meal tables as a few members of the group gathered.

"Do you really believe in this promise of unity?" Leon asked quietly, his gaze steady on Zara.

"I want to," she admitted, her voice soft yet unwavering. "But sometimes, I wonder if we're building on sand."

Leon's expression darkened slightly, but before he could respond, Estele—usually reserved but always sincere—spoke up. "Then let our dialogues, our shared truths, be the mortar that binds us together."

In the background, laughter and the gentle clinking of utensils blended with the soft hum of the settlement—a quiet chorus affirming that, despite their uncertainties, every conversation, every exchange of hope and vulnerability, wove them ever closer in this strange new world.

Jamal found Maya sitting beneath an arching tree, its blossoms glowing faintly like stars. He hesitated before joining her, the cool stone bench grounding him as he sat. For a while, neither spoke. The silence was thick, but not uncomfortable.

Finally, Jamal broke the stillness. "I think I'm starting to find my place here," he said, his voice contemplative as his eyes drifted over the softly illuminated surroundings. "But it's... complicated."

Maya turned to him, her expression searching. "Complicated how?" she asked, her voice quiet but pressing, her eyes reflecting both the moonlight and her inner unrest.

Jamal exhaled, his fingers tracing the grooves in the bench. "It's hard to think about building something new without mourning what we lost. Omari says we're preserving Earth's culture, but sometimes it feels like we're just holding onto fragments of a broken world." His words lingered in the air, carried by the faint rustle of the leaves.

Maya nodded slowly, the weight of his thoughts settling over her. "Maybe that's all we can do for now," she murmured. "But maybe... maybe those pieces are enough to build something better." Her voice was careful, as though she were testing the idea aloud—hopeful, but aware of the uncertainty that came with it.

A brief silence followed as they both turned their eyes upward. The twin moons cast a gentle glow over Noctivara's crystalline fields, their beams shimmering across the dew-laden ground.

"Do you ever think," Maya asked, her voice barely above a whisper, "that maybe the pain of loss is what makes us appreciate every small bit of beauty here?"

Jamal considered her words, then nodded. "I do. It's as if every memory, every shard of sorrow, deepens our ability to love what we have now."

Their silence deepened into something unspoken but understood—a quiet bond forged in both grief and resilience.

Later that night, Noctivara pulsed with quiet life. Bioluminescent plants glowed in harmony with the planet's subtle heartbeat, casting soft shadows that wove together beneath the light of the twin moons. In that tranquil glow, the settlers began to see Noctivara not just as a refuge, but as a place where healing could take root.

Even Maya, still tethered to the ache of loss, felt the faint stirrings of something new—possibility.

Noctivara was not merely a sanctuary. It was a canvas where fractured, resilient souls could begin to shape their futures. The gentle hum of life surrounded the settlement, a quiet reminder that beauty often rose from brokenness.

As Maya and Jamal sat beneath the arching tree, their shared presence spoke louder than words. They didn't need to voice their resolve; in every glance, every moment of quiet understanding, they made a silent promise—whatever the future held, they would face it together.

The next morning brought a subtle shift in the air. The group had been assigned tasks to integrate into the settlement, contributing to the communal effort that defined Noctivara's philosophy. Maya was assigned to the arboretum—a sprawling expanse of flora, much of it native to Earth, meticulously preserved and nurtured by the Noctivara.

The Great Divide: When Earth Lost Its Shadow

As she wandered the arboretum's winding paths, Maya couldn't help but marvel at the care taken to recreate fragments of the old world. She brushed her fingers against the familiar texture of a fern leaf, and memories of home surged forward with the whisper of each rustle. Nearby, the gentle trickle of a stream wove through the space, a quiet counterpoint to the murmur of her thoughts.

Her task for the day was to plant seedlings—new hybrids designed to thrive in Noctivara's unique soil. The Noctivara assigned to guide her was a reserved yet patient individual named Lirian. With silvery skin that shimmered under the morning sun, Lirian demonstrated the precise technique for embedding the delicate seedlings into the earth.

"You must press gently but firmly," Lirian said in a calm, measured tone as they worked side by side. "These roots are fragile now but will grow strong if given the proper care."

Maya mimicked the motion, glancing at Lirian. "Do you miss where you came from?"

Lirian paused, their hands stilling as if caught in a distant thought. "I do not know what it means to miss. My people remember, but we do not yearn. We believe that where we are is where we must be." The simplicity of Lirian's words left Maya both comforted and unsettled.

As the day unfolded, their conversation continued in quiet intervals. Maya pressed soil around a sprouting seedling and murmured, "Sometimes, I feel like every new life we plant is a silent rebellion against our loss." Lirian's gaze held a quiet understanding. "Indeed. Each seed is a promise that life persists, regardless of what has been left behind."

Meanwhile, Jamal spent his day in the cultural hub, working alongside Omari. The space—filled with relics of the past—was alive with echoes of those who had come before. Omari's steady presence was grounding, and their conversations often drifted between the practical and the poetic.

Together, they sorted through the items brought by the abductees: photographs, trinkets, and scraps of paper bearing hastily scribbled memories of the old world. One small, worn bracelet of braided leather caught Jamal's eye. Its simple design concealed the depth of its significance, the accompanying tag reading, Made by my grandmother, for strength.

Holding the bracelet delicately, Jamal murmured, "It's strange. Something so small can hold so much."

Omari looked up from his work, his expression thoughtful. "That's the nature of memory," he said, his voice soft, as if revealing a personal truth. "It doesn't need grandeur to endure. Sometimes, the smallest things carry the greatest meaning."

A moment later, another voice broke their reflective silence. "I still remember my mother's words when she made me a similar bracelet. 'Strength isn't about never breaking, but about putting yourself back together.'"

A young woman, her eyes shimmering with both sorrow and hope, stepped forward to add her own memory to the collection.

Encouraged by her openness, Jamal asked, "Do you think these tokens help us hold onto what matters?"

The young woman offered a faint smile. "They remind us who we were and who we can be, even if the pieces seem scattered."

Omari then introduced Jamal to the art of essence crafting, a practice unique to the Noctivara. "Essence crafting," Omari explained, "is not about mastering a skill. It's about expressing what cannot be spoken."

Jamal's initial skepticism faded as he tentatively tried his hand at the craft. His first creation—a small, uneven sculpture with twisting lines and curves—rested in his palm.

"It's... not great," he admitted with a rueful laugh, holding it up to examine its flaws.

Omari's smile was warm and encouraging. "It is honest. And honesty in expression is far more important than perfection."

That evening, as the group gathered around a communal fire pit, its flames shifting in an otherworldly blue hue, conversation flowed as freely as the flickering firelight. The aroma of a meal prepared from Noctivaran ingredients—a fusion of Earth-inspired dishes and exotic, alien flavors—filled the air. People took turns sharing stories; some were whispered recollections of lives left behind, while others carried hopeful visions for the future.

Maya sat quietly, her gaze fixed on the shifting fire. The murmurs of conversation around her made her feel like an outsider, an observer at the edge of a world she wasn't quite ready to step into. When Zara approached and took a seat beside her, the quiet authority of the leader's presence was undeniable.

"You're quiet tonight," Zara observed gently, her tone inviting rather than pressing.

"I'm just... thinking," Maya replied, her eyes never leaving the flames.

Zara tilted her head, studying Maya intently. "Noctivara is not Earth. It never will be. But that doesn't mean it can't become something just as meaningful. The question is whether you'll allow yourself to see it." Her voice was soft yet carried an undercurrent of conviction that stirred something deep within Maya.

Maya hesitated before responding. "It's not that simple. Earth is... was... everything to me."

Zara nodded slowly, acknowledging the depth of Maya's pain. "I understand. But sometimes, the hardest part of letting go is realizing that holding on doesn't bring it back."

A heavy silence settled between them, thick with unspoken emotions. The fire's glow cast soft shadows across Zara's face, highlighting the sincerity in her expression. For a fleeting moment, Maya almost believed there might be hope in moving forward.

As the group began to disperse for the night, Jamal lingered near the edge of the settlement. The twin moons hung low in the sky, their silvery light stretching long, contemplative shadows across the crystalline fields. He thought of Omari's lessons on essence crafting and the importance of preserving memories.

"Maybe this world can be something extraordinary," he murmured, half to himself, half to the night. "Not Earth, but something new and full of possibility."

In the days that followed, the settlers gradually found their rhythm within the community. Maya and Jamal, alongside others, began carving out roles that both honored their past and embraced the future. Yet, as they adjusted, subtle tensions simmered beneath the surface.

One morning, Maya was summoned to her first formal assembly—a gathering of representatives from various factions within Noctivara. The central chamber, an open amphitheater nestled among bioluminescent trees, hummed with quiet intensity. Noctivara delegates mingled with human settlers, their expressions shifting between curiosity and caution.

Zara stood at the center of the chamber, her presence commanding attention as she addressed the assembly. "Today,

The Great Divide: When Earth Lost Its Shadow

we discuss the integration of Earth's people into Noctivara's systems," she began, her voice steady and deliberate. "This is a partnership, not assimilation. But partnerships require effort on both sides."

A murmur rippled through the crowd. Caleb, a young man whose uncertainty was evident in his gaze, rose to speak. His voice wavered, yet his words carried undeniable urgency. "We're grateful to be here, but it feels like we've barely had time to mourn what we've lost. How can we build a future when we haven't even come to terms with our past?"

The murmurs grew louder, with several humans nodding in agreement. Meanwhile, the Noctivara delegates exchanged discreet, guarded glances. Zara remained composed, but her response was unwavering. "Mourning is a privilege Noctivara cannot afford. The survival of this settlement depends on unity and progress. Grief must not stand in the way of what needs to be done."

Maya felt the words like a physical blow. As she scanned the amphitheater, she saw the same conflict mirrored in the faces of her fellow settlers. Driven by an unshakable resolve, she slowly rose and cleared her throat.

"With respect, Zara," she said, her tone measured but firm, "grief isn't a privilege—it's a process. If we don't acknowledge what we've lost, how can we truly embrace what's ahead?"

For a long, tense moment, silence blanketed the amphitheater. Zara's gaze sharpened, her expression unreadable. "You believe mourning will strengthen us?"

"I believe it will make us whole," Maya replied, steady despite the tremor of emotion beneath her words. "You brought us here because we were broken by Earth. If we don't take the time to heal, those fractures will follow us into Noctivara."

A heavy stillness settled over the gathering. Finally, Zara inclined her head slightly. "Noted. Let us move forward."

As Maya sat down, she felt Jamal's reassuring hand on her arm—a silent gesture of solidarity.

Later that evening, as the twin moons climbed high above the settlement, restlessness pulled Maya to the outskirts of the arboretum. Drawn by instinct, she wandered into a secluded grove near a cluster of ancient trees. There, concealed in the shadows, she overheard hushed voices.

Zara was speaking with a group of Noctivara delegates.

"...Progress must be accelerated." Zara's firm voice cut through the darkness.

A tall delegate with copper-toned skin responded in a low, urgent tone. "Humans are unpredictable. We must maintain control, or their integration will fail."

Maya's heart pounded as she strained to catch every word.

"This is their sanctuary," Zara continued, her voice shifting to a softer, almost soothing tone. "But sanctuaries require structure. They'll adapt in time."

The conversation ended abruptly as the group dispersed into the night, leaving Maya trembling in the shadows. Her mind raced. What exactly did Zara mean by 'structure'? And how far was she willing to go to ensure this so-called unity?

The next day, Maya sought out Jamal in the cultural hub, where he was working with Omari, cataloging yet another batch of artifacts. The moment he saw her, concern flashed across his face.

"You look like you've seen a ghost," he remarked, setting aside a small carved piece.

Maya lowered her voice and recounted everything she had overheard. As she spoke, Jamal's expression darkened.

The Great Divide: When Earth Lost Its Shadow

"That doesn't sound like someone who's just trying to help," he said gravely. "It sounds like control—like they want us to fall in line."

Maya swallowed hard. "I don't know what to do. Zara is the one who brought us here. People trust her. But if she's hiding something..."

Jamal cut in, his tone firm. "We need to be careful. If we're going to challenge Zara—or whatever this is—we need more than suspicions. We need proof."

Maya met his gaze, a flicker of determination rising within her. "You're right. But we can't do this alone. We need allies."

Jamal glanced at Omari, who had been silently listening. "I think I know where we can start."

As dusk painted Noctivara in deep purples and golds, the three of them gathered in a quiet alcove of the cultural hub. Omari listened intently as Maya recounted fragments of the overheard conversation. His expression remained unreadable, but the concern in his eyes was unmistakable.

"There is more to Zara's plan than she has shared," Omari said after a thoughtful pause. "Leaders often carry burdens that cannot be easily explained to their people."

Jamal's jaw tightened. "Or burdens they don't want us to question."

Omari inclined his head slightly. "Perhaps. But if you truly wish to understand Zara's motives, there may be a way to learn more. The administrative center houses an archive—a repository of information about Noctivara's founding, its systems, and its governance."

Maya's eyes narrowed. "And how do we access it?"

Omari hesitated before replying, "There are certain... permissions required. But I have worked closely with the

Noctivara for many years. I believe I can grant you temporary access."

Maya studied him for a moment. "Why are you helping us?" Her voice was cautious but laced with hope.

Omari met her gaze steadily. "Because I, too, have questions. And because I believe that understanding is the foundation of true unity."

As they left the alcove, Jamal squeezed Maya's hand reassuringly. "We're in this together," he said softly.

Maya nodded, her heart a mixture of fear and determination. "We have to find out what kind of future we're really building here."

In the silent corridors of the administrative center, the three prepared to uncover the hidden archive, knowing their discovery could change everything they believed about Noctivara. Their whispered dialogue echoed against the dimly lit walls of the ancient data vault, each word bringing them closer to truths long buried. In that hushed space, where anticipation and dread coiled tightly together, Maya, Jamal, and Omari braced themselves for the revelations ahead—truths that might not only redefine their understanding of unity and control but also alter the very future of their new home.

That night, under the shroud of darkness, Omari led Maya and Jamal through the sleek, silent corridors of the administrative center. The only sound was the faint hum of energy pulsing through the walls. Moving with practiced ease, Omari's steps were measured, his movements deliberate.

They arrived at a sealed door, its surface faintly aglow. Omari pressed his palm to a small panel, the soft light casting sharp shadows across his face. With a quiet hiss, the door slid open, revealing a dimly lit chamber filled with holographic consoles and shimmering displays.

"This is the core archive," Omari said, stepping aside to let them enter. "It holds records of Noctivara's construction, governance, and integration protocols."

Maya's pulse quickened as she approached one of the consoles. The interface was unfamiliar, but Omari guided her through the process of accessing the files. "Just follow my lead," he murmured, his tone steady.

Jamal leaned over her shoulder, his brow furrowed. "What exactly are we looking for?" he asked quietly.

"Anything that explains what Zara meant by 'structure' and 'control,'" Maya replied, her voice low, tight with unease. "I need to understand if we're in danger of becoming... something less than human."

Minutes blurred into hours as they sifted through the archive. Most of the files contained technical schematics and logistical reports, their sterile language a sharp contrast to the depth of human memory. Then, at last, Maya stumbled upon a series of encrypted memos. With Omari's help, they cracked the first one.

The words made her stomach twist.

Memo 03A: Human Integration Protocols

While the humans' arrival has been successful, it is clear that their emotional and cultural baggage poses a significant risk to Noctivara's harmony. Measures must be taken to ensure compliance with Noctivara systems. Emotional regulation protocols may be necessary to prevent discord. Recommend accelerated implementation of adaptive neuro-conditioning.

Maya's hands shook as she read the words aloud. "Neuro-conditioning? Are they planning to reprogram us?" she whispered, barely audible over the quiet hum of the archive's machinery.

Omari's expression darkened, his usual calm giving way to quiet tension. "I had no knowledge of this," he said slowly, as if weighing each word. "This isn't just about integration—it's about control on a level that strips away what makes you human."

Jamal's voice dropped, thick with anger. "This isn't just about control," he said. "This is erasure. They're willing to strip away our memories, our emotions… everything that makes us who we are."

A surge of fury ignited within Maya, sharpening into a grim clarity. "Zara's vision for Noctivara isn't about freedom—it's about forced conformity. If we don't act now, we won't just lose our home; we'll lose ourselves."

As they emerged from the archive, the cool night air struck Maya's skin, sharp and bracing—a stark contrast to the stifling tension inside. Overhead, the stars burned bright, a silent reminder of just how far they were from Earth and the fragile precipice on which their future now teetered.

Jamal broke the silence as they moved through a narrow passageway toward the settlement's edge. "We can't let this go unnoticed," he said firmly. "If Zara catches wind of what we've found, she'll come after us. We need to be sure. We need to be ready."

Maya's pace slowed as she reached the settlement's boundary, where the artificial lights faded into the vast darkness beyond. "If Zara finds out…" she began, her voice steady but low, "everything we've built here will be twisted into something unrecognizable."

Omari studied her, his luminous Noctivara eyes reflecting the faint glow of the perimeter lights. His voice was measured, but beneath it lay an unmistakable edge of warning. "Caution is wise," he said. "But do not wait too long. Zara does not leave loose ends untied."

Maya held his gaze, her pulse quickening under the weight of his words. "We'll be careful," she promised, her voice resolute. "But we'll be ready. We have to tell the others—they need to know what's at stake."

Jamal nodded. "They deserve the truth. This is about more than survival. It's about who we are. We can't let them erase us."

Omari exhaled slowly, his expression unreadable. "Then our next step is clear. We must gather evidence and prepare to share it with—"

The next morning, Maya awoke with a singular focus. Challenging Zara's vision would take more than whispers in the shadows. It would require strategy, courage, and a network of people who believed in something greater than themselves.

She spent the day moving through the settlement, quietly reaching out to those she trusted. Caleb was the first to stand with her. That afternoon, he arrived at her door, eyes burning with renewed passion, a notebook clutched tightly in his hand.

"I've been thinking about what you said," Caleb declared the moment he stepped inside, his voice charged with conviction. "About standing up for what makes us human. I want to help. I can't sit back while they erase our past."

Maya welcomed his urgency. "I'm glad you're here, Caleb," she said. "We need to move quickly. There are others who feel the same—people who remember, who still cherish the stories and traditions of Earth."

Together, they worked late into the afternoon, compiling names and contacts. By evening, they had gathered a small group in the backroom of Aisha's modest home. The room, its walls covered in papers marked with Noctivara script and human translations, pulsed with quiet determination.

Aisha, a linguist whose work bridged the understanding between species, addressed the group with calm authority. "This settlement wasn't built on survival alone," she said, her voice steady yet resolute. "We came here with stories, traditions, and languages. If we allow Zara to erase that, we won't just lose our humanity—we'll lose the very essence of who we are."

A murmur of agreement spread through the room. Maya stepped forward, scanning the faces before her. "We can't let Zara dictate what Noctivara becomes," she declared. "The Noctivara gave us this opportunity, but it's up to us to define what it means. We have to protect our identity—not just for ourselves, but for the generations that follow."

Caleb leaned forward, his expression thoughtful. "But how do we fight back? How do we resist someone with this much power?"

A heavy silence settled over the room as Maya absorbed the question. Then she squared her shoulders. "We start small. We grow strong. And when the time comes, we make our voices impossible to ignore."

Determined glances flickered between the group. "We need to document everything," Aisha suggested softly. "Every memo, every protocol that exposes their plan. That's our proof."

Caleb nodded. "And we have to do it quietly. If Zara catches wind of this, she'll shut us down before we have a chance."

Maya's gaze hardened with resolve. "We'll be careful. But we must also be bold. Our future depends on it."

That night, after the rally, Maya retreated to the solitude of the waterfall. The roar of cascading water drowned out the distant hum of the settlement, offering her a rare moment of introspection. She sank onto a moss-covered rock at the edge, gazing into the shimmering pool below. Her reflection wavered, distorted by the rippling surface—much like the uncertain future she now faced.

She placed a hand over her stomach, feeling the gentle stirrings of new life—a quiet, undeniable reminder of what was at stake. "You deserve better," she whispered, her voice trembling with raw emotion. "We all do."

Bathed in the soft glow of moonlight, Maya allowed herself a quiet conversation with her own heart. "Zara envisions a Noctivara where everything is controlled, where the chaos of our humanity is stripped away. But how can we exist without our stories, our emotions... our very souls?"

A breeze carried her words into the night, and in her mind, she heard the voices of those who stood beside her. *We remember because it makes us who we are,* Aisha's steady tone echoed in her thoughts. *And every story, every tear, every smile adds color to our existence.*

Maya closed her eyes, letting the rhythmic thunder of the waterfall ground her. Caleb's passionate plea, Jamal's unwavering resolve, Omari's measured warnings—they all wove together, their words a quiet symphony in her mind. "I will fight for us," she vowed softly. "For my child, for every soul who left Earth to build something new. I will not let our humanity be erased."

The moons climbed higher, their silver light dancing across the water. Noctivara might have been built by the Noctivara, but its soul, Maya knew, would be shaped by those courageous enough to dream of something greater. "I'm ready," she whispered, her words carried away on the cool night air.

In the days that followed, the clandestine network solidified. Secret meetings were held in hushed corners, whispers passed between trusted allies, and evidence of Zara's plans was carefully gathered. With each meeting, Maya's resistance grew—not in aggression, but in unwavering defiance.

During one such gathering in the quiet early hours, Caleb confronted a worried settler. "We can't let our history be wiped clean," he said urgently. "Every memory, every tradition—it's our strength. Without them, what are we?"

The settler hesitated, their voice unsteady. "I'm scared. I came here hoping for a new beginning, but now… now I fear we're losing ourselves in the process."

Caleb placed a steady hand on the settler's shoulder. "We'll fight this. We're not alone. We have each other, and together, we will protect what makes us human."

And so, with each conversation and every shared story, the movement grew—a quiet but determined resistance against a future of imposed uniformity.

As the day of the planned rally approached, Maya gathered with her core group one last time. "This is our moment," she said, her voice both gentle and fierce. "Tomorrow, when the settlement convenes, we will speak our truth. We will demand that our humanity, our past, and our stories be preserved. We will not remain silent."

Jamal, seated nearby, added, "This isn't just about resisting control—it's about reclaiming our identity. We must remind everyone that to be human is to embrace both joy and sorrow, memory and hope."

Omari, ever the steady presence, offered his quiet support. "Remember, truth is our light in the darkness. Let it guide us as we step forward together."

That final conversation was filled with unwavering resolve, each voice a declaration of purpose. And as night fell once more, Maya returned to the waterfall—not to mourn what had been lost, but to draw strength from the unyielding rhythm of life.

Gazing into the reflective pool, she spoke softly into the night, as though entrusting her hopes to the water. "Tonight, I am not alone. I am part of a collective heart that beats with memory, with resistance, and with the fierce desire to truly live."

Her words merged with the steady cascade, a vow carried by the water's eternal flow. "For our past, for our future, we will stand together. And no matter the cost, we will protect the essence of who we are."

Above her, the moons shone brighter than ever, casting their silver glow upon the water's surface. And beneath their quiet light, Maya felt the fire of revolution kindling within her—a force ready to burn through the shadows of control and reignite the brilliance of the human spirit in Noctivara.

Chapter 6: Survivors Saving Survivors

A hush settled over Noctivara's central promenade as Maya and Jamal made their way toward the Council Chamber. The air carried the faint scent of engineered florals, cool and crisp against their skin. Overhead, iridescent vines spiraled gracefully around vaulted archways, their bioluminescent tendrils casting shifting, dreamlike patterns upon the polished floor. The living mosaic pulsed in harmony with the city's central power grid, each subtle flicker a reminder of the forces at play beneath the surface.

Though they had walked this path countless times before, today each step felt heavier, laden with the weight of recent revelations and unspoken fears. The Council Chamber, nestled at the heart of Noctivara like a sacred vow, was known not only for its serene, almost ethereal architecture but also for the heated debates that had defined its history. Towering windows framed the city's lush alien flora—broad-leafed trees in hues of pale blue and soft pink, clusters of glowing fruit swaying in an artificial breeze, and delicate winged creatures darting between branches, their movements swift and watchful.

Inside Maya's mind, memories and emotions collided. The whispers surrounding the Noctivara's rescue of the Black diaspora, the growing tension over cultural erasure, the quiet burden of her own secret pregnancy—it all swirled like fragments of a half-remembered dream. With every step, her

The Great Divide: When Earth Lost Its Shadow

pulse quickened. The weight of what awaited them inside the chamber settled deep in her chest, a mix of apprehension and resolve.

At her side, Jamal glanced at her. "You okay?" he murmured, his voice low but threaded with genuine concern. The simple question, barely above a whisper, carried the full weight of their shared uncertainties.

Maya forced a small, grateful smile, though it barely masked the turmoil beneath. "As okay as I can be," she said, her tone steady despite the storm within. She nodded toward the looming chamber doors, their surfaces etched with faint symbols that glowed under Noctivara's bio-lights. "What about you?"

Jamal ran a hand over his close-cropped hair, his expression betraying the strain he tried to hide. "I'm... trying not to overthink it," he admitted. "We survived Earth and built a new life here. I just want to make sure we don't lose what makes us who we are."

Together, they reached the towering entrance. With a soft hiss, the doors parted, breaking the silence as they stepped inside the circular meeting hall.

The chamber's centerpiece was a mosaic floor that shimmered in pastel hues, its surface inlaid with precious stones and alien minerals, each detail a tribute to both artistry and survival. Along the walls, glowing inscriptions recounted the story of Noctivara's founding and the Noctivara's solemn vow to protect those who had once been cast aside. High above, a domed ceiling arched in sweeping panels, simulating a sky tinged with lavender dusk—a quiet echo of Earth's lost sunsets.

Seated in curved rows around the hall were representatives of Earth's Black communities, a gathering of people who had once been scattered across continents. Their attire ranged widely—from traditional prints imbued with ancestral echoes to practical suits and casual modern wear. Each face reflected resilience, a quiet defiance against displacement and loss.

At the heart of the assembly stood Zara, the imposing Noctivara leader. Draped in a flowing robe of silver-black fabric that shimmered with Noctivara's ambient light, she exuded an almost otherworldly composure. As Maya and Jamal entered, Zara lifted her gaze. Her neutral expression shifted, softening—just slightly—into acknowledgment.

For a fleeting moment, the eyes of everyone in the chamber met, as though silently affirming the truth none could deny: their fates were now irreversibly entwined.

A soft hum—like the distant murmur of a sacred chant—signaled the start of the session. Zara raised her hands, palms outward in an inviting gesture that contrasted with the austere grandeur of the room.

"Today, we gather to confront the weight of our shared pasts and the possibility of a unified future," she began, her voice clear and melodic, carrying both hope and an unspoken warning. "Neither will come without struggle."

A ripple of acknowledgment moved through the council. Maya and Jamal took their seats in the front row, exchanging measured nods with Elder Simone—a Haitian matriarch whose wise eyes had witnessed many trials—and Nia Sarpong, a poised representative from West Africa. Nearby, Adewale, a fiery youth leader from Nigeria, sat with arms folded tightly, his expression set in a mask of skepticism that spoke volumes without a single word.

The Great Divide: When Earth Lost Its Shadow

Zara's gaze swept over the assembly with steady intensity. "We Noctivara have observed Earth for decades," she said, her tone measured. "In doing so, we recognized your resilience—but also your oppression. As Earth's ruling powers once believed forced assimilation would tame you, we intervened to prevent a collapse that would have echoed far beyond your atmosphere."

Across the hall, a few heads dipped in quiet approval. Others, however—like Adewale—bristled at the word intervention, as though it was a wound too raw to touch.

"Your presence here is no accident," Zara continued. "But let me be clear: our actions were not without consequences."

As the council listened with rapt attention, Zara's tone softened, shifting to something more personal. The cool detachment in her eyes gave way to a quiet sorrow.

"We, too, were once fractured by a cruel caste system that slowly eroded our identity," she confessed, her voice faltering only slightly. "For centuries, those among the Noctivara who resisted conformity were systematically eradicated. By the time we rose in rebellion, our planet was scarred beyond repair. We had no choice but to flee, carrying with us not only our lives but a vow—to spare others from suffering our fate."

For several long moments, silence settled over the chamber. Some council members leaned forward, drawn in by the raw honesty in Zara's words. Fatou Ndiaye, a Senegalese historian, quietly dabbed at her cheeks with a handkerchief, her eyes brimming with unshed tears. She had long studied the parallels between Earth's oppressed and the Noctivara's struggles—and now, hearing them spoken aloud, she felt those wounds laid bare before her.

In that charged atmosphere, a flash of memory seized Maya.

For a breathless instant, she was back on Earth during its final days, standing on a crumbling city street. Protests raged beneath acidic rain, desperate voices crying out for clean water, for fair resource distribution. Smoke choked the skyline, distant fires blurring the horizon, while ominous shadows loomed overhead—silent harbingers of the collapse to come. She had known, even then, that no system could truly save them. The realization had been as bitter as it was inevitable.

The memory faded as swiftly as it had surged, leaving Maya with a visceral understanding of Zara's words.

Zara's voice, now thick with emotion, carried through the chamber. "We recognized in your planet the same cruelty that nearly destroyed us," she continued. "Your liberation was essential—not only for your own survival but for the balance of the galaxy. For if oppression is left unchecked, it spreads like a virus, infecting all it touches."

Almost as if on cue, the atmosphere in the chamber shifted.

Nia Sarpong rose, the gold embroidery on her dress catching the soft mosaic light. Her voice was measured, yet unwavering. "We must also address the manner in which you 'liberated' us," she said. "By removing Black cultural contributions from Earth, you not only inflicted chaos on a dying planet but also denied us the agency to shape our own destiny. Is this truly different from the oppressors we fled—those who made decisions for us without our consent?"

A murmur rippled through the chamber. Some council members nodded in agreement, while others exchanged troubled glances. The weight of the question seemed to reverberate off the ancient walls.

Zara inclined her head slowly. "We believed your culture was being exploited, commodified in ways that would erase its true value," she replied. "Removing those contributions was an attempt to preserve them from further misuse. But I do not deny the moral burden of that decision. We never intended to replicate the very injustices we sought to end."

Adewale, unable to contain his anger, shot to his feet and slammed his hand against the table. "But you did!" he shouted, his voice ringing through the cavernous hall. "You decided on our behalf, uprooted us, and stole from Earth. Calling it preservation is no different from the tyranny we fought against! If you truly wanted to help, why not empower us to decide our own fate?"

A wave of subdued agreement swept through the chamber.

Maya's heart pounded as the voices around her rose with raw anger and pain. She glanced at Jamal, whose eyes were dark with concern, then returned her gaze to the speaker. The intensity in the room was palpable—a collective wound that refused to heal.

Zara's expression softened, a glimmer of regret flickering across her otherwise impassive features. "The collapse of Earth left us little time for negotiation," she said quietly. "The ruling powers were consolidating control in ways that threatened your very survival. We acted quickly—perhaps too quickly—for the sake of immediate preservation."

Sensing the conversation teetering on the edge of an impasse, Maya took a deep breath and rose to her feet. Beneath her, the mosaic floor pulsed with an almost sentient light, as if reflecting the gravity of the moment.

"We cannot deny that Earth was in desperate straits," she began, her voice steady despite the storm inside her. "But Adewale's point is clear—the absence of consent is a wound that will not simply heal. Our culture, our heritage, is not something to be hidden away or decided for us by others."

She scanned the room, locking eyes with each council member in turn. "If the Noctivara truly wish to help, they must step back and allow us to determine how we rebuild our culture. We must have the freedom to decide what remains, what is preserved, and what evolves."

Jamal joined her at the front, clearing his throat before speaking with quiet intensity. "I propose we create a Living Archive—a comprehensive repository that not only collects all the art, science, technology, and history taken from Earth's Black communities but also serves as a dynamic center for debate, innovation, and evolution. No more gatekeepers. We will own our past and shape our future on our own terms."

A hush settled over the chamber. Some council members leaned forward, eyes alight with interest; even Elder Simone's normally stoic face betrayed a flicker of hope.

In that charged silence, Omari, who had been observing quietly from the side, murmured, "So the diaspora controls it—not the Noctivara."

Jamal nodded emphatically. "Exactly. We can accept the help offered by the Noctivara, but it must be on our terms. We decide our future. No more paternalism. Our culture is ours to shape."

The Great Divide: When Earth Lost Its Shadow

For several long seconds, no one spoke as Maya and Jamal's proposals settled over the room. Then, the chamber erupted into a flurry of voices. Some members praised the idea of a Living Archive, calling it a beacon of hope; others demanded specifics. How would it be governed? Who would have access? How could they ensure the archive wouldn't be manipulated by outside forces?

Fatou Ndiaye, her eyes glistening with unshed tears, spoke in a hushed, trembling voice. "How do we guarantee that our heritage is governed by us, free from external interference?"

Caleb, a determined African-American organizer, leaned forward, his voice both calm and fervent. "We must be mindful of internal power struggles," he cautioned. "Our history is rich, but it is also complex. We need clear guidelines to prevent one faction from dominating another."

Adewale, still burning with indignation, pushed back. "The archive must be completely free of Noctivara involvement," he insisted. "If they continue meddling, our culture will be diluted beyond recognition."

Maya's pulse hammered as the voices rose around her, reverberating through the chamber's vaulted ceiling. She became acutely aware of the pressure in her abdomen—a private reminder of her own future—and the raw weight of responsibility. Steadying her breath, she clenched and unclenched her fists, willing herself to stay composed.

Near the mosaic, Zara stood in silence, the bioluminescence of her attire shifting from cool green to a deep, solemn blue, mirroring the gravity of the discussion. Finally, she raised a hand, her voice calm yet unwavering.

"We will open every database we have," she declared. "You will have full control over the Living Archive. This is not an empty gesture—it is the only way to address the mistakes of our past."

In the lull that followed, Omari stepped forward, drawing curious and expectant glances from the assembled council. He had long been a quiet, steady presence in smaller gatherings, but rarely had he spoken so boldly in the main council. His expression was measured—neither blind in loyalty to the Noctivara nor entirely aligned with Earth's diaspora.

Clearing his throat softly, he began, "If I may offer a suggestion: I have been studying the technology the Noctivara used to store Earth's cultural contributions. It is far more advanced than anything we have seen—a system that fuses data with partial organic computing. With the proper oversight, this technology can be integrated into a dedicated facility here on Noctivara—one managed entirely by the diaspora."

Jamal leaned forward, intrigued. "Are you saying we can do this ourselves?" he asked quietly, hope flickering in his eyes.

Omari nodded. "Yes. The Noctivara have the data, but they do not have the right to keep it hidden from you. With my guidance—and the expertise of those here—the diaspora can shape how and when these cultural assets are reintroduced. We can decide what is preserved, what is celebrated, and how it evolves."

Maya studied Omari carefully. In his steady gaze, she saw not only his technical expertise but also a quiet empathy that resonated with her own struggles. *We are all carrying secrets— pain, hope, and dreams alike,* she thought.

A small cluster of council members, including Adewale, Elder Simone, and Nia Sarpong, pressed him further, their

The Great Divide: When Earth Lost Its Shadow

voices merging into a respectful yet urgent inquiry about the logistics and oversight of the proposed facility. Omari answered each question with calm precision, reinforcing the notion that true control over their heritage was no longer a distant possibility—it was within reach.

As the debates ebbed and flowed, the atmosphere shifted once more when Zara stepped forward to address the assembly. Her tone darkened, and the council quieted, each member keenly aware of the weight in her words.

"There is more you need to know," she began, her voice heavy with unspoken gravity. "We did not act on Earth's behalf without risk. Our intervention was not without opposition—from other galactic forces that see our 'reparations' as a threat to their established order."

A palpable unease spread through the room. The quiet murmur of voices faded into tense silence.

Maya's stomach twisted with worry. Their struggle was no longer confined to Earth—it stretched into the vast unknown. If Noctivara's fate was entangled with unseen cosmic forces, what did that mean for the future of the diaspora? She shot a troubled glance at Jamal, whose eyes mirrored her unease.

Zara pressed on, her voice sharpening with urgency. "We do not say this to frighten you, but to prepare you. If you choose to build a strong cultural presence—if you create this Living Archive—it will not only serve as a record of your heritage but also as a beacon. And in the vast arena of galactic politics, a beacon can attract both allies and enemies."

A soft murmur rippled through the assembly.

A woman from the Caribbean diaspora spoke, her voice unsteady. "So we're not just up against Earth's old order. We must contend with entire star systems?"

Zara bowed her head in quiet empathy. "It is possible. But know this: we Noctivara stand by you. We will not abandon you should conflict arise—though you must be prepared to defend what is rightfully yours."

The tension peaked as Elder Simone rose, leaning on a beautifully carved wooden staff etched with the artistry of Haitian tradition. Her voice, though gentle, carried the weight of hard-won wisdom.

"I cannot deny my gratitude for being alive," she began slowly, "but if this intervention thrusts us into a cosmic struggle, we must be absolutely certain that we shape our own destiny—rather than become pawns in someone else's game."

A low rumble of agreement spread through the chamber.

Caleb adjusted his glasses with quiet determination before standing. "We must proceed with the Living Archive," he declared. "Our cultural survival depends on our ability to reclaim our heritage and decide our future. If that means drawing unwanted attention, so be it. We did not escape Earth only to be silenced by new oppressors."

At that, voices erupted once more—some urging caution to avoid external aggression, others insisting that bold action was the only path to true liberation.

Beneath them, the mosaic floor pulsed with an urgent glow, mirroring the rapid beating of their collective hearts. Overlapping voices, impassioned yet measured, filled the domed space as the council divided along lines of hope, fear, and defiant resolve.

Maya clenched her jaw, the crushing weight of leadership pressing down on her. She could not let rising panic splinter them now.

Before she could speak, Adewale slammed his hand on the arm of a seat, the sharp impact echoing like a gavel.

"If we cower, we might as well have never left Earth!" he roared.

His words sliced through the noise, silencing the room in a brief, charged moment. Every soul present was left to confront the raw truth of their choices.

Throughout the debate, as voices collided and intertwined, Maya's mind wavered between the present and the past. She found herself slipping into memories—glimpses of protests on Earth, the distant echoes of demands for justice in streets that had long since faded into history. These recollections stirred something deep within her, a fusion of sorrow and determination. Each moment of remembrance fueled her resolve, pushing her to lead not just with unwavering strength but with the compassion that the future demanded.

As the session came to an end, the atmosphere remained charged—the council was divided, yet bound by a common fate. The decision was final: a Living Archive would be created, and the diaspora would reclaim the cultural legacy that had been taken from them. At that moment, Maya's eyes burned with fierce determination—a silent vow that, no matter the cost, their heritage would be preserved, and their future shaped on their own terms.

The chamber's heavy doors slowly swung shut behind them as the session concluded, and the assembled council dispersed into the corridors. Each step carried the lingering echoes of heated debate and the weight of an unspoken promise—a promise that would soon be tested.

Seizing the moment amid the stunned silence that followed the heated debate, Maya rose slowly, her posture straight yet trembling with the intensity of her convictions. Her voice, though unsteady at first, gathered strength with each word.

"We can't ignore the risks," she declared, her eyes blazing with determination. "But fear alone cannot define us. We are not the same scattered communities Earth left behind. We are survivors—strong, resourceful, and resilient. We have made it to this new world not by chance, but by sheer will."

Her words, steady yet charged with raw emotion, filled the chamber as she turned to Zara. "We will build the Living Archive—on our own terms. We will keep learning, forge alliances where we can, and stand firm when necessary."

At that moment, a subtle flutter in her abdomen reminded her of the life growing inside her—a quiet promise of the future that steeled her resolve. I'm not just doing this for us, she thought. I'm doing it for the next generation, for the child who will inherit our struggles and our hope.

Her tone softened as she added, "We must remember: we are now the architects of our own culture." A murmur of cautious agreement rippled around the table. Adewale met her

The Great Divide: When Earth Lost Its Shadow

gaze, his expression measured before he gave a firm nod. Elder Simone lowered her carved staff—a subtle but unmistakable sign of approval amid the lingering tension.

Sensing that both progress and tension had reached a boiling point, Zara called for a short recess. The formal session paused, and council members broke off into smaller, quieter clusters. Overhead, the luminous mosaic dimmed slightly, as if the chamber itself exhaled in relief at the temporary reprieve.

Maya and Jamal slipped through a carved archway onto a secluded balcony. Outside, Noctivara's sky had deepened into a velvety twilight, its celestial expanse awash with swirling, nebula-like clouds. Along the balcony ledge, soft, luminescent flowers emitted a low, soothing hum—a gentle counterpoint to the intensity they had just left behind.

Jamal leaned against the cool railing, exhaling slowly. "That was... intense," he murmured, his tone edged with both exhaustion and lingering adrenaline.

Maya rubbed her temples as if trying to ease the strain of the day and nodded. "I knew it would be challenging, but I never imagined so many layers—the trauma of Earth, the burden of the Noctivara's intervention, and now the shadow of potential galactic threats." Her voice was quiet but carried an unyielding strength.

For a moment, Jamal's gaze lingered on her midsection—a silent acknowledgment of the secret she carried—before returning to her face, concern flickering in his eyes. "And you," he said softly, "handling all of this while expecting a child... You're stronger than you know."

Maya half-laughed, half-sighed. "I just hope I don't break before we see this through," she admitted, her tone laced with both humor and vulnerability.

A soft footstep announced Omari's arrival. He stepped onto the balcony with quiet grace and offered a small, apologetic bow. "I'm sorry to intrude," he said, his voice low and sincere. "I just wanted to check—are you both all right?"

Maya managed a faint smile. "We'll survive. That's what we do," she replied, her voice steadier now.

Omari's gaze lingered on the horizon before returning to them. "I believe in what you're trying to build here," he said quietly. "I want to help ensure that the diaspora truly controls the data—and, ultimately, the future of that archive."

Jamal studied Omari's face, searching for hidden motives in the soft glow of the balcony's lights. After a long moment, he replied, "We could certainly use your expertise—but that means trusting you deeply."

Placing his hand on the railing, Omari met their eyes. "I understand. I'll earn that trust, if you'll allow me."

Above them, the alien night parted to reveal twin moons— one a pale silver, the other tinted turquoise—casting shifting patterns across the balcony floor. For a few serene moments, the three stood in silence, letting the cosmic beauty soothe their turbulent thoughts.

When they re-entered the council chamber, it was clear that the recess had cooled some of the earlier tempers. Zara and a few Noctivara advisors stood near the mosaic, quietly conferring as council members gradually resumed their seats. Subdued murmurs filled the space, reverberating off the domed ceiling and blending with the soft patterns of projected constellations.

Elder Simone raised her staff and gestured for attention. "We have conferred amongst ourselves," she announced, her voice calm yet carrying the force of collective resolve. "Most of us agree to proceed with the Living Archive—provided we establish oversight committees to ensure that no single faction or individual dictates its content."

Nia Sarpong added, "And we expect the Noctivara to provide material and technical support, then step aside. Should we see any sign of interference, we reserve the right to lock you out of the archive entirely."

Zara inclined her head in acknowledgment. "We accept these terms," she said quietly, "and we want your culture to flourish on your terms, not ours."

A modest ripple of agreement followed. Adewale's expression remained guarded, but he voiced no further objections. Maya felt a quiet relief bloom inside her as she exchanged a lopsided smile with Jamal—a silent affirmation that, for now, they had reached a fragile accord.

With the major points settled, the council shifted its focus to drafting frameworks and ironing out the technical details of the Living Archive. Some members hurried to outline charters, while others debated the best way to integrate Earth's lost breakthroughs—from fiber optics to long-forgotten manuscripts—into the archive. The soft glow of the mosaic pulsed steadily, mirroring the shift to a more measured, though still charged, atmosphere.

Amid the flurry, Omari stepped forward to address the assembly. "If I may add something personal," he began, his voice firm yet measured. "There is a part of my identity that I have long kept hidden. My mother was half-Noctivara, half-human, taken from Earth long before the mass evacuations. I am a child of two worlds, and that heritage compels me to help. But I understand if that makes some uneasy."

A weighted silence settled over the chamber as several council members exchanged glances. Fatou Ndiaye frowned in deep thought, while Adewale's jaw tensed, his expression unreadable. Yet no one rose in protest.

Elder Simone, tapping her staff lightly against the floor, spoke with quiet authority. "We have no quarrel with your heritage, Omari. If you are sincere in supporting our autonomy, we welcome your contribution."

Omari exhaled slowly, a mix of relief and residual anxiety in his breath. "Then I promise to help integrate the archive's interface in a way that guarantees diaspora sovereignty. All I ask is that you grant me the trust to prove my commitment."

Jamal's gaze softened, and he offered a quiet, reassuring smile. "Trust will be earned on both sides," he said. "Thank you, Omari."

With the formal debate concluded, Zara declared the session closed. Delegates began filing out in small clusters—some still debating details in hushed tones, others exchanging guarded smiles. Though tension lingered, it had shifted from an impasse to a shared challenge—one they had all agreed to confront together.

The Great Divide: When Earth Lost Its Shadow

Maya remained by the glowing mosaic, watching the swirling lights reflect against the gentle curve of her belly. Slowly, she placed a palm over it, feeling the quiet rhythm of her heartbeat align with the subtle pulse beneath her feet. In that still moment, she imagined the future of her child in this alien yet hopeful world.

A soft, measured voice interrupted her thoughts. Zara stood quietly behind her. "Your burdens run deep, Maya," she said with quiet compassion. "But I see in you the strength of countless ancestors—resilient and unyielding."

Maya offered a faint, grateful smile. "Sometimes I wonder if I'm only strong because I'm too scared to show weakness," she admitted softly.

Zara's gaze, illuminated by the ambient glow, was steady yet kind. "Fear can be a guide—if you let it push you toward vigilance rather than despair," she replied.

Maya turned her eyes toward the grand windows, where the sky stretched vast and unfamiliar, a silent, bittersweet reminder of the Earth they had lost. "Maybe we'll create new constellations here," she murmured. "New stories to honor what we've lost." Her voice carried the weight of both promise and prayer.

Night had finally settled over Noctivara, wrapping the city's living architecture in a tranquil hush. Bioluminescent flora pulsed in gentle, rhythmic waves, mirroring the planet's own subtle energy currents. The council had dispersed, yet the decision to build the Living Archive burned brightly in every heart—a commitment to reclaim stolen legacies and shape a future on their own terms.

Maya walked slowly along a high skywalk connecting the council chamber to a residential wing. Below, floating gardens shimmered with exotic flowers in soft pastels, their fragrance carrying a delicate blend of citrus and an indefinable sweetness. She paused at the railing, letting the cool breeze temper the lingering flush on her cheeks as she sifted through the day's tumultuous events.

Her mind replayed the faces from the council—the fierce determination in Adewale's eyes, the tempered pragmatism in Nia's expression, and Elder Simone's guarded yet hopeful gaze. She thought of Zara's luminous figure, burdened by both authority and guilt, and Omari's earnest promise to help. Every word, every exchange, stirred within her a complex mix of pride and trepidation.

A step behind her, Jamal appeared, offering a weary yet genuine grin. "Couldn't sleep either, huh?" he said softly, his voice carrying the weight of exhaustion with a glimmer of hope.

Maya exhaled slowly. "Not a chance," she murmured with a bittersweet smile. They stood side by side at the railing, their gazes drawn to the glowing gardens below. In the distance, a hidden waterfall cascaded onto luminous lily pads—a serene contrast to the storm of thoughts in her mind.

"You did good today," Jamal said, his voice low and steady. "You held firm when the council could have easily splintered."

Maya leaned into him slightly, grounding herself in his quiet presence. "We all did our part," she murmured. "Even Adewale, with all his anger, reminded us that we must not forget our pain. That anger is part of our story—just like survival, resilience, and hope."

Jamal nodded slowly, his gaze tracing the unfamiliar constellations above. "It's strange," he said, "to think these stars aren't the same ones we once saw on Earth. But maybe that's the point. We're creating something new beneath them."

Maya's thoughts drifted to the child growing inside her and the legacy they would leave for future generations. "We have a lot of work ahead," she whispered, "but there's hope. And we're not alone."

Together, they stood in companionable silence, allowing the quiet rhythms of Noctivara to soothe their weary souls. Far below, the cosmos gleamed as if promising that even in darkness, a new light would rise. In that moment, Maya thought, We are survivors saving survivors. And with that, she silently vowed that their future would be etched in the luminous halls of Noctivara—a future built on unity and defiance against all forms of oppression.

Chapter 7: The Fractured World

The acrid stench of smoke hung thick in the humid air, while the distant wail of sirens wove into the cacophony of anger and despair. The camera lingered on a young girl clutching her painted sign, as if her heartbreak encapsulated the world's sorrow. Her wide, tear-brimmed eyes locked onto the lens—pleading, demanding answers no one could provide.

The world had seemed ordinary enough, perhaps too preoccupied with its routines to notice the first whispers of something amiss. The morning the disappearances began was unremarkable—except for the strange stillness that settled over entire neighborhoods. Schools, workplaces, hospitals—entire institutions ground to a halt as the truth came into focus. Black communities, from sprawling urban centers to remote villages, had vanished overnight. No warning. No trace. Just an eerie, suffocating silence where life had once thrived.

Governments scrambled to respond, issuing statements filled with platitudes and empty assurances. Scientists debated theories—some suggesting biological phenomena, others pointing to radical technology. Fringe theorists seized the moment, spinning tales of alien abduction and shadowy cabals. But in the days that followed, the cracks in society's carefully constructed facade began to widen.

The disappearance wasn't just personal—it was systemic. Businesses reliant on Black labor and ingenuity faltered. Entire

The Great Divide: When Earth Lost Its Shadow

industries faced a void of talent, creativity, and expertise. Hospitals lost skilled physicians and nurses. The entertainment world dimmed in the absence of its brightest stars. Communities were left hollowed out, their foundations stripped away. And as the reality set in, the world began to grasp a truth it had long refused to confront.

But this unraveling didn't occur in isolation—it was merely the latest chapter in a long history of scapegoating and exploitation that had always placed Black communities at the center of both blame and burden. For centuries, they had been dismissed as disposable yet depended upon as indispensable. When crises arose, they were the first to be sacrificed, the designated culprits for society's failures.

During Reconstruction in the United States, when Southern economies floundered after the Civil War, freed Black individuals were blamed for the region's poverty, even as their labor underpinned the agricultural recovery. In Europe, during economic downturns, African immigrants were scapegoated for rising unemployment and social unrest, despite their contributions to rebuilding war-torn nations. And in modern times, public health crises and economic recessions have disproportionately devastated Black communities—while society either turned a blind eye or, worse, assigned blame to those most affected.

This pattern of scapegoating wasn't just social—it was systemic. Black individuals were forced into positions of servitude and subjugation, their contributions erased from history even as they laid the foundation for global innovation and progress. The institutional caste systems that emerged placed Black communities at the bottom—not by accident, but by design. They were tasked with rebuilding after every collapse, sustaining entire industries, and generating wealth they were rarely allowed to share.

And now, with their sudden disappearance, the fragility of those systems was laid bare. The world, which had thrived on the exploitation of Black labor, creativity, and ingenuity, found itself gasping for survival without them. What had long been treated as disposable had proven to be essential. Their absence wasn't just felt—it was seismic, a reckoning for a global society that had long relied on exploitation without accountability.

The consequences extended far beyond industries and economies. Without Black teachers, cultural custodians, and healers, the very soul of the world seemed to dim. In their absence, a stark truth surfaced: this wasn't just about what was missing—it was about what had always been taken. The disappearances weren't random; they were the culmination of centuries of marginalization, masked as progress.

But history had revealed something else: Black communities had always rebuilt in the face of destruction. From the ashes of slavery, they birthed cultural renaissances. After decades of disenfranchisement, they fought for and reshaped democracy. The world might have ignored their value in life, but now, it was about to learn the cost of their absence.

And this time, those left behind refused to be silent. Across cities and villages, the burden of history ignited a growing resistance. The fires of protest burned not only for those who had vanished but for the centuries of injustice that had led to this moment. This time, those who had been scapegoated would not let the world forget. Their absence was the reckoning, but their legacy would be the uprising.

The Great Divide: When Earth Lost Its Shadow

On the streets of Washington, D.C., the protests swelled in both size and intensity. What began as candlelight vigils had erupted into riots. Anger flooded the streets as people demanded answers from leaders who had none. National Guard troops patrolled the city, their presence an ominous reminder of the state's fragility. The National Mall, once a symbol of unity and progress, had become a battleground of ideologies and desperation.

A Black protester—once a well-regarded community organizer before the disappearances—took to the makeshift stage erected near the Washington Monument. His voice boomed through a megaphone, cutting through the clamor.

"They told us we were nothing! They told us we were disposable! But look around you—what happens when you take away the so-called 'nothing'? The world collapses! Our absence is their reckoning!"

Cheers and chants erupted, surging through the crowd like wildfire. But beneath the fervor, fear simmered. The words resonated with those who had lost loved ones, yet the absence of answers gnawed at their hope. Where had everyone gone? Were they alive? Was this a form of divine punishment—a cosmic reckoning for centuries of injustice?

Social media became a breeding ground for speculation. Hashtags like #WhereAreThey and #BringThemBack trended alongside a deluge of misinformation. Some posts went viral, claiming grainy footage of UFOs hovering over predominantly Black neighborhoods before the vanishings. Others spread pseudo-scientific theories about mass teleportation events triggered by secret government experiments.

A particularly insidious theory blamed the disappearances on the victims themselves. "They left because they wanted to," a prominent pundit sneered during a televised debate. "After all, why wouldn't they? They've been telling us for centuries they're sick of our world."

But the devastation was undeniable. Entire economies teetered on the edge of collapse. Fashion industries that thrived on Black culture struggled to find relevance. The tech sector, once propelled by Black innovation, faced stagnation. Even the food supply chain faltered, as agricultural hubs reliant on Black farmers and workers crumbled under the strain.

Amid the chaos, a chilling pattern began to emerge. Surveillance footage, satellite images, and intercepted communications pointed to an unsettling synchronicity in the disappearances. They hadn't been random, nor were they geographically isolated. It was as if an unseen force had meticulously orchestrated the exodus.

Back at the protest, the journalist wiped her face with the sleeve of her jacket, smearing soot across her cheek. Sarah Collins—an investigative reporter known for her relentless pursuit of the truth—had spent six months uncovering classified documents, interviewing whistleblowers, and infiltrating covert government meetings.

Standing before the camera, she took a steadying breath and spoke directly to her audience.

"Despite the silence from world leaders, my investigation has uncovered a series of classified documents hinting at global experiments involving 'dimensional rifts.' Governments across the world may have known about these phenomena—and their

The Great Divide: When Earth Lost Its Shadow

potential consequences—for decades. But instead of addressing the risks, they buried the evidence. The question we must ask ourselves now is: What are they hiding? And is it too late to undo the damage?"

As Sarah's words reached millions, chaos exploded around her. Protesters shoved against riot shields as police advanced. Tear gas canisters arced through the air, their hissing release punctuated by panicked screams. Sarah gestured for the cameraman to follow as she ducked into an alleyway, her voice trembling as she signed off.

"This is Sarah Collins, reporting live from Washington, D.C., where the fight for truth—and for those we've lost—continues."

Across the globe, the repercussions of the disappearances were inescapable. Schools teetered on the edge of closure as teacher shortages crippled districts. Churches that had once been the beating heart of their communities now sat in eerie silence. And in nations that had long prospered from the exploitation of Black labor, history pressed down like an unrelenting specter, suffocating under its own weight.

In Lagos, the marketplace was a ghost of its former self. The once vibrant stalls, alive with color, sound, and movement, now stood hollow and abandoned. A lone vendor, his face etched with grief, lingered beside an empty stall. It had belonged to a woman who sold handwoven baskets, her laughter as much a part of the market as the goods she peddled. But now, like every other Black soul in the city, she was gone. As he rearranged his wares, he muttered under his breath, "She always said the world couldn't go on without us. Maybe she was right."

In Detroit, a nurse locked the doors of the hospital where she had once worked tirelessly. Without staff to treat patients or power to sustain equipment, the building was little more than a tomb. She taped a note to the entrance: We tried. Her hands trembled as she stepped back, taking in the emptiness of the streets. Entire neighborhoods had vanished overnight, leaving behind only unanswered questions—questions she wasn't sure she had the courage to ask.

In Rio de Janeiro, a friend stood before the crumbling remains of an apartment complex, calling his best friend's name into the void. He had been among the brightest students at the local university, driven by the dream of building a better future. But now, like so many others, he is gone. The silence that followed was a devastating confirmation.

In a sprawling London mansion, a billionaire tech mogul stood before an empty boardroom, staring at the vacant seats where his executives had once strategized. The past six months had eviscerated his company's workforce, leaving his innovation pipeline barren. His assistant shifted beside him, gripping a tablet filled with bleak financial reports.

"Do you think they'll come back?" he asked, his voice betraying desperation.

The assistant hesitated, her response edged with quiet resignation.

"Would you?"

Back at the protest, the young girl with the sign stood motionless as the crowd surged around her. Amid the chaos, her small figure remained impossibly still, a fragile island in a sea of unrest. A nearby photographer crouched low, capturing a

The Great Divide: When Earth Lost Its Shadow

shot that would soon become iconic: her tear-streaked face framed by the desperate plea, We Miss You. Please Come Back.

Her step-mother had vanished in the initial wave of disappearances. In the weeks that followed, her father lost his job, their home, and, eventually, his will to fight. Now, the sign was all she had—a lifeline in a world that no longer made sense.

As night fell over Washington, D.C., fires burned unchecked, casting flickering shadows across the city's scarred streets. Somewhere in the darkness, a faint hum rose—a sound imperceptible to most but undeniable to the few who could feel it. It was the sound of something shifting, something awakening. The world had been brought to its knees, but the story was far from over.

The faint hum of the servers filled the cramped basement, a stark contrast to the furious clicks of keyboards and the rustling of papers. Ethan leaned back, dragging his hands through his unkempt hair. The cold glow of the monitors cast sharp shadows on his face, highlighting the exhaustion, determination, and guilt etched into his features. The sheer magnitude of what they were uncovering loomed over him like an unrelenting storm cloud.

Across the desk, Liam's eyes flicked over his screen, his expression grim as he pieced together the fragments of a conspiracy that had shattered their world. Stacks of old government files, faded photographs, and encrypted data drives cluttered the space around them—a chaotic mass of secrets no one was ever meant to unearth.

"This doesn't make sense," Ethan muttered, breaking the silence. "How does something this massive stay hidden? There had to be leaks, whistleblowers, someone who tried to stop it."

"They probably did," Liam replied, not looking up. "And they were probably silenced. You think the kind of people who orchestrate this leave loose ends?"

Ethan exhaled sharply, frustration crackling beneath the surface. "It's just—this can't be real. Sacrificing entire communities? How do you even begin to justify that?"

Liam's voice was low, laced with quiet fury. "You don't justify it. You rationalize it. To them, it's numbers on a spreadsheet, Ethan. Lives reduced to statistics, labeled as 'acceptable losses.' That's how they've always operated."

Ethan hesitated, his fingers hovering over his keyboard as doubt took hold. "And what exactly are we hoping to find?" he asked, his voice nearly pleading. "A smoking gun? A confession?"

Liam finally looked up, his jaw set. "We're looking for the one thing they can't explain away. Proof that they knew this would destroy the world and did it anyway. It's not enough to expose this—we need evidence so damning they can't spin it."

Ethan swallowed hard and returned his attention to his screen, the tension between them thick enough to cut with a knife. His cursor hovered over a folder labeled Operation Concord: Final Parameters. With a deep breath, he double-clicked. The screen filled with text—cold, clinical language that outlined an unthinkable reality.

"Liam," Ethan said, his voice tight. "You need to see this."

Liam rolled his chair closer, his brow furrowing as he scanned the document. It detailed a series of secret meetings between Earth's most powerful leaders and an alien species referred to as the Noctivara. The text was devoid of emotion, each line more horrifying than the last. But beneath the list of participants, one directive stood out like a death sentence:

"Proceed with population destabilization to preserve elite control. Technology and resources to be provided as compensation."

Liam's voice broke as he read the words aloud. "They... they planned this. They bargained with those things. Traded millions of lives for their own survival."

Ethan's hands shook as he scrolled further. Another file appeared—Internal Memorandum: Collateral Impact. His stomach turned as he read its contents.

"Projected economic collapse in sectors reliant on Black labor, creativity, and innovation. Estimated timeline: six to eight months. Recommended action: consolidation of resources to prioritize elite infrastructure and survival protocols."

The document ended with a single line that burned itself into Ethan's mind:

"Sacrifice necessary for long-term survival. Focus resources on global elite stabilization."

Ethan shoved back from the desk, his chair scraping loudly against the floor. His chest tightened, his breath coming in short, shallow bursts. "They knew," he said, his voice raw with guilt. "Maya tried to warn me. She saw it coming—what this system was capable of. And I dismissed her. I told her she was overreacting."

iam stood, placing a steadying hand on Ethan's shoulder. His voice was calm but firm. "You're here now. That's what matters. We can't undo what they've done, but we can make sure the world knows the truth."

Ethan nodded, his jaw clenching as his resolve solidified. "We have to expose this. Every file, every memo. People need to know what really happened."

Liam hesitated, shadows flickering in his eyes. "You know what happens if we do this, right? They'll come after us. These people don't play by the rules. They'll kill us if they have to."

Ethan met his gaze, unwavering. "Let them come. If we don't do this, no one will. I don't care what happens to me—this has to stop."

Liam studied him for a moment before nodding slowly, a trace of admiration surfacing beneath his concern. "Alright," he said. "Then we do this together."

They turned back to their screens, the weight of their task pressing down on them. The air in the room pulsed with tension—charged with fear, defiance, and something else: a quiet but undeniable sense of purpose. As they worked, the brutal calculations and callous justifications laid bare in the files only reinforced their determination.

For the first time, they felt like they were fighting back. But deep down, they knew the real battle was only beginning.

The theater groaned under the burden of its years, its ornate moldings cracked and faded, a silent witness to time and neglect. The air hung heavy with tension and the faint scent of mildew. Yet, within its decaying walls, something else stirred. Beneath the broken chandeliers and peeling paint, hope smoldered like the last embers of a dying fire, waiting to be rekindled.

Jean-Louis stood center stage, his silhouette framed by the soft glow of a lone spotlight. The murmurs of the audience faded as he raised a steady hand, commanding their attention. Faces from every walk of life stared back at him—immigrants, laborers, activists, survivors. They were bound by grief, but also by something far more powerful: the need to fight for a future that was slipping through their fingers.

His voice, deep and resolute, cut through the silence like a blade.

"We gather here not because we are weak, but because we are strong. Stronger than the systems that have tried to erase us. Stronger than the fear they use to divide us."

He paused, letting his words settle over the room. In the front row, a young woman in a hijab, her cheeks streaked with tears, nodded solemnly. An elderly man clutched his cane with renewed grip, his eyes glinting with determination.

Jean-Louis pressed on, his voice swelling with emotion.

"Yes, we have suffered an immeasurable loss. Entire communities—gone. Loved ones taken from us without a trace. But we cannot allow that loss to define us. We owe it to them, and to ourselves, to stand tall. To resist. To rebuild."

The crowd murmured in agreement, a rising hum of collective resolve filling the space.

Jean-Louis's expression softened as he spoke of Jamal, his late partner.

"Jamal always said our strength is in our togetherness. He believed in the power of community, in the idea that we could build something greater than ourselves. He gave his life for that belief." His voice wavered, but he didn't falter. "Let us honor his legacy—not with tears, but with action."

Thunderous applause erupted, reverberating through the battered walls. As Jean-Louis scanned the faces before him, he saw more than just grief. He saw something he hadn't witnessed in months: hope. His words had planted a seed. But he knew that seeds did not grow on their own. They needed care. And protection.

Even as the audience erupted in applause, a darker scene unfolded behind the curtain. In a sleek, modern conference room across the Atlantic, Earth's elite convened in secret. The polished glass table mirrored their cold expressions as they analyzed reports detailing Jean-Louis's growing influence.

A young operative entered the room, holding a tablet. "The campaign is live," she announced, placing it on the table. The screen displayed a fabricated news article, its headline blaring: Jean-Louis: The False Prophet? Financial Scandals and Hidden Agendas.

The silver-haired man at the head of the table smirked as he skimmed the article. "Perfect. By the time they realize it's fake, the damage will be done. Perception is everything."

A woman in an impeccable gray suit crossed her arms, her expression sharp. "This man is dangerous," she said. "He's uniting them. If he succeeds, it won't be long before they start challenging our authority."

Another member of the group leaned forward. "What about infiltration? We have someone close to him, don't we?"

"In progress," the operative replied. "They'll begin sowing doubts within his leadership team by week's end. We're also monitoring key allies for weaknesses—past mistakes, hidden scandals, anything we can exploit."

The woman in gray let a thin smile curve her lips. "Good. If we fracture his inner circle, his movement will collapse from the inside."

The Great Divide: When Earth Lost Its Shadow

The silver-haired man steepled his fingers, his gaze cold and unyielding. "Jean-Louis is a symbol, and symbols hold power. But even the most revered symbols can be tarnished. Deploy the usual strategies—disinformation, propaganda, infiltration. Turn his allies against him."

The operative nodded, taking notes on her tablet. "We've already seeded stories questioning his motives. But if he continues gaining momentum, more... direct measures may be necessary."

A slow smirk crept across the silver-haired man's face as he tilted his head. "Good. Keep the pressure on. We don't need to destroy him outright—just cast enough doubt to stall his progress." He leaned back in his chair, his voice steady yet laced with menace. "Time favors us. Let them believe they're winning. When the moment is right, we'll remind them where real power resides."

At the center of the table, a holographic display flickered to life, casting an eerie glow as it projected a map of Jean-Louis's expanding influence. Red dots pulsed over strongholds—Paris, Lagos, São Paulo. A board member gestured toward the area with the densest concentration. "If his reach extends much further, we may have to escalate."

The silver-haired man's smirk wavered, his expression hardening into cold calculation. "Then let's ensure it doesn't." His fingers tapped idly against the surface of the table. "We don't need to destroy him outright—just cast enough doubt to slow him down. Time is on our side."

Back at the theater, Jean-Louis convened with key leaders from various communities. Gathered around a worn wooden table backstage, voices clashed in heated debate.

"This isn't just about survival," argued Aisha, a young activist with piercing eyes. "It's about justice. If we don't hold them accountable for what's happened, we're only ensuring history repeats itself."

Marco, a grizzled union leader, exhaled sharply, shaking his head. "Justice is a luxury we can't afford right now. Survival comes first—food, shelter, protecting the people who are left."

Jean-Louis raised a hand, cutting through the argument. "Both of you are right," he said evenly. "Justice and survival aren't at odds. But we won't achieve either without unity. If we let these disagreements divide us, we've already lost."

The room stilled, but the tension lingered. Jean-Louis leaned forward, his voice steady yet resolute. "We don't have the time or privilege to turn against each other. The systems that shattered our communities are banking on our division. Every second we spend arguing is another second they use to tighten their grip. If we don't stand together now, we'll fall apart."

A hush settled over the group. Slowly, nods of reluctant agreement spread through the room. Aisha and Marco exchanged a glance, then gave a quiet, mutual acknowledgment.

The meeting ended with a renewed sense of purpose. Jean-Louis stepped outside for a breath of air, the cool Parisian night wrapping around him like a cloak. The city was quieter than it had been in years, its usual hum subdued by the ongoing turmoil.

The Great Divide: When Earth Lost Its Shadow

He gazed at the Eiffel Tower in the distance, its lights dimmed to conserve energy. In its shadow, he could almost hear Jamal's voice—steady, warm: "Keep going. You're doing the right thing."

Jean-Louis whispered into the night, "I hope you're right."

By morning, the plans set in motion during the summit began taking shape. Community leaders coordinated resource-sharing efforts, established underground networks to evade government surveillance, and launched a media campaign to counter the elite's disinformation.

But as Jean-Louis's advocacy shifted from grief to action, so too did the threats against him. That night, a shadowy figure lingered near the theater, a camera lens catching the faintest glint in the darkness.

Jean-Louis knew the road ahead would not be easy. The forces he opposed were powerful, ruthless, and relentless. But as he stepped back onto the stage, facing a growing movement of the defiant and determined, one thing was clear: he would not back down.

And neither would they.

The neighborhood bore scars that told the story of its pain—burned-out buildings, shattered windows, and streets overrun with weeds. The silence was suffocating, broken only by the distant hum of a generator and the occasional clatter of debris caught in the wind. Elena stood in the middle of it all, the air thick with the ghosts of a once-vibrant community.

Her hands tightened around the files Liam and Ethan had sent her, their edges crumpled from her grip. The words inside haunted her—cold, calculated plans that reduced lives to mere statistics. She had spent her career championing policies she believed would drive progress, never realizing that the foundations of her efforts had been built on exploitation and erasure. Now, the truth seared through her like a brand on her conscience.

An elderly woman emerged from a nearby building, her gait slow but deliberate. Her face, etched with lines of age and grief, was a map of resilience. A faded headscarf framed her stern expression, and her weathered hands clutched a cane carved with intricate designs. Her gaze locked onto Elena—unflinching, sharp.

"You didn't see us when we were here," the woman said, her voice clear and cutting. "You didn't care to look. Now you see us because we're all that's left."

Elena's throat tightened. For a moment, she couldn't find her voice. The woman's words struck like a hammer, shattering the fragile justifications she had clung to for so long. She had been blind—willfully blind—choosing the comfort of ignorance over the discomfort of facing a broken system.

"I didn't mean—" Elena started, but the woman raised a hand, silencing her.

"You didn't mean?" The elder's laugh was bitter, a harsh sound laced with years of pain. "You didn't mean to ignore the voices? To pass the laws that pushed us out? To build a future you called progress while we stood here, shouting that we were being erased?"

"I didn't understand..." Elena tried again, but her voice wavered. "I thought I was helping. I believed I was making things better for everyone. I didn't see—"

The Great Divide: When Earth Lost Its Shadow

"No," the woman interrupted, her eyes narrowing. "You didn't want to see. You saw enough to know it wasn't your problem. You saw enough to turn your back."

Elena felt the sting of the words, each one a blade slicing through the excuses she had told herself for years. She thought of Maya—how she had judged her, dismissed her pain, all while fighting tooth and nail for Ethan. She had assumed Maya was just bitter, unwilling to understand Ethan's sacrifices. But now, she saw the truth: Maya had been carrying a burden Elena had never even tried to acknowledge.

"You're right," Elena admitted finally, her voice barely above a whisper. "I didn't see. I ignored the warnings, dismissed the voices shouting for justice. I told myself it wasn't my problem, that I was doing enough. But I was wrong."

Her words faltered as she felt the weight of their stares—the woman's, Maya's, and the unrelenting gaze of her own conscience. Memories crashed over her like a tide: every policy she had supported, every vote she had cast, every speech she had delivered. Each had seemed rational at the time, necessary even. But now, standing amid the ruins of lives she had unknowingly helped dismantle, she realized that necessity had been an excuse.

"I want to help," she said, her voice breaking. "I know I don't deserve your trust, but I'm asking for the chance to earn it. Not with words. With action."

The elder woman tilted her head, her expression unreadable. She stepped closer, the wood of her cane tapping softly against the cracked pavement. "Wanting is easy," she said. "Doing is hard. Are you ready for that?"

Elena's mind flashed to a memory—Maya sitting across from her at the bar, shoulders hunched with a weariness Elena had once mistaken for bitterness. Ethan had been pacing nearby, frustration carved into every tense movement. They hadn't just been arguing about strategies or policies; it had been something deeper, something Elena hadn't fully grasped at the time.

"She's holding us back," Ethan had said, his voice low but taut with anger. "We don't have time for doubt."

Maya's retort had been instant, her tone sharp. "Holding you back? I've been breaking myself to keep us moving forward, and you can't even see it."

"You're not the only one sacrificing," Elena had interjected, trying to mediate. "We all have something at stake."

Maya had let out a bitter laugh, her eyes blazing. "Oh, do you? Because while you've been sitting in offices and signing papers, I've been out there. Talking to people who lost everything. Fighting for those who have nothing left to lose. You think you're helping? You're just adding more to the pile we're already carrying."

Elena had felt the sting of Maya's words but brushed it off, telling herself Maya was simply overwhelmed. She had turned back to Ethan, offering him unwavering support, too focused on the mission to see the cracks forming beneath Maya's feet.

Now, standing in the ruins of lives she had unknowingly helped dismantle, those words returned with searing clarity. Maya hadn't been bitter—she had been exhausted, fighting a battle Elena had barely acknowledged. And when Maya had needed someone to listen, someone to lighten the crushing burden she carried, Elena had chosen the easier path. She had sided with Ethan, with plans that now haunted her.

"I am," Elena said, her voice trembling with a mix of remorse and resolve. "Whatever it takes. Not because I want forgiveness. I know I may never earn that. But because it's the only thing left to do."

The elder woman studied her for a long moment, her gaze probing, as though searching for the truth beneath Elena's words. Finally, she nodded. "Good. Then start by listening."

The elder led Elena to what remained of the community center—a hollowed-out building that still bore the faint traces of its former purpose. Faded murals stretched across the walls, their colors dulled by time. A bulletin board, cluttered with old flyers, clung stubbornly to its past, even as the world outside had moved on.

Inside, a small group of people sat in a circle—survivors who had refused to give up despite the odds. Their conversations hushed as the two women entered, and all eyes turned to Elena.

"This one says she wants to help," the elder announced, her tone neutral but heavy with meaning. "But first, she needs to understand."

A middle-aged man with a wiry frame and an unyielding gaze leaned forward, elbows resting on his knees. His skin was sun-weathered, his accent edged with the cadence of the Southwest. "Understand what?" he asked. "That we've been abandoned? That the systems she served were built to crush us? Or that we're here, fighting every day just to survive while people like her profit?"

Elena met his glare, her stomach twisting under the weight of his accusation. "I do understand that now," she said, her voice steady despite the knot in her throat. "I've seen what's happening—the supply routes being blocked, the communities left to fend for themselves, the cover-ups. I know I was part of the problem, but I'm here to be part of the solution."

A younger woman with cropped hair and a scar running across her cheek scoffed. Her voice carried the clipped vowels of the Midwest, but her sharp cheekbones and almond-shaped eyes spoke of a heritage often erased in stories like these. "The solution?" she echoed, disbelief thick in her voice. "You think you can undo what's been done? That pretty words and promises will bring back the people we've lost? The homes we'll never get back?"

"No," Elena said quickly, turning toward her. "I know I can't undo the past. And I'm not asking you to trust me, not right away. But I can fight for what's next. I can use my voice, my position, my resources to help rebuild—on your terms, not mine."

Silence settled over the room, heavy and uncertain. Elena's words hung in the air like something fragile, something waiting to be tested.

The man leaned back, crossing his arms as he studied her, his expression a mix of weariness and measured skepticism. "And what happens when it gets hard?" he asked. "When the people you used to work with—the ones who built these systems—turn against you? When they call you a traitor, or worse?"

Elena's shoulders squared, the fire in her eyes steady and unflinching. "Then I'll keep going," she said. "Because I should have done it long before now. I thought I understood sacrifice. I thought I knew what it meant. But now I see I only knew the version of sacrifice that was safe for me, comfortable. I can't promise I won't make mistakes, but I can promise I won't run. Not this time."

The Great Divide: When Earth Lost Its Shadow

A man in the back of the circle, his dark eyes framed by wiry curls, spoke for the first time. His voice was soft but firm, carrying the weight of lived experience. "Words like those are easy to say when you've always had something to fall back on. My abuela used to say, 'When the winds change, some houses fall faster than others.' So tell me, Elena—what happens when you're the one falling?"

Elena's chest tightened. "I'll stand up," she said, her voice steady. "Because I should have stood up for others when I had the chance. Now, the only way forward is to carry this burden and keep moving."

The elder woman, who had been watching in silence, stepped closer, her cane tapping softly against the cracked floor. "Words are easy, child," she said. "But actions are heavy. Are you ready to carry them?"

Elena nodded, her hands curling into fists at her sides. "I am," she said. "Tell me what to do."

The elder handed her a map, its surface covered with markings—supply routes, safe houses, key meeting points. "This is what we have left. Guard it with your life. And when the time comes to defend it, we'll see if you're really ready."

Elena accepted the map, feeling its weight as if it were made of stone. "I won't let you down."

For the first time, the elder's gaze softened. "It's not about letting us down," she said. "It's about standing up when it matters. Redemption isn't about wiping the slate clean—it's about carrying the burden and walking forward anyway."

As the group laid out their plans—organizing supplies, connecting with other survivor communities, and strategizing ways to expose the conspiracy—Elena listened intently. Each conversation carried the weight of survival and resistance: rationing dwindling resources, scouting safer routes, and keeping their efforts hidden from watchful eyes. Every word was a reminder of the lives she had failed to protect, but it was also a call to action.

The elder woman watched Elena carefully before leaning in. "If you're going to be one of us, you'll need to carry your share of the load. Words are a start, but actions build trust."

"I understand," Elena said, her voice steady. "Tell me what to do."

The wiry man who had spoken sharply before softened slightly as he slid a worn notebook across the table. "Here. Names of contacts—people who've helped us before. Some of them might still be alive. Some... might not." His voice caught for a brief second, but he pushed forward. "If we can reconnect with them, we have a shot at keeping the supply lines open."

A younger woman—her cropped hair damp with sweat from the stifling heat—pointed to a hand-drawn map spread across the table. "This road here," she said, tapping a line with her finger. "It's too close to their patrols. We've lost three runners already trying to get through."

Elena studied the map, her mind sorting through options. "What about this route?" she asked, tracing an alternate path that skirted the danger zone. "It's longer, but it avoids the choke points."

The younger woman hesitated, then glanced at the elder. "It could work... if we can spare the extra fuel."

The elder nodded thoughtfully. "It's a risk, but a calculated one. We'll need someone to test it."

The Great Divide: When Earth Lost Its Shadow

"I'll do it," Elena said before she could second-guess herself.

The room fell silent. Eyes turned toward her. Finally, the wiry man spoke again, his voice edged with grudging respect. "You've never run a supply line before, have you?"

Elena shook her head. "No. But I've planned enough to know how they work. And if I'm going to be part of this, I need to understand what it's like for the people risking their lives every day."

The elder's gaze lingered on Elena—sharp but no longer unkind. "All right," she said. "We'll send a runner with you—someone who knows the route and can show you the ropes."

The younger woman smirked. "Don't slow us down."

"I won't," Elena replied, her voice firm.

The elder handed her a separate map, this one marked with key locations—supply routes, safe houses, meeting points for resistance cells. "This is what we have left. Protect it. Expand it. And when the time comes, use it."

Elena took the map, feeling its weight as if it were made of stone. She had spent years in offices, surrounded by aides and advisors, her decisions filtered through layers of bureaucracy. Now, she stood among the very people she had failed, tasked with something far greater than any policy she had ever signed.

As she rolled up the map, the wiry man spoke again, his voice quieter now. "One more thing. If you're going to do this, you need to understand—it's not just about running supplies or following orders. This is about hope. Every person you meet on this route is holding on by a thread. Every successful delivery is a reminder that they're not alone. Don't lose sight of that."

Elena nodded, the weight of his words sinking in. "I won't forget."

As she stepped toward the door, the elder called after her. "One last thing." Her voice held a softness now, an edge of something close to faith. "Helping us won't erase what you didn't do before. Redemption isn't about wiping the slate clean—it's about carrying the burden and walking forward anyway."

Elena turned back, meeting the woman's gaze. "I know," she said, her voice steady. "And I'll carry it."

Elena's journey was only beginning, but as she walked through the ravaged neighborhood, she felt something unexpected—a spark of hope. For the first time in years, she wasn't running from the truth. She was running toward it.

Her footsteps echoed in the silence, each one a reminder of the burden she carried. *You're not the same person you were,* she thought. *You can't be. Not after everything you've seen. But will they believe that?*

Her hand brushed against the map in her pocket. The lines and markings weren't just directions—they were lifelines, fragile connections holding together the remnants of a shattered world. *Don't mess this up. They're counting on you now. No excuses.*

The files in her hands crinkled as she tightened her grip, their contents etched into her memory. For years, she had seen people as numbers, statistics that could be bent, balanced, or ignored depending on the goal. Now, each page felt heavier than steel, every figure tied to a life she had overlooked until it was too late. *How many lives did I measure and discard? How many people paid for my decisions?*

The Great Divide: When Earth Lost Its Shadow

But this wasn't about guilt. It couldn't be. Guilt was paralyzing, and she couldn't afford to stand still anymore. It's not about what you've done; it's about what you're going to do. Keep moving. Keep fighting.

The elder's words surfaced in her mind, steady as a drumbeat: "Redemption isn't about wiping the slate clean—it's about carrying the burden and walking forward anyway."

She slowed as she reached the edge of the neighborhood, the silhouette of the community center fading into the distance. Turning back, she felt a pang of uncertainty. Will they ever really trust me? Do I even deserve that trust?

But then another thought rose, quieter but firmer: It doesn't matter. Trust isn't the goal. Doing what's right is.

She clenched the files in her hands, her determination hardening. The road ahead would be brutal. There would be failures, setbacks, and sacrifices. But for the first time, she understood—redemption wasn't about erasing the past. It was about carrying it forward and choosing to act anyway.

As she faced the unknown, she drew in a steadying breath. This was only the first step, but for the first time, she was ready to take it—and keep going.

Ethan tightened his grip on the phone as the wind howled around him, cutting through his jacket like a blade. The flash drive in his pocket felt heavier than it should, a tangible reminder of the responsibility he carried. Below him, waves crashed against jagged rocks, their relentless force at odds with the stillness of the moment.

"I hope you know what you're doing, Ethan," Jean-Louis said, his voice edged with both concern and admiration. "The

Noctivara aren't just playing games. If what we've uncovered is true, this isn't just about Earth anymore."

Ethan's jaw tightened as he replayed the files he and Liam had unearthed. The Noctivara's influence stretched deep, their technology entangled in Earth's survival. But the truth was darker than anyone had imagined. The disappearances of Black communities weren't just collateral damage—they were the first step in something much bigger. The directives from the elites weren't just a betrayal of their own people. They were part of a pact.

"Jean-Louis, we've spent months reacting to what they've done. It's time we stop playing defense. The Noctivara think we're too fractured to fight back, and Earth's leaders think we're powerless. They're wrong."

Jean-Louis sighed heavily. "And you think exposing these files will change that? You've seen how quickly they bury the truth."

Ethan's gaze drifted toward the horizon, where the setting sun bled across the sky in streaks of orange and crimson. "The truth isn't just in the files. It's in the people. The ones who disappeared, the ones who are still here. If we show the world what's really happening, it won't just be anger—it'll be action. The kind they can't suppress."

Silence stretched on the other end, the weight of Jean-Louis's thoughts thick even through the static. "And what about the ones who disappeared?" he asked quietly. "Do you really think you can bring them back?"

Ethan swallowed hard, the question hitting him like a blow. He thought of Maya—her laughter, her fire, the way she had believed in him even when he couldn't believe in himself. The memory of her smile pushed him forward, even as the odds loomed impossibly large.

He could still hear her voice on the night she left for the protest. "You're better than this, Ethan," Maya had said, her eyes burning with both determination and frustration. "You talk about justice, but when it comes time to act, you freeze. What are you so afraid of?"

"Losing you," he had whispered—too quietly for her to hear.

Now she was gone, and all that remained was the emptiness where she had been. Ethan clenched his fists, the ache of her absence settling deep in his bones. He wouldn't fail her again. Not this time.

"I don't know," he admitted. "But I have to try. If the Noctivara are responsible, then there has to be a way to reverse it. And if there's a way, I'll find it."

Jean-Louis's voice softened. "You're taking a dangerous path, Ethan. You're not just going up against Earth's elites—you're challenging something far bigger. And you'll be doing it alone."

Ethan shook his head, a faint smile tugging at the corner of his mouth. "Not alone. You'll be here, fighting for the people who are still standing. And I've got Liam. Besides..." He reached into his pocket, pulling out the flash drive and holding it up to the fading light. "I've got everything I need."

As Ethan ended the call, a low hum vibrated through the air. His eyes narrowed, scanning the sky. At first, he thought it was a distant aircraft—until he saw it. A sleek, dark shape hovered just beyond the cliff's edge, its surface absorbing the fading light.

It wasn't human.

Ethan's pulse quickened. He had seen images of Noctivara technology in the files, but nothing had prepared him for the sheer presence of it. The craft seemed to pulse with an unnatural energy, its smooth edges defying logic and gravity.

A beam of light flickered to life beneath the vessel, cutting through the dusk. It didn't just scan—it lingered, pulsing with an energy Ethan could feel deep in his chest, like the resonance of a distant drum. A faint vibration rippled through the ground beneath his feet. Then, a sound—a low, guttural hum—emanated from the craft, reverberating through the air as if speaking to the Earth itself.

Ethan froze, unsure whether the sound was real or imagined, but its presence clung to the night long after the craft vanished into the clouds.

The words from the files echoed in his mind: *Technological compensation will ensure compliance.*

Ethan shivered. What exactly had Earth's leaders bargained for? And at what cost?

His chest rose and fell in uneven breaths as he stared at the empty sky. The message was clear. They were watching.

As night fell, Ethan made his way back to the small cabin where Liam was waiting. The glow of a single desk lamp cast long shadows across the room, stretching over the clutter of maps, files, and hastily scrawled notes. Outside, the world was eerily quiet—the kind of silence that carried the weight of anticipation.

Inside, Liam hunched over his laptop, fingers flying across the keyboard. He glanced up as Ethan entered, his eyes tired but

The Great Divide: When Earth Lost Its Shadow

resolute. "You sure you want to do this? Once we hit 'send,' there's no going back."

Ethan slid the flash drive into the computer, his hand steady. "There was no going back the moment they took Maya. The moment they took all of them." His voice was calm, but the words scraped against raw wounds. Maya. Her name had once meant home. Now, it was a reminder of everything he had failed to protect.

Leaning against the table, Ethan exhaled sharply. The files before him—the evidence they had spent months collecting—felt heavier than they should have. They were proof of the Noctivara's manipulation, their cold, calculated eradication of millions. But for Ethan, it wasn't just about justice. Or even revenge. It was about redemption.

You should have listened to her sooner, his thoughts whispered, relentless. She saw the cracks long before you did. You called it paranoia. Told her to trust the system. And now she's gone because you couldn't see what she was fighting against.

He swallowed hard, the guilt pressing against his ribs like a vice. But guilt wasn't enough—not anymore. He couldn't change the past, couldn't take back the moments he had dismissed her fears or the nights they had argued about priorities. But he could fight for the future. He could fight for her.

"She used to tell me," Ethan said suddenly, his voice quieter, "that people like us—people who try to play by the rules—never win against systems like this. She said the only way to fight back was to burn it all down and start over."

Liam raised an eyebrow, pausing his work. "Sounds like she was smarter than both of us combined."

"She was." Ethan's lips twitched with the ghost of a smile. But the moment passed, and his face hardened once more. "I thought I could keep her safe by staying inside the lines, by not pushing too hard. And now the lines don't even exist anymore."

Liam studied him for a moment, then nodded. "You're here now. That's what matters."

Ethan wasn't sure he agreed.

What if it's too late? What if even this isn't enough to bring her back—or to deserve her if she does come back?

The thought cut through him, sharp and relentless, but he shoved it aside. There was no room for doubt now.

"This isn't just about exposing what they've done," Ethan said, his voice firm. "It's about making sure it never happens again. If we fail—if we let them keep their grip on this world—then everything she fought for was for nothing."

Liam nodded, his fingers poised over the keyboard. "Alright. On your mark."

Ethan took a deep breath, the weight of what they were about to do settling over him like a gathering storm. He thought of Jean-Louis, rallying the people who had been left behind, his voice slicing through the despair like a beacon. He thought of the millions who had been stolen away, their absence an unhealed wound in the world. And then he thought of Maya—not just the woman he loved, but the fighter she had been. Her fire. Her defiance. Her refusal to surrender, even when he hadn't seen what she was truly up against.

She would have done this without hesitation. She would have risked everything to make them pay.

He clenched his jaw. *I owe her that much.*

"They think they've won," he said quietly, his voice steady. "Let's show them they haven't."

"Enter," Ethan commanded.

Liam pressed the key.

The files began uploading, the progress bar creeping forward like a slow, steady heartbeat. A simple keystroke, yet Ethan felt the weight of it ripple through him. This wasn't just about striking back at the Noctivara—it was a declaration. Of defiance. Of hope. Of love.

As the upload neared completion, Ethan exhaled slowly, his hands braced against the table.

This is for you, Maya. For all of us. I'll keep fighting. No matter what it takes.

Far above the Earth, in the void of space, the Noctivara watched. And somewhere, in the vast unknown, a spark of rebellion ignited—a spark that would soon become an inferno.

Ethan closed his eyes, the weight of everything pressing down on him. In the silence of the room, he whispered into the darkness, the words carrying a quiet, desperate hope.

"I'm sorry, Maya. I'm sorry I wasn't enough when it mattered. But I'll make it matter now. I'll make it count. I promise."

Chapter 8: Bridging the Divide

A faint glow of turquoise vines lit the cobblestone paths leading to the Council Chamber, casting a soft, rhythmic light that pulsed in time with the city's central power grid. Vendors in hover-carts lined the walkways, selling spiced teas, fresh fruit genetically adapted to Noctivara's controlled climate, and handcrafted jewelry inspired by African, Caribbean, and Pacific motifs. Parents guided curious children, some pausing to admire mechanical sculptures that whirred and clicked—a tribute to the diverse makers who had shaped Noctivara into a living archive of old Earth traditions fused with advanced technology.

Near a raised platform, a small group of musicians played a blend of steelpan and electronic strings. Their music drifted through the corridors in a soothing, rhythmic hum, while overhead, the arched ceiling projected holographic patterns of an Earth sunset—a reminder of the skies their ancestors once knew.

Yet tonight, something felt off. Whispers wove through the crowd, carrying rumors of an imminent council decision about "helping Earth." Others murmured about unexplained fluctuations in the power grid. A few anxious glances flicked upward toward the shimmering outlines of Noctivara's floating walkways. Even the children, usually boisterous, clung closer to their parents.

The Great Divide: When Earth Lost Its Shadow

Maya paused briefly at a vendor's stall, buying a small cup of hibiscus-infused tea. The vendor, an elderly woman with a turban adorned in intricate beadwork, gave her a knowing nod. "Word travels fast, child," she said in a hushed voice. "Everyone suspects the Council is deciding something big tonight."

"They might be right," Maya replied, forcing a faint smile. The vendor pursed her lips in concern but said nothing more.

Moments later, Maya squared her shoulders and stepped into the Council Chamber, where holographic stars shimmered overhead. The lively energy of the corridors dissolved at the threshold, replaced by the heavy hush of impending decisions. Tonight, normalcy would end—and choices with far-reaching consequences would begin.

The Council Chamber of Noctivara was as much a place of ceremony as it was of governance. Even the massive oval conference table—carved from obsidian and shot through with veins of organic fiber-optic light—reflected the city's fusion of tradition and technology. Above, the curved ceiling simulated a night sky teeming with digital constellations, each one reminiscent of the cultures that had once named them on Earth.

Yet beneath the chamber's beauty, tension coiled thick in the air. Tonight, there were no illusions of peace. Tonight, no one gazed at the artificial stars with wonder. Every set of eyes was fixed either on the obsidian table or on Maya, who stood at its head, her arms rigid at her sides. The copper filaments braided into her hair caught the light each time she turned to address a council member.

Above the council chamber, holographic windows flickered, revealing the faces of Indigenous leaders still on Earth: a Cherokee elder with long silver braids and worry lines etched deep into her cheeks; the Mapuche representative, eyebrows knitted in frustration; an Australian Aboriginal advocate struggling to maintain a calm facade. Their transmissions arrived with intermittent static, making them appear as though they were slipping in and out of reality. Though their images were half-broken, their words were crystal clear:

"We need your help."

Each time the words repeated, a ripple of discomfort passed around the table. They needed help—and if Noctivara didn't give it, there might be no one left to ask again.

Maya sucked in a breath, willing the trembling in her chest to settle. She was used to speaking in front of crowds; back on Earth, before the abduction, she had been a community organizer. But tonight was different. The fate of an entire city—perhaps an entire civilization—rested on her next words.

She cleared her throat. "We were not saved by the Noctivara just to hide up here, away from Earth's problems," she began, keeping her voice steady. "We were saved, allegedly, to build something new—something that can resist what destroyed our old world." She let the words settle before continuing. "If we refuse to help those who remain, then we forfeit the right to call ourselves a refuge."

A charged silence followed. The small audience surrounding the table was a study in contrast. Jari, dressed in a razor-sharp suit, leaned back in his seat, fingers laced together, scrutinizing Maya as though she were an anomaly under examination. Jamal sat to her right, his posture rigid, shoulders locked with tension. Across from them, Kiona—an elder strategist from the Pacific Islands—rested her chin on folded hands, her expression unreadable, weighing every word. Zara

The Great Divide: When Earth Lost Its Shadow

stood just beyond the circle, silver irises glinting with unreadable thoughts.

For a moment, no one spoke. The only sounds were the low hum of Noctivara's ventilation system and the faint crackle of the holograms overhead.

Finally, Jamal broke the silence, his voice edged with both challenge and plea. "Even if we want to help, Maya, you know the risks. Our resources are stretched thin. Even our Noctivara tech can't guarantee safe passage to Earth and back. One mistake could expose our location."

Maya pressed her palm flat against the obsidian surface of the table. A faint swirl of colored light responded beneath her fingertips. "You think Earth's elites don't already know? If they find a reason to come after us, they will. War is coming, whether we act or not."

A murmur rippled through the council, voices overlapping in half-formed arguments. Jari lifted a hand, his tone smooth but firm. "War might come," he said, "but why accelerate its arrival? Noctivara's survival depends on secrecy and strength. If we reach out now, we could be lighting a beacon that draws every threat in the galaxy to our doorstep."

Maya's gaze flicked across the table to Jahi. His posture was so still it was almost unsettling, his head tilted slightly as he listened. He was the only one who had yet to speak.

Why won't he say something?

It was said that Jahi had once sat in the secret rooms where Earth's fate was decided, that he knew more than anyone about why the Noctivara had chosen to save them.

Maya forced her attention back to Jari. "So you're content to watch them suffer?" she challenged. "When we have the means to offer real, tangible support?"

Jari's expression remained collected. "Content? No. But if we die in the process—if the entire population of Noctivara is wiped out—then no one is saved, Maya. Not them, not us."

A metallic scrape cut through the chamber as Idris, a former scientist from Lagos, shifted in his seat. "We're not helpless," he said. "We have advanced med-bays, starship prototypes, stealth capabilities. If we're systematic, there's a chance we can rescue people without revealing our entire city. Or at least buy them time."

Jari waved a dismissive hand. "A chance is not a plan."

"Better a chance than cowardice," Idris muttered.

Zara cleared her throat, drawing all eyes. She stood poised with an almost eerie grace, her silver irises reflecting the overhead lights. "I've advised you on the Noctivara perspective as best I can. But you must understand: the power structures on Earth remain hostile. If you engage, they will respond with force."

Jamal's lips pressed into a tight line. "We're already fugitives in their eyes." Then, more softly, just loud enough for Maya to catch, "If we do nothing, the guilt might destroy us from within."

A hush fell over the chamber. Even the holographic figures from Earth seemed to sense the tension across light-years. Maya scanned the room—Kiona, Jari, Jamal, Idris, Jahi... all of them were either scowling or lost in thought.

She exhaled, then squared her shoulders. "Then we can't let fear rule us," she said, her voice ringing through the chamber. "Are we so afraid to lose what we've built here that we'll condemn others to die?"

Silence followed, thick and unyielding, broken only by the soft hum of Noctivara's life-support systems. Her words lingered in the air, pressing down on each listener with the weight of a moral imperative they could no longer ignore.

While the council wrestled with moral dilemmas, Jahi closed his eyes, letting the murmur of debate fade. In the darkness of his mind, another room took shape—a memory from Earth, three days before the Great Abduction.

He had stood on the periphery of a war room buried deep beneath what had once been Washington, D.C. The air was thick with the scent of stale coffee, recycled ventilation, and the quiet rancor of final negotiations. Around a large oak table sat the last major world powers, their representatives clinging to the fractured remnants of a collapsing civilization. Their suits were neatly pressed, but their eyes carried the exhaustion of too many losses.

At the center stood Kethis, a Noctivara emissary—tall, willowy, his skin so pale it verged on opalescent. His voice cut through the tension like a scalpel. "Your planet is in terminal decline," he said in English, though his strange, layered tones suggested he spoke on multiple frequencies at once. "You have neither the will nor the resources to halt ecological and societal collapse."

No one argued. They already knew it was true. Jahi saw it in their silence—the quiet, bitter acceptance. But he saw something else too: relief.

They're hoping the Noctivara will save them, he realized.

An American defense official rose, adjusting the hem of his uniform, his movements practiced, composed. "And what exactly are you proposing?" he asked, feigning calm.

Kethis folded his elongated fingers together, the joints bending in ways that seemed unnatural to human eyes. "We will remove those who must be preserved," he said. "A partial evacuation."

A twist of unease tightened in Jahi's gut. He could feel it—something monumental, something not entirely altruistic.

Preserved.

The American official's mouth twitched. "And how do we decide who must be preserved?"

Kethis's alien eyes swept the room. "The Noctivara have already decided. We will take the people who have borne the brunt of your planet's injustices—people systematically oppressed, enslaved, and brutalized. We will take Black communities and relocate them to a place where they can thrive."

He said it so simply, as though it were the only logical answer to a cosmic equation.

Jahi's breath caught. He was grateful that so many would be saved—his own family, his neighbors.

But something in the official's cold stare curdled his blood.

"You mean you'll take all of them?" the official pressed carefully. "Including, for instance, children of mixed heritage? People who only have partial—"

Kethis's tone turned icy. "Blackness is not what you define it to be."

A hush fell over the room. Some officials exchanged uneasy glances. Jahi saw fear and hostility flicker across faces that had clung to power their entire lives. Then, a European representative, voice tight, asked, "And what of the rest? Will you also evacuate them?"

Kethis paused. "We cannot. Your planet must complete its collapse. The system itself cannot be salvaged."

The official exhaled sharply. "So you'll leave us to die?"

"You'll be left to your own devices," Kethis corrected smoothly. "The Noctivara do not interfere on a scale that violates cosmic equilibrium. However, we have... uses for some of you."

The finality in his words lingered, settling like a heavy stone in the hush that followed.

And that was when Jahi understood the truth. The Noctivara were not coming as saviors. They were selecting who survived based on an alien sense of morality, or balance, or reparation. And the rest were expendable.

When the meeting ended, Jahi was among the few who truly grasped the magnitude of the arrangement. The officials weren't outraged by the injustice. They were outraged by their lack of control. They would allow the abduction to happen, accepting it as the lesser evil—clinging to the hope that they could bargain for their own salvation later.

That same helpless fury surged back into Jahi's chest as he recalled stepping out of the war room, shadows stretching long across the corridor floor.

The Noctivara wanted to isolate us. Study us, maybe. But Earth's leaders let them do it.

The buzz of the council's arguments pulled Jahi out of his recollection. The memory dissolved, and he was back in Noctivara. The hum of hidden machinery replaced the hush of subterranean corridors. He inhaled, feeling the artificial breeze circulating through the council chamber's climate controls.

Around the table, the debate raged on.

"We have to act," Idris insisted. "We can at least send medical supplies, coordinates to safe zones—hell, even a drone team to gather intel."

"And if that draws an Earth fleet we can't repel?" Jari shot back. "Are you willing to watch Noctivara burn for a maybe?"

Kiona raised a hand. She was one of the quieter members, but when she spoke, people listened. Tiny shells and beads woven into her long hair clacked softly as she addressed the room. "This isn't just about Earth," she said. "It's also about the Noctivara. They gave us technology, but they never revealed their true intentions. If Earth's elites secure new allies—alien or otherwise—what's to stop them from turning on us? The next war may not be fought in the shadows. It could be on our front doorstep."

Zara's gaze flicked to Maya, then to Jahi. "You must realize that if you intervene, you accelerate their timeline. Earth's old powers may already be forming alliances—unions meant to reclaim what they believe is theirs."

Jamal interlaced his fingers, leaning forward, his elbows pressing into the table. "So we sit and wait for them to come for us? That's your solution?"

Zara inclined her head. "I'm advising caution. The real question is—what do your values demand?"

A heavy silence settled over the chamber. Every person in the room could feel it: the clash of two opposing forces—the moral obligation to save lives versus the undeniable risk that doing so could spell their own destruction.

Maya met Jahi's eyes again. There it was—that fleeting look, something almost imperceptible. But she saw it. A trace of regret. He knew something. Something he wasn't saying.

Why won't he speak? she wondered. *What else does he know?*

She drew a shaky breath and turned her focus back to Jari. "We don't need a full-scale operation. Let's start small—five, maybe six people. They can make contact with pockets of survivors and assess whether extraction is even possible."

Jari's skepticism was tangible. "That's a plan without details. Who goes? What resources will they have? What's the timeline for return? And how do we ensure we don't expose Noctivara's location?"

Idris spoke up. "A stealth dropship, cloaked with Noctivara tech. We land under cover, gather intelligence, and leave. If the risk is too great, we abort. Minimal time on the ground, minimal chance of detection."

Jari's gaze swept the council, weighing their reactions. "That's a tall order. We'd have to slip in and out unnoticed—no satellites, no drones, no Earth-based starships tracking us. And if Earth's elites have already acquired advanced weaponry from other off-world sources... we may be walking straight into a death trap."

Maya tightened her fist. "But if we do nothing, entire communities could be annihilated or enslaved by whichever faction seizes power first. And we'll have stood by—again."

A hush fell over the council, the weight of her words settling heavily in the air. Through the expansive windows, Noctivara's floating walkways shimmered under artificial starlight, an intricate network of progress and survival. The city stood as proof of what they could accomplish when left to build in peace. Yet, in that moment, their achievements felt fragile—like crystal, poised to shatter under the slightest pressure.

"Let's put it to a vote," Kiona said gently, though her voice carried steel. "We can refine the details if the majority agrees in principle."

A quiet exchange of glances followed. One by one, the council members offered small nods—some hesitant, others resolute. Even Jari leaned back slightly, a subtle sign of acquiescence.

"Fine," he muttered. "Let's vote."

Before the process could begin, a distant chime reverberated through the chamber. The overhead lights dimmed for half a second—an electrical disturbance that sent a ripple of unease through the room. Maya frowned. Such malfunctions were rare in Noctivara, where the infrastructure was meticulously maintained. She glanced at Zara, who returned a knowing, yet unreadable look.

"Power fluctuation?" Idris asked, fingers already tapping across his personal holopad. "I'll check the grid."

Maya inhaled deeply, forcing herself to push aside the creeping sense of unease. That could be addressed after the vote.

She squared her shoulders. "All in favor of sending a small scout and potential rescue team to Earth, raise your hands or submit your vote electronically. We proceed if we have a majority."

Silence blanketed the chamber as the council cast their votes. A holographic display flickered to life above the table, showing the tally in real time: green for "Yes," red for "No."

- Maya: Yes
- Jamal: Yes
- Idris: Yes

- Kiona: Yes
- Zara: Abstained, though her posture suggested quiet reservation rather than opposition.
- Jari: No, his scowl deepening.
- Two other council members: One Yes, one No.

They held their breath, hearts pounding in unison. The final count blinked in neon light: 5 in favor, 3 against, 1 abstention.

Maya's chest tightened, then released. It passed.

Jari exhaled a resigned sigh. "Then so be it." His voice was oddly hollow.

Zara inclined her head, her silver eyes drifting toward the artificial sky. "You have chosen," she murmured.

Beyond the chamber walls, another flicker rippled through the city's lights—a subtle but undeniable sign that forces beyond Noctivara's control had already begun to stir.

Less than an hour after the vote, Maya slipped away from the Council Chamber under the guise of checking logistical issues. In truth, her destination was the med wing. She moved briskly down a corridor bathed in soft, rhythmic lighting, each pulse aligned with the city's artificial day-night cycle.

Her heart pounded louder with each step, though it wasn't just the weight of the council's decision pressing on her. In the privacy of her own mind, another battle raged—one she hadn't spoken of yet. As she passed a polished metal panel, her reflection caught her eye. The worry lines on her forehead, the rigid set of her jaw—she had always been strong, unshakable. But tonight, fear had begun creeping into her gaze.

The med wing's sleek doors slid open as she approached, revealing a spacious chamber lined with diagnostic pods and data screens. The air carried a faint antiseptic scent, softened by a floral undertone—an attempt to make the space feel less sterile. A few late-shift staff moved quietly, adjusting holographic readouts or restocking supplies.

Dr. Seema, clad in a pale lilac coat, noticed Maya's entrance and met her with a warm, knowing look. She had been overseeing Maya's checkups ever since suspicion first arose. "Maya," she greeted, voice gentle but steady, ushering her toward a private alcove. "I take it you're here for an update?"

Maya nodded, her throat tightening. She followed Dr. Seema into a discreet, glass-walled cubicle fitted with a single diagnostic bed and a large projection screen. The frosted glass hummed as it turned opaque, sealing them in privacy.

A moment later, Maya sat at the edge of the bed, working to steady her breath. Dr. Seema lifted a handheld scanner, positioning it just above Maya's abdomen. A soft blue glow radiated from the device, and within seconds, swirling lines of color appeared on the screen—biometric readings, nutrient levels, and other vital data.

"How is it?" Maya whispered.

Dr. Seema's lips curved into a small, reassuring smile. "So far, everything appears normal—healthy, even. You're roughly eight weeks along, give or take. Our technology can only approximate Earth's measurements, of course."

Maya exhaled a trembling breath. That meant the child had been conceived just before — the London trip where she and Ethan had parted ways, unsure if they would ever see each other again. She pressed a hand to her abdomen. To the untrained eye, nothing had changed. But she felt it. A new life.

"What... what about the risk factors?" she asked, thoughts racing. "The city's gravity is slightly different, the atmospheric composition—"

"Noctivara's environment is remarkably stable, especially compared to a post-collapse Earth," Dr. Seema reassured her. "Your stress levels, however, are concerning. Your hormone fluctuations indicate extreme strain."

Maya let out a hollow laugh. "I'm about to plan a covert mission to Earth—one that might plunge us into war with forces we don't fully understand. Stress is unavoidable."

Dr. Seema rested a hand on Maya's shoulder. "Then find ways to manage it. For your sake—and your child's."

A knot tightened in Maya's stomach. The word "child" still felt unreal. "I'm not sure I'm ready," she whispered. "I didn't think I'd ever have the chance to—" She stopped, her thoughts drifting to Ethan—his unwavering belief that they could build something better from the ruins.

"You have time," Dr. Seema said gently, returning the scanner to its charging station. "Not much, perhaps, but enough to decide your path."

Maya nodded, though her mind churned with questions. How could she fight for Earth while carrying a life inside her? And how could she not fight—when so many others were in danger?

Just then, the lights in the med wing dimmed for half a second, accompanied by a faint beep echoing through the corridor. Dr. Seema frowned. "Power fluctuations again? That's the second time tonight."

Maya's pulse quickened. "It happened in the council chamber too."

"Strange," Dr. Seema murmured, tapping a console to check the city's power grid. "Everything looks stable now, but those dips shouldn't last this long."

A staff member rushed in, eyes wide with urgency. "We're getting reports from the sensor station. There's an unidentified energy signature near our outer perimeter."

Maya shot to her feet, her heart pounding. An unidentified energy signature could mean a Noctivara vessel—or something else entirely. She locked eyes with Dr. Seema. "Keep me updated," she said briskly before dashing toward the door.

As she rushed down the corridor, her free hand instinctively found its way to her abdomen. Her world had just become infinitely more complicated, but she had no time to dwell on it. Duty called, and it called loud.

Jamal was already at the sensor station when Maya arrived, his posture taut with tension. The station formed a semicircle of holographic screens, overlooking Noctivara's sprawling cityscape through a tall, reinforced window. Technicians moved with hushed urgency, adjusting controls, zooming in on external camera feeds, and analyzing energy readings.

Maya's gaze drifted to Jamal's clenched fists. He always carried an undercurrent of intensity, but tonight it hummed like a live wire. She stepped closer, resting a hand lightly on his shoulder. "Any news?"

Jamal flinched slightly, as if yanked from deep thought. "We picked up an anomaly just outside the city's sensor range. It's gone now, though."

The lead technician, a short woman with silver braids, turned from her console. "It was only visible for about twelve seconds. Some kind of phase shift? Possibly a cloaked ship scanning us."

Maya forced a steady breath. "No visual confirmation?"

The technician shook her head. "Only these spikes in the electromagnetic spectrum. It doesn't match Noctivara cloaking—or anything from Earth, as far as we know."

Jamal ran a hand over his face. "So either something else is out there, or we've got a sensor glitch."

His tone carried an edge, and Maya sensed something deeper behind his unease. She lowered her voice. "You okay?"

He hesitated. For a moment, it seemed like he might dismiss the question. Then, exhaling slowly, he let the strain show in the rigid set of his jaw. "I was thinking about... Jean-Louis."

Maya's brow furrowed. She knew fragments of Jamal's past—the man he'd loved, left behind when the abductions began. "You think he's still on Earth?"

"He was supposed to come with me," Jamal said, his voice hollow. "We had a plan—to meet near the port, just before the Noctivara ships finalized the evacuation. But he never made it. I don't know if he was captured, if he joined a resistance group... or if he's... gone."

Maya squeezed his shoulder gently. She opened her mouth to offer reassurance, but the words faltered. How could she promise anything about a world she hadn't seen since the abductions? After a pause, she finally found her voice. "We'll find out," she said softly. "This mission we're planning—it might give you answers."

Jamal nodded grimly. "And if those answers lead me to a choice I can't handle?"

Maya's chest tightened. She thought of her own secret—the child she carried—and how suddenly, so many choices had become heavier. "Then we help each other carry it. That's the only way."

Before Jamal could respond, the overhead speakers crackled to life:

"All council members, please report to the main observation deck immediately."

Maya and Jamal exchanged a brief, uneasy glance. He let out a shaky breath, pushing his personal turmoil aside. "Sounds urgent."

Without another word, they turned and hurried toward the exit. As Maya stepped past a dimming monitor that displayed the city's perimeter, she hesitated. No movement now. But the memory of that anomaly lingered—coiled in the back of her mind like a predator waiting for the right moment to strike.

By the time Maya and Jamal reached the main observation deck—a large platform near the top of Noctivara's central spire—the rest of the council was already assembled. Floor-to-ceiling windows offered a sweeping view of the city's luminous walkways and floating biodomes. Normally, the sight inspired pride and hope. Tonight, the air was thick with unease.

Kiona was the first to speak, stepping forward with her hands clasped. "The vote is confirmed: we will send a small, covert mission to assess conditions on Earth."

Idris tapped a holopad on his wrist, projecting a diagram of a sleek, arrowhead-shaped craft. "I've been developing a prototype dropship—Project Ebony. It's a Noctivara-human

The Great Divide: When Earth Lost Its Shadow

hybrid design, optimized for stealth. If we push through final checks, it could be ready in two days."

Jari, arms crossed, studied the blueprint with narrowed eyes. "I'd prefer more time to test its cloak under real conditions."

Maya stepped forward. "We may not have more time. An unidentified anomaly near our perimeter suggests we've already drawn attention. Whether it's the Noctivara, Earth factions, or something else, I don't want to give them the chance to strike first."

A wave of uneasy nods swept through the group.

Zara, still lingering at the edge of the assembly, spoke up. "If you're going in two days, you need to be precise in selecting your team. Military experience, stealth expertise, diplomatic skill. One or two scientists to collect samples—if you want a full assessment of Earth's condition."

Jamal exhaled. "I have infiltration training from my time leading protest movements—covert communication, sabotage, that sort of thing."

Idris nodded. "And I can handle field diagnostics. My background in exobiology might be useful if Earth has mutated pathogens or... new environmental factors."

Maya's gaze lingered on Jahi, who stood silent, hands folded behind him. "You haven't said if you'd be willing to join," she prompted, her tone measured. "Your knowledge of the Noctivara and Earth's leadership could be invaluable."

For a moment, Jahi remained quiet, his eyes drifting over the distant lights of Noctivara as if searching for an answer. When he finally spoke, his voice was barely above a whisper. "I will join, if you'll have me."

Jari's mouth set into a grim line, but he didn't argue. He simply gave a curt nod. "We're taking a massive risk. But if we do this, at least we're stacking the deck in our favor."

Maya forced a small smile. She wished she could feel triumphant, but the storm of emotions within her refused to settle. "All right. In two days, we launch Ebony on a reconnaissance mission. Meanwhile, we'll work around the clock to finalize pre-flight checks and gather resources."

Kiona raised a brow. "And if we confirm that Earth is... salvageable? We return with a larger rescue force?"

"That's the idea," Maya said, though deep down, uncertainty gnawed at her. Earth might be in ruins. Its people could be too scattered, too heavily controlled, or too far gone to save. Still, hope was all they had.

Overhead, the lights dimmed for half a second before stabilizing. A murmur of concern rippled through the group.

Jari frowned. "The power disruptions are getting worse. Could be mechanical. Or sabotage."

Zara's silver eyes glowed faintly as she interfaced with her personal device. "I'm detecting no immediate infiltration inside the city's grid. It could be external interference. Someone might be scanning for our location, probing the outer force fields."

Uneasy glances passed through the group.

Maya cleared her throat. "Regardless, we have to prepare for the worst. Jari, can you reinforce the city's defenses? Maybe recalibrate the sensors to detect whatever is causing these anomalies?"

"I'll do what I can," Jari replied. "I'll coordinate with the security division."

"Then let's get to work," Maya said. She cast one last look over her shoulder at the gleaming towers below, each one a reflection of how far they had come—*and how far they could still fall.*

Hours later, the clock neared what passed for "night" in Noctivara. The artificial sky overhead dimmed to a deep purple hue, speckled with projected stars. Despite the programmed day-night cycle, the city rarely slept—especially now.

Jamal wandered along a narrow walkway lined with luminescent vines. These genetically modified plants emitted a soft blue glow, their DNA spliced with Earth coral to survive in air. The effect was both eerie and beautiful, casting an aquatic shimmer across the path.

He needed solitude—or at least the illusion of it. Guilt gnawed at him like a living thing, relentless and insidious. Every step echoed the fears that had haunted him for years: What if Jean-Louis is alive and waiting for me? What if he hates me for leaving? What if he never thought of me again?

"Couldn't sleep either?"

Jamal turned to see Omari approaching. A sudden rush of memory seized him, pulling him away from the sensor readouts he had been reviewing. His mind snapped back to a storm-swept street in Port-au-Prince, the night he and Jean-Louis had stood at the heart of a protest against forced labor camps.

The rain had lashed sideways, but Jean-Louis had stood tall, gripping a megaphone, his voice defiant over the downpour:

"We are not a broken people! We stand for the ones they've silenced. We stand for hope!"

Jamal remembered the roar of the crowd, the electric charge of unity—even as armed drones loomed overhead. And he remembered the moment the march dispersed, Jean-Louis grabbing his hand, pressing a quick kiss to his cheek, whispering, "We don't stop. Not ever."

Then the abductions had begun. In the chaos, they'd made a desperate pact: rendezvous at the old airstrip if they got separated.

Jamal had raced there at dawn, his heart hammering, scanning the horizon for Jean-Louis. But he never came. Minutes later, the Noctivara ships swallowed the sky, taking Jamal and thousands of others away.

Now, standing in Noctivara with its polished metal walls and the soft hum of technology, Jamal's heart pounded as if it were still that stormy night. Is Jean-Louis still down there, still fighting? Still waiting for me?

His fist slammed against the console, frustration twisting with longing. A part of him dreaded returning to Earth. Another part ached for it—because it was the only way to find out if Jean-Louis had survived. Or to finally learn the truth if he hadn't.

Omari, one of the city's stealth specialists, had joined him without a word. He was someone who understood infiltration—someone who understood him. Over time, they had formed a quiet bond, one that lingered in the space between duty and longing.

Jamal forced a smile, but it didn't reach his eyes. "Yeah. My mind's too full."

Omari fell into step beside him. "You're going on the Earth mission, right?"

"That's the plan."

They walked in silence, the glowing vines casting soft shadows across their faces. Jamal felt the quiet warmth of

Omari's presence and hated himself for it. I shouldn't be this close to anyone, he thought. Not when I can't even face my past.

Finally, Omari spoke, his voice low. "Look, I know you're torn about going back. But maybe that's exactly why you need to go. To find answers."

Jamal's chest tightened. "Answers... or heartbreak."

Omari stopped, gently turning Jamal by the shoulder to face him. Their eyes met, and for a fleeting moment, Jamal felt an overwhelming urge to close the space between them. Then came the guilt, sharp and immediate. "Omari—"

"It's okay," Omari said softly, though his voice carried emotions he didn't fully name. "You don't owe me an explanation. But I want you to know something."

Jamal's pulse hammered. "What?"

Omari hesitated, as if measuring whether the truth was worth the risk. Then, quietly, "I'll be here when you get back. No matter what you find on Earth. If you—if you need someone."

Something in Jamal's chest cracked and mended all at once. He inhaled, feeling the sting of unshed tears. With a shaky exhale, he nodded. "Thank you," he managed, barely trusting his voice to hold steady.

Before either could say more, a sharp crackle came from Omari's comm device. He raised it to his ear, listened, then met Jamal's gaze. "We need to get to the docking bay. Idris wants us to run final checks on Ebony now."

"Right." Jamal cleared his throat, forcing his emotions back down. "Let's go."

They moved in unison, the luminescent vines swaying gently behind them. For a brief moment, Jamal glanced over his shoulder, and a phantom image surfaced—Jean-Louis standing in the rain, voice fierce, shouting that they should never give up.

Then he turned away, centering himself on the present—on Omari's steady footsteps beside him, and on the mission that might finally bring him peace... or shatter him completely.

Night in Noctivara was a time of illusory peace—but not tonight.

Alarms blared across the city, sirens that few residents had ever heard, because until now, Noctivara had never truly been discovered. The sound was a high-pitched wail that cut through the stillness like a scalpel through flesh.

Maya stood on the main observation deck, her heart hammering. But this time, it wasn't a council debate that filled the space—it was raw, unfiltered panic. Council members, technicians, security officers, and stunned onlookers crowded around the massive windows, eyes locked on the sky.

At first, Maya saw nothing. The horizon stretched in front of them, an expanse of artificial starlight and the distant outlines of Noctivara's biodome clusters. Then—reality itself seemed to distort, rippling as though something unseen was bending space with an invisible hand.

A hush of dread spread through the deck. Jamal appeared at Maya's side, his breath ragged, while Omari, Jahi, Jari, and Idris pressed in close. Zara stood apart, her silver eyes glowing with intensity.

Slowly—like ink dissolving into water—the shape of a colossal vessel emerged. It didn't simply appear; it bled into existence, its surface devouring light rather than reflecting it. Maya's mind struggled to comprehend the scale—it dwarfed even the largest Noctivara craft. For a moment, she had the chilling sensation that the night sky itself was vanishing.

The Great Divide: When Earth Lost Its Shadow

Then came the hum.

A low, bone-deep drone reverberated through the air. It was neither the Noctivara's melodic hum nor the mechanical roar of Earth-made engines. This was something else—something ancient, something vast. A sound that spoke of awakening.

Chaos ignited across the observation deck. People shouted half-formed questions:

"Is it scanning us?"

"Are the weapons powered?"

"How did it find us?"

Maya's pulse slammed in her throat as she tried to seize control of the spiraling panic.

"Zara?" she barked. "Can you interface with them? Gauge who they are?"

Zara shook her head, her expression grim. "I'm running every frequency, every protocol we know. There's no response. It's as if—" She hesitated, searching for the right words. "As if it's deliberately bypassing our technology. Overriding it."

Idris was hunched over the controls, his fingers flying across failing systems. "We're losing city-wide feed. The power surges are escalating. Our scanners are offline. I can't get a reading on the ship's composition or armaments."

Maya forced herself to take steady breaths. "Then we rely on visual assessment. Keep emergency power running. Evacuate non-essential personnel from high-risk zones."

A sudden wave of static tore through the observation deck's speakers. Every holographic display flickered once before dissolving into a chaotic haze of distortion. The massive glass windows trembled—not from impact, but from something deeper, something unseen. A force that scraped against the very foundation of the city.

Then—silence.

A voice that wasn't a voice curled through the air, vibrating through metal and bone alike:

"You are not alone."

The words resonated in every corner of the deck, sinking into every cell of Maya's body. They weren't simply heard. They were felt—coiling around her thoughts, invasive and intimate.

For a split second, no one moved or breathed. Then, the nearest consoles sparked and died. Lights across the city wavered. Beyond the windows, the ship loomed closer—or perhaps it simply expanded, blotting out every star.

Jahi muttered under his breath, "What in all the cosmos...?"

Jari's face was pale, his expression grim. "This is no Noctivara vessel."

Zara's voice trembled—something Maya had never heard before. "We don't know who it belongs to. Or what it belongs to."

A heavy silence followed, broken only by the ragged breathing of those gathered. Maya gripped the railing so hard her knuckles turned white. She swallowed hard, feeling the weight of the unborn child she carried. *Is this how it ends?* The thought threatened to choke her. *Have we been found just to be destroyed?*

The ship hung there, a silent monolith against the sky. Another wave of that bone-shaking hum rippled through the city. This time, arcs of blue-white energy crackled across the outer walkways, shorting them out. One of the floating bridges collapsed on one side, sparks flying as it dangled precariously.

Screams erupted in the distance. Maya's heart lurched. "We have to stay calm," she called to the council. "We have to maintain order."

Jari barked out orders to the remaining security teams with functional comms. Kiona rallied city medics to stand by. Idris cursed under his breath, frantically tapping a control panel that refused to respond. Jamal clenched his jaw, his face set in tense determination.

For a moment, the voice returned. Or perhaps it was only an echo in their minds:

"You are not alone."

Then, the massive vessel began to move—not away, but around, circling Noctivara's perimeter. In the pulsing city lights, it looked like a wound in the sky—an absence of reality itself. A chill raced down Maya's spine. Whatever was aboard that ship was studying them, scanning them in a way more invasive than any sensor technology. Just like the Noctivara once did. But this felt even deeper, like it was peeling back layers of them, reading them at a level beyond mere data.

"We need Ebony ready now," Jamal hissed at Idris, who nodded numbly. "We might have to evacuate—or at least attempt contact from outside."

"Are you insane?" Jari snapped. "That thing could swat our little ship down in an instant."

Jamal's eyes blazed. "Better than standing here, waiting for it to crush us. Or do you want to watch while it tears the city apart?"

Maya felt the tension rising, pushing them toward panic. She forced herself to breathe, to think. "We can't just flee," she said firmly. "We have thousands of people here. We need to protect Noctivara. We have to negotiate—or defend ourselves. But we do something."

Zara tried again, sending transmissions through every frequency. Still, nothing but static. The ship wasn't responding—either by choice or because it was simply beyond their ability to reach.

Then, without warning, the hum ceased. The arcs of energy vanished. For an instant, the city seemed to exhale a collective sigh of relief.

And just as swiftly, that relief shattered when a different voice crackled through the static—this time mechanical, clipped, unmistakably Earth-based:

"This is Earth Fleet Vessel *Emergence*. Do you copy?"

A stunned hush followed.

Earth Fleet? But Earth's last known fleets had been disorganized remnants of private militaries, fractured warbands held together by desperation and scarce resources. And then there were the rumors—the whispered alliances with unknown alien powers. Did this "Emergence" belong to the monstrous shadow looming over them, or was it a separate threat entirely?

Maya's mind reeled. She glanced at the other council members and saw her own confusion mirrored in their faces. Jamal stood rigid, his jaw clenched—a man reliving the day Earth's forces had turned against them.

Zara's silver eyes shimmered with something Maya couldn't name. Fear, perhaps. Or recognition. "We... we should respond."

Jahi stepped forward, tension rippling through his frame. "If that's an Earth Fleet ship, how did it find us so quickly? And who are they allied with?"

The Great Divide: When Earth Lost Its Shadow

Maya inhaled shakily. "We have no choice but to find out."

She stepped toward one of the few consoles still partially operational. Her hands trembled as she keyed in a transmission line, isolating the incoming signal. Lips dry, she leaned toward the mic.

"This is Noctivara. We read you, Emergence. State your intentions."

Silence stretched.

Just as she began to think there would be no answer, a burst of static crackled through the speakers. Then, a voice—harsh, clipped, utterly devoid of warmth:

"Surrender your city and its population. By order of the Earth Restoration Authority, you are harboring stolen property—the abducted. Compliance will ensure your survival."

Jamal's breath hitched. "Stolen property?"

Maya's stomach twisted. Rage and fear collided in her chest. Around her, the council wore expressions of disbelief, revulsion, fury. Abducted? That was how they saw it—that the Noctivara had "stolen" Black people from Earth, and now they wanted them back?

She turned to the window, her gaze locking onto the massive silhouette beyond the glass. The Earth Fleet had given their demands, but who held the true power here? Was the vessel in the sky their warship, or were they merely its instruments? The lines of control had blurred beyond recognition.

Her fingers curled into fists. She had led her people this far, had fought to carve out a future in the void. And now—

A war had come for them. And it had many faces.

Slowly, she turned from the window, her gaze sweeping across the council—Jamal, Jari, Jahi, Idris, Zara, Kiona. She was searching for something. Resolve. Commitment. The fire that told her they would not bend.

A small, secret weight pressed against her awareness—the life within her, the child not yet born. A future not yet shaped.

Maya swallowed hard. We won't surrender. That truth burned within her, hot as molten steel. But how did they fight something this vast?

Behind her, the alien ship loomed, an impassive titan in the sky. In front of her, the council waited, the weight of Earth's ultimatum hanging between them like a guillotine. Outside, Noctivara's lights wavered—almost as if the city itself trembled.

She turned to the console again. When she spoke, her voice was steady, even as her heart pounded against her ribs.

"Noctivara does not surrender. We will protect our people. We will protect our future."

A distorted hiss of static preceded the response.

"Then you have chosen war."

And as the final words dissolved into silence, the massive ship overhead pulsed with arcs of swirling energy once more—signaling a conflict that would not only consume Noctivara, but unravel everything they thought they knew about Earth, the Noctivara, and the forces lurking in the abyss.

Chapter 9: The Next Step

Noctivara's Council Chamber glowed with an almost sacred radiance. Overhead, the simulated sky displayed a soft twilight—purple hues streaked with shimmering veins of light, reminiscent of an aurora. Around the long, polished conference table—carved from black marble embedded with bioluminescent fibers—Council members and key advisors sat rigid, their expressions heavy with the weight of the decision before them.

Maya stood at the head of the table. The quiet hum of hidden machinery occasionally interrupted the stillness, but for the most part, silence—thick as fog—pressed against the room, settling over them like an unspoken omen. She drew in a measured breath, one hand drifting unconsciously to her abdomen—a protective gesture. Only a few present knew of her pregnancy, but with each passing day, the knowledge felt heavier.

"We've been circling this decision for weeks," she said, her voice laced with exhaustion from too many sleepless nights. "The Indigenous communities still on Earth are outnumbered and in grave danger. Their leaders have risked everything to survive in secrecy, and now, they've finally reached out for our help."

A low murmur swept through the chamber. At the far end of the table, Jari—one of the more cautious council members—shifted uncomfortably, arms crossed over his chest in a defensive knot. Idris, a scientist from Lagos, leaned forward as if to speak, but before he could, Maya pressed on.

"We have two choices," she continued, her gaze locking onto each member in turn. "Either we take action—commit to rescuing them before Earth's forces close in—or we sit back and hope the situation resolves itself."

Jamal cleared his throat. Seated at Maya's right, he had grown increasingly restless as the debate stretched on. "Maya, you know I respect what you're trying to do," he said, his voice edged with hesitation. "But... are we truly equipped to pull off a large-scale rescue? Noctivara's resources are finite. We're barely a nation—certainly not a force capable of standing against Earth's militarized factions."

The concern in his voice mirrored the tension in his posture—shoulders tight, brow furrowed, as if he were wrestling with his own conscience. *He's afraid we'll lose everything we've built here,* Maya thought. *And he's not wrong to worry.*

She exhaled slowly, forcing steadiness into her voice. "And what are we if we don't act?" Her gaze swept the table, pausing on Jari's unreadable expression, Kiona's solemn nod, and finally, Jamal's conflicted stare. "If we turn our backs while others suffer, we become complicit in their destruction. We—the ones torn from Earth—understand better than anyone what it means to be abandoned."

A ripple of agreement passed through the room, laced with lingering doubt.

Idris finally spoke, his soft-spoken tone measured yet firm. "We do have a stealth vessel in development—Ebony. It's been tested in smaller operations, but never on a scale like this."

In the corner, where the artificial twilight cast silver glints in her eyes, Zara raised a hand. The room stilled. Though not a

The Great Divide: When Earth Lost Its Shadow

council member, she carried knowledge from the Noctivara side of things—knowledge they could not afford to ignore.

"I must warn you," she said evenly, "Earth's elites are no longer content to leave you in peace. They've continued developing weapons specifically designed to track and intercept Noctivara ships—and, presumably, any derivative technology you're using here."

She paused, letting the words settle like an unspoken verdict. "What was once a standoff is turning into a confrontation. Reports indicate Earth already has at least one operational prototype weapon. And from what I've gathered, the ruling factions don't just want to stop you—they want to erase you. Any trace of your independence."

A ripple of anxious whispers spread among the council. Maya felt a sharp twist of dread in her stomach. She glanced at Jamal, whose lips had pressed into a thin, unreadable line. He exchanged an uneasy look with Omari, seated a few chairs away, arms crossed, eyes scanning the room as if searching for reassurance.

Jamal's voice was low but urgent. "If they can track Noctivara ships, they can track ours. If we go in—whether for reconnaissance or full-scale evacuation—we risk exposing Noctivara's location."

"That's the crux of it," Jari said quietly. "We risk everything for a moral cause."

Maya couldn't stop the flash of frustration in her eyes. "And what else are we if not a moral cause?" She pressed a hand to the table, leaning forward. "We were stolen from Earth because the old powers saw us as expendable—and the Noctivara saw us as necessary. We built Noctivara to prove we deserved to exist on our own terms. Now, we have a chance to help others facing the same fate. I won't stand by while they're hunted and destroyed."

Silence stretched, thick with the weight of choice.

Finally, Kiona, an elder strategist from the Pacific Islands, cleared her throat. "We can plan this carefully—limit the mission's scope, use Ebony's stealth systems, coordinate with allies on Earth who can shield our movements. But it will demand unwavering commitment from everyone in this room. Once we begin, there's no turning back."

Idris adjusted his glasses, his eyes flicking between council members. "The question is: do we vote now, or do we need more data?"

"There's no more time," Maya said. Straightening, she steeled herself. "I'm calling for a final decision. Either we move forward with this rescue—fully aware it places us on a collision course with Earth's new powers—or we close our borders, stay hidden, and let the chips fall where they may."

The hush that followed was almost suffocating. The council exchanged glances that ranged from terror to quiet resolve. One by one, they pressed their palms against the holographic interface before them, casting their votes.

Green or red—yes or no.

Maya held her breath as the tallies appeared midair—swirling orbs of light converging at the center of the table. A slow bloom of green overtook red, winning by a handful of votes.

She exhaled, relief tinged with dread. It had passed.

But the burden of that choice pressed against her chest like an iron weight. They were about to provoke a hornet's nest—and Earth's hornet was bigger, angrier, and more prepared than ever.

The Great Divide: When Earth Lost Its Shadow

After the vote, the Council Chamber emptied into the massive corridor, its arching walls pulsing softly with luminescent strands. Outside, Noctivara's bustling core awaited—hundreds of people moving with purpose, some deep in work, others lingering in quiet conversation. News of the Council's decision spread at lightning speed, carried across whispered exchanges and illuminated public message boards.

Maya stepped into the corridor, flanked by Jamal on her right and Zara on her left. Omari trailed a few steps behind, his gaze sweeping their surroundings with quiet vigilance. They paused near an alcove carved into the corridor, where the hum of foot traffic granted them a moment of relative privacy.

"That was a narrower margin than I'd hoped," Maya admitted, her voice low. "We have to keep unity strong if we're going to see this mission through."

Zara's silver-flecked eyes flicked to passersby. "Unity will be difficult to maintain if people learn Earth's new weapon can pinpoint us. Fear will paralyze them."

Omari folded his arms, his stance subtly protective. "Better they know than be kept in the dark. Let them prepare. If we hide the truth and get ambushed, the panic will be worse."

Jamal let out a slow breath, rubbing the bridge of his nose. Fatigue crept into his voice. "Maya, about the resource allocations—I wasn't trying to undermine you in there. I'm just... worried. We've poured everything into stabilizing this city, and now we might have to divert all of it into a mission that could blow up in our faces. Literally."

Maya's gaze softened. "I know. And I respect that concern. But we can't let fear of losing what we have stop us from doing what's right." She let the words settle, watching the flicker of doubt in Jamal's eyes. "We'll prepare as thoroughly as possible."

Zara's posture straightened. "I need to gather updated intel. My contacts say Earth's elites are already mobilizing. I'll meet you at the Ebony docks in two hours. We need to confirm the ship's stealth capacity under the latest threat parameters."

Maya nodded. "Agreed."

As Zara turned to go, Jamal placed a hand on Maya's shoulder. He cast a glance at Omari, then back to her. "Can we talk somewhere private?" he asked quietly.

Maya studied the tension in his expression, the way the weight of the decision lingered on him. "Of course."

Omari, reading the unspoken cue, gave a small nod and stepped away, though his gaze lingered on Jamal. Once he was gone, Jamal steered Maya into a quieter side passage branching off from the main corridor.

The walls here were covered in intricate patterns of glass and etched metal, forming a living record of resilience—scenes of African diaspora, Caribbean revolutions, Pacific Islander heritage, and more. A mosaic of shared histories, stitched together in defiance of erasure.

Jamal stopped near an image of a Haitian freedom fighter brandishing a broken chain. He inhaled unsteadily. "I know how important this mission is. But part of me can't stop thinking about how fragile everything we've built really is. If we fail—" He exhaled sharply, pressing his lips together.

Maya offered him a faint, knowing smile. She had known Jamal long enough to recognize the battle waging within him—the push and pull of moral conviction against personal fear.

"If we fail, then we face war sooner than we'd like," she said, her voice steady. "But if we do nothing, we lose ourselves. We lose the reason Noctivara exists at all."

Jamal nodded, though his gaze dropped to the floor. "I just... need to be sure we've thought this through."

"And we have. We will."

Her hand drifted once more to her lower abdomen, an instinctive gesture. A quiet storm of emotions churned within her—fear for her unborn child, resolve not to let that fear define her choices. "Trust me, I'm not stepping into this lightly."

Jamal exhaled, nodding again before giving her shoulder a firm but gentle squeeze. "All right. Let's do it, then."

By late afternoon—according to the city's precisely maintained day-night cycle—Maya found herself in the vast docking bay dedicated to Project Ebony. Overhead, arc-shaped lights cast a crisp white glow across the hangar floor. Technicians in navy-blue jumpsuits moved with practiced efficiency, loading supply crates and fine-tuning delicate instrumentation.

At the heart of the activity sat Ebony—a sleek, midnight-black vessel with elegantly arched wings. At certain angles, the craft seemed to dissolve into the shadows of the hangar, its stealth hull partially engaged.

Near one of the landing struts, Idris crouched over a handheld console, fingers moving swiftly across the interface. He glanced up as Maya, Zara, and Jamal approached.

"The stealth nodes are integrated, but we're struggling to balance the power draw," he said, rising to his feet and motioning for them to follow him inside. "We have to account for the risk of Earth's new sensor arrays. If they can track partial Noctivara tech, Ebony's standard cloak might not be enough."

Inside the vessel, the corridors were compact, lined with high-level instrumentation. Idris led them toward the small command cockpit at the front, where holographic displays flickered with diagnostic readouts in real time: hull integrity, atmospheric compatibility, sensor profiles.

Jamal ran a hand over one of the control panels. "How close are we to operational readiness?"

"Close," Idris replied, pulling up a schematic. "I've got a plan to add a second-phase diffuser. It breaks up Ebony's energy signature into smaller, randomized pulses, hopefully scrambling Earth's sensor sweeps. But we need more time to test it."

Zara skimmed the readouts, eyes narrowing. "Time is a luxury we don't have."

Maya frowned, pressing a hand to the back of the pilot's seat. She pictured the Indigenous families still hiding on Earth, crouched in concealed enclaves, waiting for an escape that might never come if Ebony wasn't ready.

"Do your best to accelerate the schedule," she said to Idris. "We can't fly blind, but we also can't afford to wait forever."

He nodded, tension tightening his expression. "We'll do what we can."

They stepped off the ship, descending the short ramp onto the hangar floor. Around them, dozens of cargo crates were stacked against the walls, their labels stark and utilitarian—Medical Supplies, Nutrient Rations, Tactical Gear. At the far end of the hangar, Kiona stood in discussion with a small security team, her stance firm as she outlined infiltration strategies in case Ebony had to land in hostile territory.

Maya approached, and Kiona acknowledged her with a curt nod.

The Great Divide: When Earth Lost Its Shadow

"If Earth's new weapon can pinpoint Noctivara-based signals, we may need to rely on low-tech stealth on the ground as well," Kiona said. "Minimal hover activity, minimal emissions. We land Ebony far from any Earth stronghold, then approach the Indigenous camps on foot or with small rovers."

"It's a risk," Maya admitted. "But so is staying up here while they get wiped out."

Kiona's gaze flicked to a crate labeled Communications. "We'll have short-range comm units that bounce signals between rovers, reducing the risk of detection. But that means we'll be mostly in the dark if something goes wrong. No immediate backup from Noctivara."

Maya nodded, the weight of the mission settling in her chest. They were risking isolation, stepping into Earth's shadow while it bristled with new weaponry.

We can do this, she told herself. *We have to.*

Far below, on the battered surface of Earth, the night sky glowed—not with stars, but with the distant, restless burn of industrial fires. Clouds of ash drifted across the moon, shrouding the skeletal remains of what had once been a thriving metropolis. Beneath its crumbling skyline lay a hidden encampment—the only home Ethan had left—tucked within the remnants of an abandoned subway network, where layers of concrete and steel provided meager protection from aerial scans.

Ethan crouched in a half-collapsed maintenance tunnel alongside Liam, a wiry, sharp-eyed operative with a knack for infiltration. The flickering glow of a handheld flashlight revealed ghostly remnants of graffiti—protest slogans and half-finished murals from a world that felt like ancient history.

"You sure the data vault's still active?" Liam murmured, voice barely above a whisper. Dust motes swirled in the air. "The whole building could've caved in by now, for all we know."

Ethan pressed a thumb drive deeper into his jacket pocket. "Intelligence says they moved the entire data center underground. We access it through the metro lines. If we're lucky, we can hack in without setting off alarms."

They crept along, water dripping from overhead pipes. Every muffled footstep echoed, amplifying the claustrophobic hush. Finally, they reached a heavy metal door, its surface unnervingly new against the decay around it—reinforced, fortified. Liam pried open a small control panel, wires sparking as he connected a homemade hacking device.

Ethan stood watch, heart pounding. His thoughts drifted, unbidden, to Maya—to the moment they were torn apart when the Noctivara evacuation descended. *I can't lose her again. Not when we just found hope.* The memory threatened to pull him under, but he forced it away. *Focus. This is the only way to warn her if Earth is planning an attack.*

A subdued click sounded, and the door slid open. They stepped inside, the corridor ahead lined with towering servers. Fluorescent lights buzzed overhead, casting a sterile glow. The air was thick with the scent of overheated circuits and long-settled dust. So much data—possibly Earth's last reservoir of strategic knowledge—stored right here.

"Keep an ear out," Liam whispered, making his way to the largest server. "I'll pull what we can."

Ethan hovered near the entrance, every muscle taut, ears straining for any sign of movement. The steady hum of cooling fans filled the silence, broken only by the occasional beep of an unseen system running diagnostics.

"We're clear," he whispered back.

Liam's fingers flew across the console, lines of code streaming too fast to track. Then the overhead lights flickered, just once—but sharply enough to make Ethan's breath hitch. Had they tripped a silent alarm?

No sirens. No rushing footsteps.

Then Liam froze. A pop-up window flashed across the screen, its red-bordered text making his eyes widen.

"We hit the jackpot," he breathed. "They're developing something called the ANTARES Array. It's classified top-secret—an anti-Noctivara weapon." His voice dropped lower, tension coiling in his words. "But it doesn't just track them. It can calibrate for any energy signature derived from Noctivara tech."

Ethan felt dread settle like a stone in his gut. "That means Ebony," he whispered, his breath shallow. "Or any ship from Noctivara." His throat went dry. "So if Maya tries to come here—"

"She'll fly straight into a trap," Liam finished, his fingers flying over the console as he downloaded the files. "They've already tested it in the Arizona wastelands—successful hits on high-altitude targets."

Ethan felt his blood run cold. The mental image of Maya surfaced unbidden—her fierce brown eyes, her determined stance. *She's not just risking herself*, he thought, recalling the weight in her voice the last time they spoke. *She's carrying our future.* He exhaled shakily. "We have to warn her. We have to find a way to reach her."

Liam yanked the thumb drive free and stashed it in a hidden pocket. "Let's move before they realize we're here."

They hurried back through the corridor, hearts hammering against their ribs. Halfway to the door, the overhead lights flickered again. A distant alarm began to wail, its sound dampened by the thick walls but unmistakable.

"Too late," Ethan muttered. "They know we're here."

Liam shot him a tense look. "You got your route?"

Ethan nodded sharply. "Tunnel 14. Let's go."

They sprinted, their footsteps echoing in the confined space, their breath tight with urgency. Behind them, the data vault buzzed with agitation—systems reacting, protocols engaging. Guards might already be closing in. Sirens might be summoning drones. But Ethan ran faster, adrenaline propelling him forward, fear sharpened by the single, unshakable need to warn Maya.

If Earth unleashed the ANTARES Array, they would shoot down any rescue attempt before it even began.

And that would mean *no more second chances.*

Ethan and Liam ducked into a hidden bunker—a cramped storeroom connected to the subterranean rails by a narrow hatch. The place reeked of old grease and mildew. Dim emergency lights pulsed intermittently, casting jagged shadows over the battered table and scattered supplies: ration packs, torn bedrolls, a handful of dented weapons.

Panting, Liam locked the hatch behind them. "We lost the guards, for now. They won't stop searching, though."

Ethan nodded, his chest still tight from the sprint. He pulled out the thumb drive and slid it into a small portable

The Great Divide: When Earth Lost Its Shadow

reader. The shaky holographic interface blinked to life, lines of text and schematic images flickering.

"Here it is... the ANTARES Array," he muttered. "Looks like a ground-based energy weapon with satellite support. Its entire function is to detect and neutralize Noctivara-based vessels in orbit or atmosphere."

Liam let out a sharp breath. "They've basically built a giant snare for anyone using Noctivara stealth."

Ethan scrolled further, his expression darkening. "They're planning to finalize testing in a matter of days. If Maya or anyone from Noctivara arrives during that window..."

"It'll be a slaughter." Liam ran a hand through his sweat-dampened hair. "What do we do now?"

Ethan paced the cramped space, his mind a storm of calculations and worst-case scenarios. *I have to warn her. She couldn't come anywhere near Earth until they disabled or evaded the Array.* His pulse thundered as he thought of Maya—the warmth of her hands, the fierce determination in her gaze. *We've already lost too much—*

He turned sharply to Liam. "We need to get this intel to Maya. And we need to find a way to sabotage or block the ANTARES Array before her ship enters Earth's airspace. Otherwise, it's over."

Liam shrugged in resignation. "Easier said than done. That facility is buried deep in what used to be Arizona—now it's an armed fortress. The only reason we got these files is because they were transferring them from a central server."

Ethan's voice trembled with urgency. "I'll do it. Whatever it takes. I can't let her walk into that kind of ambush." He set the reader down on the table. "We could broadcast a coded message from one of the old orbital relays. I know it's risky, but if I can piggyback on some dormant satellite link—"

Liam cut him off with a shake of his head. "That's a guaranteed way to light up every sensor they have. They'll pinpoint your location in minutes."

"Then I'll just have to be faster," Ethan said, his jaw tightening. "I can't lose her again. Not when there's still a chance." He exhaled, forcing down the rising panic. "You don't have to come with me if it's too dangerous."

Liam half-laughed, his voice edged with bitter amusement. "If we don't warn them, none of us will have a future anyway. I'm in."

An unspoken understanding passed between them. They were about to gamble their lives on a slim chance to avert disaster. Ethan's mind flickered to the truth he had only begun to grasp—Maya wasn't just risking herself. She was carrying new life within her, a child she hadn't even had time to tell him about properly.

I won't fail this time, he vowed silently. *I won't let Earth's elites steal her future.*

Back in Noctivara, the hour grew late, and the city's ambient lighting dimmed to mimic twilight. Maya sat in a secure briefing room with Zara, Idris, and Kiona, the four of them hunched over newly collated data—transmissions Zara had intercepted from uncertain sources in Earth's orbit.

Zara tapped a console, pulling up a scrambled text feed. "I managed to decode partial messages referencing an 'Array' on Earth. The gist: it's a planetary defense system designed to shoot down Noctivara ships."

Idris let out a low whistle. "That lines up with what we've heard. Earth's spent the last few years consolidating under a new authority, pouring resources into advanced weaponry."

Kiona's expression hardened. "That means Ebony might not be safe, even with the new diffuser. If they can track our power signature, we're sitting ducks."

Maya's pulse spiked with cold dread. "Do we know how soon it'll be operational?"

"Within days," Zara said simply, her silver-flecked eyes catching the dim light. "And from what else I've decoded, Earth's factions have also formed alliances with... someone else. Possibly an offshoot of the Noctivara or a different alien race entirely."

Maya felt the blood drain from her face. "You're saying Earth might have an offworld ally now? One that wants us destroyed?"

Zara nodded, tension evident in the way she pressed her lips together. "It's not clear who or what they are. Only that Earth's leaders struck a bargain—offering assistance in exchange for technology to expand their military power."

Idris clenched his fists. "Which means we can't assume Earth is technologically behind. They might already be ahead in certain areas."

A heavy silence settled over the group, broken only by the faint hum of the city's ventilation system. Finally, Maya exhaled. "We can't delay. If we do, the Array will go live, and the Indigenous communities we're trying to save could be wiped out by Earth's new regime before we even reach them."

Zara's gaze flicked to the side. "There's something else. If we fail—or if Ebony is shot down—it will confirm that Earth's new weapon works. That alone could push them to launch a broader strike against Noctivara."

The weight of the decision pressed against Maya's chest. If they acted, Earth might retaliate. If they did nothing, Earth's growing power could still lead to their destruction. Either way, the future of Noctivara—and my child—hangs in the balance.

She straightened, her voice steady despite the turmoil in her chest. "We launch immediately. Ebony's diffuser has to hold long enough to get us through. Let's hope we have allies on the ground who can help us take out or evade the Array once we're there."

She pushed back from her seat, the others following suit. As she turned to leave, Zara rested a hand briefly on her shoulder. "Be mindful. Earth's not the same place we left."

Maya met her gaze, her expression grim. "Neither are we."

A day later, the Ebony hangar buzzed with urgent activity. Cargo containers were sealed, final diagnostic checks completed, and a small crew assembled for the voyage. Maya stood near the base of the ramp, issuing final instructions to Kiona, who would remain behind to oversee Noctivara's defenses.

"You'll have full emergency authority in my absence," Maya said, tapping a secure datapad. "Keep an ear out for any sign that Earth might try a preemptive strike."

Kiona bowed her head solemnly. "Stay safe out there. Return quickly."

Maya nodded, offering a brief embrace before stepping back. As she turned, she spotted Jamal approaching, his gear bag slung over one shoulder, tension lining his face.

The Great Divide: When Earth Lost Its Shadow

"All set?" she asked.

He gave a curt nod. "As ready as I'll ever be."

A few steps behind him, Omari lingered, his expression unreadable but weighted with unspoken concern. He would remain on Noctivara, coordinating infiltration data from afar. His eyes met Jamal's in a fleeting exchange—something unspoken, but understood. Jamal adjusted his bag and forced a half-smile.

Idris strode forward, carrying a case of scientific instruments. "We'll need these to assess Earth's atmosphere. If it's degraded further, the route to the Indigenous camps might be toxic or irradiated."

"All the more reason not to linger," Maya said, steadying herself against the surge of apprehension in her chest. Her child's future rested in her hands, and she was about to place herself in the crosshairs of Earth's deadliest weapon.

The Ebony's side hatch hissed open, casting a cool blue glow onto the hangar floor. They stepped inside, finding their places in the compact but efficient cockpit. Idris secured himself at the science station, Jamal took the co-pilot's seat, and Maya settled into the pilot's chair with practiced ease. Behind them, Selene—a quiet but lethal infiltration expert—took her position at the systems console.

As the hatch sealed, the engines rumbled to life with a low, steady hum. Over the comms, Zara's voice crackled through.

"Your route is clear, Ebony. We'll monitor for any trace signals that could compromise you. Good luck. Remember, Earth is on high alert."

Maya tightened her grip on the control yoke. "Acknowledged, Zara. We'll keep comm usage minimal once we're in range. See you soon."

With a gentle lurch, Ebony lifted off, ascending through the hangar's open flight path. Lines of shimmering navigational data traced their trajectory, guiding them upward. Through the forward canopy, Noctivara's domed skyline spread out below, a constellation of lights against the void.

A familiar ache settled in Maya's chest. Her home. Her people. The fragile future they represented.

I will bring us all back, she vowed silently. *No matter what it takes.*

Ebony exited Noctivara's protective orbit smoothly, the stealth field pulsing faintly around the hull. A scattering of distant stars and cosmic dust framed the vast emptiness ahead, but the ship's instruments painted a more intricate picture—gravitational anomalies, old satellite debris, and stray waves of cosmic radiation.

Jamal monitored the sensor arrays, his fingers poised over the controls. He cast sidelong glances at Maya, catching the tension in her set jaw. "We're still clear. No sign of Earth's new weapon range yet."

Idris sifted through layers of spectral data, his expression tightening. "We'll be entering Earth's atmosphere near what was once southwestern North America—where some of the last Indigenous enclaves have been reported. Air quality's questionable. We'll need rebreathers on standby."

Maya nodded curtly. "Selene, keep the diffuser modulated. We can't let the cloak slip." She forced herself to steady her breathing. Just a few more minutes to atmosphere entry.

A sharp alarm pierced the cockpit.

The Great Divide: When Earth Lost Its Shadow

Jamal's eyes flicked to the readout. "We've got a ping. Something's sweeping for us—some kind of long-range sensor."

Maya's heart jolted. "Already?"

Selene's fingers danced over the controls. "I'm boosting the diffuser. It's pushing back, but the amplitude of that scan is massive. This might be the ANTARES Array. They're searching the entire approach corridor."

A bead of sweat traced down Maya's temple. "We can't outrun a planetary array. We have to stay under the radar. Descend faster."

She guided Ebony into a steeper angle. The hull shuddered as they skimmed Earth's outer atmosphere, heat building against the ship's exterior.

Jamal gripped his harness. "Careful. Too fast, and we'll generate more heat. Their satellites might pick us up on infrared."

A bitter laugh slipped from Maya's lips. "Damned if we do, damned if we don't." She eased back on the throttle, threading the needle between speed and stealth.

The moment they pierced the cloud layer, Ebony lurched. Murky skies, tinted a sickly orange by pollution, stretched endlessly around them. The sensors flickered wildly as the ship's stealth systems strained against the atmospheric interference.

Maya's gaze flicked to the world below—a scarred wasteland where nature had once thrived. Once-majestic mountains now stood stripped bare by resource extraction. Valleys lay scorched from wildfires. Rivers, once lifeblood, had withered to mere trickles.

Earth wasn't just hostile. It was dying.

Idris scanned the terrain, his fingers moving swiftly over the controls. "The Indigenous camps are hidden, but I'm picking up a faint energy signature about twenty kilometers north of our planned landing zone. Could be them."

Maya nodded, adjusting the flight path. "We'll set down in the desert. Then we approach on foot or with minimal hover support." She exhaled slowly, lowering her voice. "Everyone, get ready. We're about to see what Earth has turned into."

As Ebony glided lower, a sudden pulse of light flared on the horizon—a bright, rhythmic glow cutting through the thick haze. Jamal's screen blared a warning: high-intensity energy discharge, dangerously close to their position.

Selene cursed under her breath. "That's the Array. It's firing in wide arcs, hoping to clip anything it pings. They must've caught a fluctuation in our cloak."

Heat coiled in Maya's chest. *This is it.* "Brace for turbulence. I'm taking us down fast."

The craft shuddered, a high-pitched whine rattling their seats as Maya wrestled with the controls. The stealth field wavered at the edges, struggling to compensate. If they didn't land now, the next volley might lock onto them.

Warning lights flared red.

With a final push, Maya forced Ebony through the roiling dust, the ship plunging until it struck the cracked earth with a bone-jarring thud.

For a long moment, no one moved. The engines wound down, settling into an uneasy hum. Outside, the wind howled against the hull, driving sand in restless waves, a haunting whisper of Earth's fury.

Maya exhaled sharply, unbuckling her harness, her pulse still racing. "We made it."

Jamal let out a breath, shaking his head. "So far."

Idris rechecked the scans, tension easing from his shoulders. "No direct hits from the Array. We got lucky."

Maya rose to her feet, legs unsteady but her resolve unwavering. "Luck and skill. Now we find those communities—and figure out how to stop that weapon before it turns us into dust."

They lowered the ramp into a world of stinging winds and dusky light. The desert stretched endlessly, its barren expanse broken only by the jagged skeletons of petrified trees and rusting vehicles half-buried in sand. Overhead, the sky looked bruised—swathes of red and gray locked in perpetual twilight. A faint acrid scent of chemicals clung to the air, thick and unforgiving.

Maya stepped out first, rebreather in place. Each inhale felt dense, as if Earth's very atmosphere resisted their return. Jamal and Idris followed, eyes scanning the horizon with practiced precision. Selene remained inside Ebony's hatch, monitoring signals with quiet focus.

No one spoke. Only the wind howled across barren dunes. Then, in the distance, a brief movement—a group of figures picking their way toward the ship, rifles raised in cautious readiness.

Maya's pulse kicked up. Are these Earth soldiers? Or allies?

Idris lifted a hand. "Wait. They're not in uniform. Possibly Indigenous scouts."

As the figures closed in, a tall, broad-shouldered man at the front lifted his rifle skyward in a non-threatening gesture. "You came," he called, voice muffled by a face covering.

Maya lowered her guard slightly, stepping forward. "We did. We're here to help. Is there a place we can talk?"

The man gave a wary glance past her, toward Ebony's hull. "We have a hideout, but we need to move fast. Earth's patrolling drones aren't far."

A prickle of urgency ran down Maya's spine. "Lead the way."

They fell into step with the group, trudging across the ever-shifting sands. Half a kilometer later, they reached a rocky outcrop beneath which a concealed entrance lay hidden from aerial scans. Their guide pulled back a camouflage sheet, revealing a descending stairwell.

"Down here," he said. "Hurry."

The moment they ducked inside, a distant rumble echoed overhead—a telltale sign that the Array might be cycling up another shot. Maya's muscles coiled tight. *We can't keep Ebony grounded if that thing is sweeping the skies.* She imagined the destruction it could unleash, the countless lives teetering on the brink—including her unborn child's.

As they ventured deeper into the dimly lit refuge, the reality of what they were fighting for hit her. Families huddled in corners, elders marked by time and hardship, children with wide, fearful eyes. Silence spread as more people noticed their arrival. Some faces flickered with cautious hope; others shone with tears. A few held skepticism, their expressions edged with wariness.

And then, at the heart of it all, Ethan stood.

His eyes—red-rimmed from too many sleepless nights—locked onto hers. Relief crashed over him like a tidal wave, his entire body tensing as if bracing against the weight of disbelief.

Maya froze.

The Great Divide: When Earth Lost Its Shadow

For a heartbeat, the world around them faded. She found herself staring at a face she had never thought she'd see again—a piece of her past, now standing before her.

Ethan staggered forward, nearly tripping over scattered crates. Maya took a trembling step toward him. His expression was raw, laced with anguish, desperation, and an unshakable resolve.

A ragged breath escaped her lips. *It's him. Truly him.*

"Maya," Ethan choked out, his voice cracking. "Thank God."

She managed a shaky smile. "Ethan..." Words failed her. She reached out, touching his arm lightly, as if to confirm he wasn't a dream.

"I have intel," he said quickly, his voice taut. "The Earth forces—they've built a weapon. The ANTARES Array. It's fully operational. They're scanning for any sign of a Noctivara-based vessel in orbit or atmosphere."

Maya nodded, her throat tight. "We know. We barely slipped by."

"They'll upgrade it soon," he continued, his eyes darting to Jamal, Idris, and the others behind her. "If you're planning an evacuation, you have to move now—and sabotage that array."

His words tumbled out in a rush. The raw panic in his eyes was unmistakable. But beneath it, she caught something else—an almost frantic relief that she was here, alive, carrying the future he never got to share.

She steadied herself, the weight of responsibility pressing in from all sides. "Then we do it. We get these communities out. And we destroy or disable that weapon. Because if we don't—"

Ethan nodded grimly. "They'll annihilate all of you. And any chance at a new world will die with you."

A hush swept through the subterranean space. Jamal exchanged a tense glance with Maya. Idris checked the readings on his handheld device, lines of data scrolling across the screen.

We're on a ticking clock, Maya thought. The unborn child in her womb felt like a promise she might never keep if they failed.

Outside, thunder rumbled again—an ominous reminder that Earth's wrath was closing in. Maya exhaled, turning to the circle of weary survivors—the half-starved children peeking around crates, the elders who had endured endless betrayals. She felt Ethan at her side, sensed Jamal's uncertainty, Idris's measured resolve, and the silent pressure of an entire planet's future resting on them.

"All right," she said, her voice echoing in the low-ceilinged chamber. "We have to act now. We'll split our forces: one team will organize an immediate evacuation—women, children, elders first. Another team will go after the ANTARES Array. We'll coordinate with Ebony's stealth once we neutralize the scanning radius."

She looked from Ethan to Jamal, from Jamal to the battered faces of the Indigenous scouts. "This is it. *We weren't just saved to survive—we were saved to lead.* If we let fear stop us now, we've already lost."

Outside, the wind howled, and a surge of static-laced thunder reverberated through the hidden refuge. Earth's new masters were preparing their next move. But so were they.

The next step had begun.

Chapter 10:
Unity in the Shadows

The wind howled through the desert canyon, its fierce cry merging with the dying light of the sun. Dust and debris swirled in chaotic whirlwinds, each particle catching the last golden rays, shimmering as though charged with memories. This stretch of Earth, once a thriving ecosystem interwoven with clear, life-sustaining rivers and rock formations that had borne witness to centuries of Indigenous history, now lay half-barren. Mighty rivers had withered to muddy trickles, and the proud, timeworn faces of the cliffs bore fresh scars—evidence of relentless weapon strikes and seismic upheavals that had forever reshaped the land.

High above the canyon floor, a Noctivara spacecraft hovered silently, a dark sentinel against the bruised sky. Its sleek silver-black hull exuded a quiet menace, its power contained yet unmistakable. Thrusters pulsed with blue ion light, momentarily illuminating the dusky air as they traced fleeting lines across the horizon. The ship's belly ramp extended downward over the canyon's edge, forming a precarious, metallic bridge between Earth's shattered terrain and the ship's gleaming interior.

Below, in the shadow of the hovering vessel, refugees moved in a controlled rush. Families with anxious eyes clung to one another; elders leaned on younger kin, their fragile steps measured yet determined. Children, some clutching blankets worn soft from years of use, shuffled forward in quiet resignation. Each footstep carried the weight of survival—a fragile hope carved from years spent hiding underground, evading a merciless Earth.

Amid the shifting crowd, Maya stood atop a red stone outcropping, surveying the throng below. She was a silhouette of unwavering resolve, clad in a lightweight protective vest and a rebreather to shield against the toxic dust storms that plagued the canyon. The wind tugged at her tightly braided hair as her sharp gaze scanned the horizon, ever watchful for the telltale signs of Earth's forces closing in. Since Ebony had landed in a concealed ravine two days ago, Maya and her team had worked tirelessly to rally the scattered Indigenous groups. Soon, a larger Noctivara vessel would arrive to accelerate the evacuation.

"Keep moving!" Maya shouted, her voice amplified through a handheld transmitter. "We hold position until the last person is safe. Anyone with injuries—head straight to the medical module!"

Her command cut through the restless murmurs, steady and unwavering. Around her, volunteers moved with practiced urgency. They guided refugees in small groups, their gestures firm but compassionate. Overhead, the ship's stark white interior lights cast sharp contrasts against the canyon's deepening twilight, revealing glimpses of its advanced technology: energy barriers flickering along the walls, stasis cots lined in precise formation, supply crates stacked in meticulous rows. Each group that crossed the threshold into the ship represented another life saved—a soul that had endured Earth's tyranny and years of hiding, now stepping into the unknown, grasping at the fragile promise of something more.

The Great Divide: When Earth Lost Its Shadow

On the canyon floor, a figure moved with purpose through the frantic crowd. Jean-Louis—once the missing love of Jamal's life—guided an elderly couple too frail to scale the final rocky stretch on their own. His steady hands and reassuring smile eased their steps as he murmured in soft French Creole, his voice rich with devotion. He had arrived unexpectedly that morning, leading a small band of guerrilla fighters determined to aid the evacuation. His presence had reignited something in Jamal's heart—an ember of hope buried beneath years of loss and longing.

From her vantage point atop the red stone, Maya caught sight of Jean-Louis just as he turned his gaze upward. A volunteer signaled for her assistance, and without hesitation, she hopped down to join them.

"Jean-Louis?" she asked, her voice carrying both recognition and urgency. She already knew his name, but she needed to hear it from him.

He gave a curt nod, eyes burning with an intensity that spoke of fierce devotion, love, and personal sacrifice.

Before more words could pass between them, a distant explosion shattered the moment. The blast sent a tremor through the canyon, rattling the ground beneath their feet.

Maya's transmitter crackled to life. "Maya, come in!" Zara's voice, calm but urgent, cut through the ambient noise. "Scouts have sighted an enemy convoy approaching from the west—could be only minutes away."

Maya's jaw clenched. She swept her gaze toward the horizon, her pulse quickening. In the far west, plumes of black smoke coiled into the sky, rising over the dunes like a warning. Earth's forces were moving faster than anticipated. She pressed the transmitter to her lips.

"Understood. We need every second we can get. Is Ebony still hidden?"

"Affirmative," Zara responded. "But be advised—the ANTARES Array may be scanning for activity. We're picking up faint signals spiking at regular intervals."

A cold dread settled in Maya's chest. The ANTARES Array—the prototype Earth weapon designed to track Noctivara ships—had haunted their operations for months. Every second spent on the ground increased the risk of detection.

"All right," she said firmly. "Keep Ebony on standby for emergency dustoff if we lose this position. But we get these people out first."

Even as she spoke, the refugees surged up the ramp, urgency driving their every step. The Noctivara craft's thrusters adjusted to the shifting load, sending gusts of turbulent air across the canyon floor. The force stirred blinding swirls of dust, forcing many to shield their eyes.

Amid the frenzy, Maya spotted Jamal pushing through the crowd below. His frantic gaze swept the sea of faces, searching.

Searching for Jean-Louis.

Beneath the main ridge, the canyon funneled into a narrow passage, its rocky walls pressing in like the pages of an ancient manuscript. Jagged formations jutted outward, casting deep shadows and creating pockets of concealment—essential hiding places the resistance fighters used during the evacuation. In one such pocket, where the wind carried the sting of dust and the acrid bite of lingering explosives, Jamal stumbled around a collapsed boulder. His pulse pounded, each frantic beat a stark reminder of the dangers closing in.

The Great Divide: When Earth Lost Its Shadow

His eyes swept across the determined faces of fellow resistance fighters, all moving with a shared urgency to ensure the evacuation's success. Thoughts swirled in his mind—memories of protests, whispered meetings in the shadows of city basements, and the relentless fire that had once fueled his every step. Yet now, in the face of immediate peril, his emotions twisted into something rawer—anticipation, fear, and a desperate hope he scarcely dared to acknowledge.

Then, through the dust-choked air, he saw a familiar stance—a tall figure clad in a threadbare jacket, hair pulled back in a no-nonsense style that spoke of long-forgotten days of resistance. The figure was guiding two limping refugees, murmuring quiet reassurances while offering steady support.

Jamal's breath caught. He didn't hesitate.

"Jean-Louis!" His voice broke with emotion as he surged forward, his body moving before his mind could catch up.

Time seemed to contract as Jean-Louis turned toward him. The chaos of the evacuation faded into the background, drowned out by the deafening thud of Jamal's heartbeat. For a single, suspended moment, nothing else existed—not the roar of the hovering spacecraft, not the threat creeping ever closer. Just Jean-Louis.

Alive.

Their eyes met, and in that instant, a thousand unsaid words passed between them. A lifetime of pain, relief, and devotion settled in the space between their gazes.

Jean-Louis's expression shifted, the rigid lines of battle-softened features melting into something unreadable—equal parts relief and sorrow. He released his grip on the refugees and, in a fluid motion, stepped toward Jamal. The distance between them vanished in an instant as they collided in a breathless embrace. The dust clung to their clothes, mingling with the lingering scents of gunpowder and sweat.

Jamal's grip tightened. "God, I thought—" His voice cracked. He had believed Jean-Louis lost forever, swallowed by the brutal upheaval of Earth's war-torn chaos. But now—against all odds—he was here.

Jean-Louis slid a hand to the back of Jamal's neck and pressed their foreheads together—a fleeting but powerful connection. "I thought the same about you," he murmured, his voice low and thick with unshed tears. "But we're here now."

A heartbeat later, the ground trembled beneath them as the distant thunder of artillery rolled through the canyon. Overhead, the shrill whine of a passing drone sliced through the smoke-laden air. The moment shattered. Instinct kicked in.

Without hesitation, they dropped into a crouch behind a jagged outcropping of rock. Nearby, a squad of resistance fighters surged forward, their faces hardened by years of struggle, their weapons trained on the west—where, any second now, the enemy convoy would emerge.

Jamal's breath came in ragged gasps. He had dreamed of this reunion countless times, but never like this—never in the midst of chaos, with danger closing in from all sides.

"We have a ship," he managed between breaths. "A safe haven in Noctivara. You can come with us—"

Jean-Louis pressed a steady hand to Jamal's cheek, a quiet reassurance amid the storm. "Shh," he murmured. "We'll talk later. Right now, we need to keep these people safe." His gesture toward the continuing stream of refugees was both a command and a plea.

Jamal swallowed hard, nodding with a mix of sorrow and reluctant acceptance. The time to talk, to unpack the weeks of

The Great Divide: When Earth Lost Its Shadow

loss and the fragile hopes still lingering between them, would come. But not now.

Now, the mission demanded everything they had.

On a rocky ledge overlooking the evacuation path, Maya had established a makeshift command post. A portable holo-map floated in midair before her, its shifting lines and contours tracing the canyon's treacherous terrain. Every gust of wind sent distortions rippling across the projection, but its data remained crucial for coordinating the evacuation and defending against the approaching enemy convoy.

Beside her, Zara appeared, her presence as steady as ever. The Noctivara leader's face was partially obscured by a specialized mask, but her silver eyes gleamed with unwavering intensity.

"Enemy convoy is five minutes out," Zara reported, her voice low and urgent. "They've deployed scouting drones—small, fast, but our jamming measures have silenced most of their signals."

Maya's gaze snapped to the holo-map, where a blinking red cluster marked the enemy's approach. "Any way we can slow them down before they reach us?" she asked, her voice edged with determination.

Zara studied the map for a beat before nodding. "We still have a few explosives from the sabotage teams. If we trigger a controlled rockslide, it could buy us time." There was a trace of cautious optimism in her voice, but the weight of their situation pressed down on both of them.

Maya's expression hardened. The risk was high, but their choices were limited. "Do it—but minimize casualties if possible. Some of those soldiers might be conscripts forced into this war." Her words were measured, firm, but threaded with empathy.

Zara pressed her lips into a thin line before signaling to a nearby group of resistance fighters. They moved swiftly, disappearing into the swirling dust as they set out to plant the charges along the cliffside. Watching them go, Maya felt the relentless pull of war's cruel choices. Violence was never the goal, but survival had left them with no other path.

Her transmitter crackled to life with an update from Kiona, who was leading the fallback line of evacuees.

"Maya, we've got a group lagging behind—people who won't make it unless we delay the enemy."

Maya's eyes darted between the map and the distant red dots creeping closer. "Hold your position as long as you can," she ordered, her voice cutting through the static. "We're stalling Earth's forces. I'll hold the ramp as long as possible. No one gets left behind."

As she issued the command, another wave of refugees surged up toward the ship. The Noctivara craft's thrusters roared, sending gusts of displaced air that mixed with the canyon's restless dust.

Amid the chaos, Maya caught sight of Jamal maneuvering through the crowd below, his head swiveling frantically. His expression was sharp with urgency, his eyes scanning every face.

Searching, perhaps, for Jean-Louis.

The canyon trembled with a deep, resonant boom as an explosion tore through the distant ridge. A violent detonation shattered the fragile calm, sending massive chunks of rock crashing onto the makeshift road below. Dust billowed skyward, swallowing the convoy's vehicles in a swirling haze of grit.

From their vantage point, Maya and Zara watched intently as plumes of debris rose over the western ridge.

"Let's hope that slows them down," Zara murmured, tapping a finger against the holo-map's display. "We might gain ten, maybe fifteen minutes."

Before anyone could respond, a piercing shriek split the air. Two Earth drones streaked overhead, releasing flare-like munitions that exploded in bursts of white-hot light. The shockwaves rattled the canyon walls, sending terrified refugees scrambling for cover. One near-miss blast unleashed a powerful gust, momentarily rocking the Noctivara craft mid-hover.

Maya cursed under her breath and grabbed her transmitter. "Pilots, hold your position! We need at least ten more minutes to load the rest of the evacuees!" Her voice was taut with urgency.

A pilot's response crackled through the static, edged with anxiety. "We're sustaining minor damage from overhead strikes. We'll hold as long as we can, but our margins are thin."

Maya's pulse pounded as she sprinted down the rocky slope, her protective vest rustling with every determined step. Dust stung her eyes and coated her tongue as she reached a group of elders huddled near a jagged outcrop. She moved swiftly, ushering them forward.

"Head toward the ramp! Don't stop—you have to keep moving!" she urged, her voice firm yet reassuring.

Across the ramp, she caught sight of Jean-Louis among a line of survivors. Just behind him, Jamal stood, his face streaked with sweat and dirt. His expression carried a weight far heavier than exhaustion. Their eyes met, and in that fleeting moment, a silent understanding passed between them. This was more than a reunion. It was hope in the middle of destruction.

Maya paused as the chaos around her seemed to slow. For a single breath, the cacophony of explosions, frantic shouts, and scrambling feet faded into the background. She pressed a steady hand against her abdomen, feeling the unmistakable flutter of life within.

You deserve a peaceful world, little one, she thought, her resolve hardening into something unshakable. I will do everything in my power to protect you.

Dust and debris thickened the air as the Noctivara ship loomed above, its engines humming a low dirge amid the chaos. Refugees poured onto the ramp in a frantic blur, their faces indistinct through the shifting haze. Beneath the ramp, in a small alcove carved by the natural rock—a fleeting sanctuary from the storm—Jamal and Jean-Louis stood together, their breaths uneven, their hearts pounding in a shared rhythm of hope and despair.

They had just helped an injured father reach the medical module. Now, in the brief lull between detonations and urgent commands, they faced each other at last.

Jamal's gaze roved over Jean-Louis's familiar features, searching for the man he had once known so well. The rugged determination in his eyes remained, though softened by the scars of time and war. Yet beneath the hardened lines of hardship, the same fierce spirit burned. They stood close enough that their breaths mingled—a collision of past and present, of longing and loss.

The Great Divide: When Earth Lost Its Shadow

"Come with me," Jamal pleaded, his voice raw with emotion as he reached out. "Don't stay here. If this fight continues, it could take everything you've ever cared for." His words trembled with both love and desperation.

Jean-Louis cupped Jamal's face in his calloused hands, his touch both tender and unyielding. "I have people here who depend on me," he murmured, his eyes shining with unshed tears. "There's an underground network ready to stand against Earth's tyranny. And now, with the ANTARES Array closing in, I can't walk away."

Jamal's throat tightened. "But you'd be safer if you left. Let Noctivara help you—let me help you—from a distance." His voice wavered with the weight of past loss and the dread of future heartbreak.

A bittersweet smile tugged at Jean-Louis's lips. "You know me too well," he whispered. "From the moment we met, you knew I wouldn't leave those who need me behind." His hand slid down to Jamal's shoulder, offering a final, lingering squeeze.

Jamal pressed his trembling hand over Jean-Louis's, as if trying to anchor himself in the fleeting moment. Memories surged through him—late-night planning sessions, whispered strategies under flickering streetlights, secret protests in the rain, and stolen kisses amid the turmoil. They had always been a team, a beacon of resistance in a fractured world.

"I can't lose you again," Jamal murmured, his voice barely steady, tears threatening to spill.

Jean-Louis leaned in, resting his forehead against Jamal's in a final, aching embrace. His next words were hushed, weighted with heartbreak. "This is where I stay. We fought side by side for so long, but now our paths must separate. Earth's people need me, and you—" He hesitated, his voice faltering.

"You have Maya, you have Noctivara... and a future beyond this battle."

A single tear traced its way down Jamal's cheek as he pleaded, "Don't say you're leaving me."

Jean-Louis's expression softened, though his resolve remained unshaken. "Don't speak of that," he whispered, his tone both tender and unyielding. "If I don't make it, you must remember what we stood for—and then live, Jamal. Really live."

The ground trembled with another distant explosion. A stray bullet sliced through the air, ricocheting off a jagged rock nearby. Instinct took over as they ducked, their hands tightening around each other in that shared moment of peril.

"Go," Jean-Louis urged, gripping Jamal's arm with sudden urgency. "Board the ship. Get to safety before it's too late."

Jamal's chest tightened painfully. His throat burned as he choked out, "Jean-Louis—" He wanted to hold on, to anchor himself to the man he'd once thought lost forever. But the battle raged on, pressing in with its unrelenting force. From the command post, Maya's voice crackled over the comms, calling for final boarding.

With a last, desperate kiss—one that tasted of salt, dust, and unspoken farewells—Jean-Louis pulled away. "I'll hold them off so more can board," he said, his voice steady despite the tremor beneath it. "Go now."

Their eyes locked one final time, a silent communion of love, loss, and all the words they would never get to say. Then, with a swift motion born of necessity, Jean-Louis turned and disappeared into the chaos, moving through jagged rocks to find his vantage point. He would fight—one last time—to ensure their people had a chance.

The Great Divide: When Earth Lost Its Shadow

Jamal stood frozen, his heart fracturing as the truth sank in. This was the moment their paths truly diverged.

Behind him, the ship's ramp pulsed with urgency as the Noctivara vessel prepared for liftoff. Blinking away tears, driven by grief and the stubborn ember of hope, Jamal stumbled forward. He would carry Jean-Louis with him—etched into his soul, a reminder of the price they had paid.

And long after the dust had settled, the weight of that sacrifice would remain.

Inside the Noctivara craft, chaos swirled like a storm barely held at bay. The narrow corridors teemed with refugees—men, women, and children crammed together, clutching meager belongings while others desperately tended to wounded loved ones. Medical modules overflowed, overwhelmed with cases of shrapnel wounds, dehydration, malnourishment, and the weakened moans of those too frail to stand. Yet amid the controlled mayhem, Maya moved with steady purpose. Her sharp eyes scanned the suffering faces as she offered calm reassurances, directing volunteers with precision, her every step unwavering despite the storm of anguish reverberating in her bones.

Then, without warning, the comm systems erupted into a burst of static. Overhead lights stuttered violently—a telltale sign of a Noctivara override, a secure communication channel rarely accessed by the refugees. Maya's pulse quickened. She knew what that meant.

Without hesitation, she wove her way to the central communications node. Suspended in midair, a shimmering holographic interface pulsed with alien luminescence, intricate symbols shifting and reforming like something alive.

In the cold glow of the projection, Zara and Omari were already at work, their faces tense with concentration as they parsed the alien script scrolling before them. The text spiraled in endless motion until Omari pressed his palm to the console. The moment his skin made contact, the holographic symbols hesitated, as if recognizing him.

Maya inhaled sharply. She had long suspected Omari harbored deeper ties to the Noctivara than he had ever admitted, but this? This was undeniable proof.

"Look at this," Zara muttered, frustration and unease threading through her voice. "We're receiving a top-priority alert from the Noctivara network." Her gaze remained locked on the data, her tone shifting to something heavier, laced with foreboding. "They've detected a partial activation of a cosmic device—possibly the Array, or something worse. They're warning us of an interstellar escalation."

Omari's normally composed expression darkened as he pressed his palm more firmly against the interface. "It's not just Earth's Array," he murmured, his voice taut with urgency. "The Noctivara suspect another faction is arming them—preparing to strike not only this planet but every world where humanity has resettled." He exhaled slowly, his fingers twitching over the console. "They fear a larger war is coming… beyond Earth, beyond Noctivara."

Maya stared at the cascading alien text, her thoughts reeling. "A… cosmic conflict?" The words felt fragile, barely forming in the wake of the revelation.

Zara nodded grimly, her eyes shadowed with concern. "Yes. The Noctivara believe that these new alliances forming on Earth might be the first moves in something far greater—a galactic power shift. Noctivara, the very idea of it, has become more than an experiment. It's a beacon." She met Omari's gaze. "A beacon that could tip the balance of power. Can you verify the data from your side?"

Omari's jaw tightened as he redoubled his efforts, his palm pressing deeper against the console. The holographic script flared in response, surging with fresh lines of text. A name emerged in the alien scrawl, stark and unmistakable—Keshu Rift.

Maya's breath hitched as Omari began translating, his voice weighted with understanding. "They're calling it the Keshu Rift—a cosmic corridor that's been contested by multiple species for centuries." His fingers flexed over the controls, decoding the shifting symbols. "And they're saying Earth's new allies may be using the Array to secure humanity's cooperation in a coming war."

His voice hung in the air like a pronouncement of something inescapable.

Something inevitable.

A cold sweat formed on Maya's brow. "So Earth's leadership has sold us out to an alien faction for advanced weaponry? And in return, they're dragging us into a war that isn't ours?" Her voice wavered between disbelief and dread.

Zara exhaled heavily, her shoulders sagging as if she could feel the crushing inevitability of it all. "It appears so," she admitted, her tone grim.

Before Maya could press further, the comm system crackled to life, carrying a voice she knew too well—Jamal's, edged with urgency. "Maya, I'm aboard. The ramp is nearly clear. We have maybe thirty seconds before we either lift off or get overwhelmed."

Maya tore herself away from the weight of the revelation, forcing her focus back to the moment. "Zara, keep decoding. Omari—do whatever you can to gather more intel on this offworld threat. We'll regroup once we're airborne." With that, she spun on her heel and rushed down the corridor, ensuring the final evacuation steps were executed without delay.

As she moved through the chaos, a part of her couldn't shake the question clawing at the edges of her mind. How would this change everything they had been fighting for? The knowledge that unseen forces were aligning against them—threatening to turn their hard-won sanctuary into yet another battlefield—only heightened the urgency of their mission.

While chaos raged within the craft, Ethan found refuge in the dimly lit cargo bay, concealed within the shadows. His presence went unnoticed, just another ghost amid the storm of evacuees. He had slipped aboard with the final group through a hidden tunnel, half-expecting to see Maya among them. Yet, when his eyes locked onto hers across the corridor, his breath hitched, and his resolve wavered. Instead of stepping forward, he remained pressed against the cold metal bulkhead, his pulse hammering in the silence.

His mind churned with thoughts long buried in the recesses of his memory. He had spent endless nights poring over schematics and encrypted data drives, desperately trying to warn them about the ANTARES Array's final stage of activation—how close the system was to reaching its peak. That

The Great Divide: When Earth Lost Its Shadow

knowledge was vital. It had cost him everything to secure the classified data now clutched tightly in his palm.

But now, as he watched Maya guide a limping elder through the corridor, the urgency of his mission clashed with something far more personal. He saw her pause momentarily at a junction, her hand pressing instinctively to her abdomen—a small, protective gesture that sent a jolt of realization through him. She was pregnant. The swell was subtle, barely discernible beneath her protective gear, but from this angle, there was no mistaking it.

Ethan's breath caught. The revelation hit like a silent explosion: she was carrying a child—his child? The thought seared through him, igniting a maelstrom of longing, regret, and unshakable guilt. He had been so consumed by his mission, so fixated on stopping Earth's betrayal, that he had failed to see the life growing inside her.

Fragments of their past flashed through his mind—a desperate, whispered conversation during the early days of the abductions, a promise made in the face of uncertainty, the fragile thread of love stretched thin by war and time. He remembered how they had been torn apart, how the weeks had dulled the memory of her laughter. And now, she stood before him, carrying a future he had never dared to imagine.

His body tensed as emotions warred within him. Every instinct screamed for him to step forward—to reveal the encrypted drive, to warn her of the impending storm. But an equal force held him back. Guilt. Fear. The quiet certainty that his presence would only complicate things. Maybe, he thought bitterly, it was better this way. Maybe she had moved on. Maybe she had chosen to leave him behind.

Slowly, he backed away, retreating into the darkness of a storage alcove, watching as Maya disappeared down the corridor, her silhouette glowing faintly under the ship's emergency lights. *I can't get in her way now*, he told himself, the ache in his chest near unbearable.

As he slumped against the cool metal, his thoughts turned down a darker path. *Did she know before she left? Had she decided to move forward without me?* The data drive trembled in his grip, a silent burden of the warnings he never got to share. But as much as it hurt, one thing remained certain: even if he couldn't be by her side, he would protect her—from the shadows, from the war that loomed ahead, from the truths he could no longer escape. No matter what it cost him.

Above the canyon, the Noctivara ship's engines roared, priming for full thrust. Inside, every corridor and hold teemed with refugees, their faces a mixture of relief, fear, and quiet determination. Medical staff from Noctivara moved swiftly, tending to the sick and stabilizing the wounded, while volunteers navigated the packed halls, handing out sealed water pouches and ration bars. Beyond the open ramp, Earth's battered skies loomed—a haunting expanse of smoky reds and oranges, a silent testament to the planet's suffering.

At the base of the ramp, Maya's gaze darted frantically across the evacuation zone, searching for any sign of Jean-Louis or the remaining fighters—any familiar face that might fortify her resolve. Instead, she saw only scattered pockets of resistance, exchanging cautious fire with the advancing enemy convoy. A stray bullet struck the ship's hull, the impact sending a sharp clang through the metal. The ramp shuddered, as though the vessel itself protested their departure.

Jamal appeared at her side, his face streaked with sweat and dust. Grief and determination weighed equally in his dark eyes. "We have to go, Maya," he urged, his voice low but firm. "Time's running out."

Maya nodded, the burden of leaving anyone behind pressing against her chest like an iron weight. But there was no choice. She pressed her transmitter. "Pilot, close the ramp in ten seconds. Prepare for immediate ascent." Her voice carried the steely command of a leader, laced with the sorrow of the decision she had no time to grieve.

A final rush of evacuees scrambled aboard. The ramp let out a long mechanical hiss before sealing shut with an echoing clank that reverberated through the canyon. Through a narrow viewport, Maya caught one last glimpse of Earth—a battlefield where resistance fighters scattered among jagged rock formations, their silhouettes fleeting against the advancing enemy. A ribbon of black smoke twisted through the sky, backlit by the dying sun.

Inside the cockpit, the pilot's voice crackled over the comms. "We're airborne." The ship jolted violently as it lifted from the surface, a tremor that sent murmurs of alarm and quiet sobs rippling through the hold. Maya gripped a nearby rail, steadying herself against the cold metal, inhaling deeply as the rhythmic pulse of the engines filled the air.

"We're detecting a significant energy spike from Earth's western quadrant," the pilot continued, his voice straining against static. "It appears to be the Array."

Maya's stomach twisted. Her jaw clenched. "Engage full stealth—evade if possible."

In the dim glow of the corridor, Ethan lingered, his gaze fixed on the cockpit door. Every instinct screamed at him to step forward, to tell Maya everything he knew about the trap waiting for them. But his feet remained rooted to the floor, paralyzed by hesitation. He watched the strain on her face—the exhaustion, the weight of command, the quiet evidence of the life growing within her. His fingers tightened around the data drive, his resolve hardening.

I must protect her—from afar, if not by her side.

High above the canyon, the Noctivara ship cut through thick, churning clouds, its sleek hull crackling with electrical static as the partial cloaking field engaged—a last-ditch effort to evade Earth's relentless sensors. For one fleeting moment, hope sparked in the cockpit as the vessel seemed to dissolve into the storm, slipping from the enemy's gaze.

Then came the sound. A deep, resonant hum—a low-frequency pulse that rattled the ship's core, as if something ancient had been stirred from its slumber. The interior lights spasmed, flashing erratically, while the hull groaned under the sudden pressure of an unseen force. Alarms blared, a cacophony of urgency drowning out every other noise.

The pilot's voice, raw with urgency, cut through the chaos. "They're firing the weapon! Massive energy surge inbound from two o'clock low! Evasive maneuvers—now!"

The ship reeled violently, pitching hard to one side. Crew members tumbled, crates slammed against the bulkheads, and cries of fear echoed through the corridors. Maya braced against a reinforced wall, her fingers digging into the cold metal as she shouted, "Hold on! Everyone, brace for impact!"

Zara's voice crackled over the intercom, slicing through the panic. "The Array's beam is locked onto our Noctivara signatures. If we can't scramble the signal in time, a direct hit is inevitable!"

Then, Omari burst into the cockpit, his expression taut with urgency. "I might be able to short-circuit the targeting system," he said, scanning the interfaces with sharp precision. "We need to generate a powerful disruptor feed—if we can override even a fraction of the Array's signal, it could buy us a fighting chance."

Maya's gaze locked onto his, her nod fierce. "Do it. Whatever it takes."

Omari spun on his heel and bolted deeper into the ship, toward a cluster of secondary Noctivara control panels. Meanwhile, in the dim recesses of the cargo hold, Ethan listened—silent, motionless. His mind raced. The data drive he carried, containing classified Earth weapon schematics, might be the advantage Omari needed. But revealing himself meant exposing a secret he had spent too long protecting. The weight of it pressed against him.

Yet as the ship lurched again, another near-miss shaking the deck beneath his feet, survival drowned out hesitation. Jaw tightening, Ethan darted after Omari, shoving aside his doubts. In that moment, nothing mattered more than ensuring they lived to fight another day.

In the cockpit, the pilot executed a sharp maneuver, pulling the ship into a near-vertical climb as the western sky darkened ominously. The once-calm horizon twisted into a turbulent vortex of storm clouds, illuminated from below by erratic flashes of orange—the unmistakable bursts of Earth's weapon discharges. The hull trembled with every pulse of energy from the Array, the ship groaning under the relentless strain of evasive maneuvers.

Maya, strapped into the co-pilot's seat, scanned the frantic readouts, her wide eyes a mix of terror and steely resolve. In the doorway, Jamal appeared, his silhouette briefly framed by the flickering glow of the control panels. He clutched a handrail to steady himself, his face pale—not just from the ship's violent jostling, but from the unbearable sorrow of his reunion with Jean-Louis earlier that day.

"How bad is it?" Jamal's voice was low, measured—an attempt at control despite the turmoil gnawing at him.

"We're close to breaking free of Earth's atmosphere," Maya said between rapid breaths. "But if the Array locks on again, we won't survive a direct hit." Her voice wavered, thick with fear and the crushing responsibility of those aboard.

Below, Earth's horizon pulsed with the eerie glow of a world on the brink—strobing bursts of apocalyptic light underscoring the relentless threat. The Array was charging again, its energy building like the slow, deliberate rise of an executioner's blade. Every second stretched unbearably, the tension coiling tighter.

Outside the cockpit, a final blast of weaponized light tore through the clouds. The ship's sensors shrieked in protest, a deafening cacophony of alarms converging in a single, harrowing warning.

"Impact imminent!" the pilot shouted, his voice barely cutting through the roar of the engines.

Maya's grip on the seat tightened, her knuckles bloodless as she fought to steady her racing heart. Not now... not like this. Then, as though summoned by sheer desperation, a surge rippled through the ship's systems. The walls lit up with glowing

The Great Divide: When Earth Lost Its Shadow

Noctivara script as Omari's override engaged. For a breathless moment, the entire craft wavered, as if suspended between dimensions—a mirage caught in the storm.

The approaching energy beam streaked past, searing dangerously close, its heat carving a trail of ionized particles off the starboard side. The ship lurched violently from the near-miss, the force rippling through its core.

For an instant, silence held. Then, as realization set in, relief spilled through the corridors—sharp, disbelieving gasps, cries of gratitude. They had survived. Barely.

Yet before that relief could fully take root, a transmission crackled through the cockpit's speakers—low, resonant, and steeped in chilling finality.

A voice, one that normally carried only the weight of high-level Noctivara commands, now bled through the static with an urgency that made the air itself feel heavier.

"They have found us. We are no longer safe. The conflict extends beyond Earth."

The signal wavered, then returned, clearer this time—each word laced with a foreboding certainty.

"All Noctivara craft—disengage from standard routes. Assemble at Sector 9-F. The resolution is at hand."

Maya's heart pounded as she absorbed the truth: a new war was unfolding—one that threatened not just their sanctuary but the vast expanse of the cosmos itself. She pictured Noctivara, the city of survivors, once a refuge, now a looming target in an interstellar struggle that eclipsed human conflicts.

Inside the cargo hold, Ethan pressed his back against the cold metal wall, his gaze heavy with unspoken turmoil. The data drive still rested in his grip, the choice to surrender it to Omari left unmade. As the ship hurtled into orbit, reality crashed down on him—Maya was pregnant. Their future, once uncertain but possible, had now been irrevocably altered. The thought of a life without her—of a fate that might never allow him to stand by her side—filled him with an unbearable mixture of sorrow and steeled resolve.

Back in the cockpit, Jamal stared at the receding planet, silent tears tracing lines down his face. Memories of Jean-Louis, of everything lost and sacrificed, clashed in his mind. The weight of it all pressed down, but before it could consume him, Maya reached out, resting a steadying hand on his shoulder—a quiet acknowledgment of their shared grief, of what had been left behind. Yet, no comfort could undo the truth. Every heartbeat in that cabin carried the weight of an ending, and yet, every ending was also a beginning—one that now stood on the precipice of a war stretching far beyond Earth, into the cold infinity of space.

With a final, desperate thrust, the ship broke free of Earth's gravity well. Through the porthole windows, the curve of their scarred homeworld shrank into the distance—a planet ravaged yet unbroken. Somewhere down there, Jean-Louis was still fighting for freedom. Somewhere beyond, in the dark reaches of space, an even greater menace awaited.

The transmission lingered in the silence, its grim urgency reverberating through the vessel. They were no longer safe.

In that moment of suspended reality, as the ship surged forward into the unknown, Jamal's tears became a tribute to lost love, and Maya's silent vow to protect her unborn child burned brighter than ever. War had come—not just to Earth, but to the entire cosmos. And every boundary of loyalty, love, and survival would soon be tested in the fire of an inevitable, all-consuming conflict.

www.ingramcontent.com/pod-product-compliance
Lightning Source LLC
LaVergne TN
LVHW021808060526
838201LV00058B/3290